EVERYBODY WAS DEAD

Everybody.

Lister had been in stasis three million years.

Three million years.

Since one drunken night outside the Marie Lloyd off Regent Street, London, every step he'd taken had led him farther and farther from home. And now he was three million *years* away. Three million years out into Deep Space. And he was totally alone.

The enormity of all this was slowly beginning to sink in when Holly, the ship's computer, dropped his final bombshell. The one about the human race being extinct.

"What d'you mean 'extinct'?"

"Well, three million years is a very good age for a species. I mean, your average genus only survives a couple of hundred thousand years, max. And that's with a clean-living species, like dinosaurs. So chances of the human race making it to the big three-oh-oh-oh-oh-oh-oh are practically nonexistent."

Much to his surprise, Lister let out a sob.

"Were you very close?" Holly asked sympathetically.

RED DWARF

INFINITY WELCOMES CAREFUL DRIVERS

Grant Naylor

A ROC BOOK

To Kath and Linda

Special thanks to Paul Jackson
for everything, to Ed Bye for
everything else and to Chris Barrie,
Craig Charles, Danny John-Jules,
Norman Lovett, Peter Risdale-Scott,
Roger Bolton, Peter Wragg and all the
Red Dwarf backstage crew.

ROC
Published by the Penguin Group
Penguin Books USA Inc., 375 Hudson Street,
New York, New York 10014, U.S.A.
Penguin Books Ltd, 27 Wrights Lane,
London W8 5TZ, England
Penguin Books Australia Ltd, Ringwood,
Victoria, Australia
Penguin Books Canada Ltd, 10 Alcorn Avenue,
Toronto, Ontario, Canada M4V 3B2
Penguin Books (N.Z.) Ltd, 182–190 Wairau Road,
Auckland 10, New Zealand

Penguin Books Ltd, Registered Offices:
Harmondsworth, Middlesex, England

Published by Roc, an imprint of New American Library,
a division of Penguin Books USA Inc. Previously published in Great Britain
by Penguin Books.

First Roc Printing, September, 1992
10 9 8 7 6 5 4 3 2 1

CONTENTS

Part One

Your own death, and how to cope with it

ONE

'DESCRIBE, USING DIAGRAMS WHERE APPROPRIATE, THE EXACT CIRCUM-STANCES LEADING TO YOUR DEATH.'

Saunders had been dead for almost two weeks now and, so far, he hadn't enjoyed a minute of it. What he wasn't enjoying at this particular moment was having to wade through the morass of forms and legal papers he'd been sent to complete by the Department of Death and Deceaseds' Rights.

It was all very well receiving a five-page booklet entitled: *Your Own Death and How To Cope With It*. It was all very well attending counselling sessions with the ship's metaphysical psychiatrist, and being told about the nature of Being and Non-Being, and some other gunk about this guy who was in a cave, but didn't know it was a cave until he left. The thing was, Saunders was an engineer, not a philosopher – and the way he saw it, you were either dead or you were alive. And if you were dead, you shouldn't be forced to fill in endless incomprehensible forms, and other related nonsensica.

You shouldn't have to return your birth certificate, to have it invalidated. You shouldn't have to send off your completed death certificate, accompanied by a passport-size photograph of your corpse, signed on the back by your coroner. When you're dead, you should be dead. The bastards should leave you alone.

If Saunders could have picked something up, he would

have picked something up and hurled it across the grey metal room. But he couldn't.

Saunders was a hologram. He was just a computer-generated simulation of his former self; he couldn't actually *touch* anything, except for his own hologramatic body. He was a phantom made of light. A software ghost.

Quite honestly, he'd had enough.

Saunders got up, walked silently across the metal-grilled floor of his sleeping quarters and stared out of the viewport window.

Far away to his right was the bright multi-coloured ball of Saturn, captured by its rainbow rings like a prize in a gigantic stellar hoop-la game. Twelve miles below him, under the plexiglass dome of the terraformed colony of Mimas, half the ship's crew were on planet leave.

No planet leave for Saunders.

No R & R for the dead.

He caressed his eyelids with the rough balls of his fingers, then glanced back at the pile: the mind-bogglingly compli-cated Hologramatic Status application form; accident claims; pension funds; bank transfers; house deeds. They all had to be completed so his wife, Carole – no, his *widow*, Carole – could start a new life without him.

When he'd first signed up, they both understood he would be away from Earth for months on end, and, obviously, things could happen; mining in space was dangerous. That was why the money was so good.

'If anything happens to me,' he'd always said, 'I don't want you to sit around, mourning.' Protests. 'I want you to meet someone else, someone terrific, and start a new life without me.'

What a stupid, fat, dumb thing to say! The kind of stupid, fat, dumb thing only a living person would ever dream of saying.

Because that's what she was going to do now.

Start a new life – without him.

Fine, if he was *dead* dead. If he'd just taken delivery of his shiny new ephemeral body and was wafting around in the ether on the next plane of existence – fine.

Even if there was no life after death, and he totally ceased to be – then again, absolutely fine.

But this was different. He was dead, but he was still here. His personality had been stored on disc, and the computer had reproduced him down to the tiniest detail; down to his innermost thoughts.

This wasn't the deal. He wanted her to start a new life when he was gone, not while he was still here. But of course, that's what she'd do. That's what she *had* to do. You can't stay married to a dead man. So even though she loved him dearly, she would, eventually, have to start looking for someone else.

And . . . she would sleep with him.

She would go to bed with him. And, hell, she would probably enjoy it.

Even though she still loved Saunders.

She would, wouldn't she? She would meet Mr Terrific and have a physical relationship.

Probably in his bed.

His bed! Their marital bed. His bed!

Probably using the three condoms he knew for a fact he had left in the bedside cabinet.

The ones he'd bought for a joke.

The flavoured ones.

His mind ran amok, picturing a line of lovers standing, strawberry-sheathed, outside his wife's bedroom.

'No!' screamed Saunders, involuntarily. '*Noooooo!*'

Hologramatic tears of rage and frustration welled up in Saunders' eyes and rolled hologramatically down his cheeks. He smashed his fist down onto the table.

The fist passed soundlessly through the grey metal desk top, and crashed with astonishing force into his testicles.

5

As he lay in a foetal position, squealing on the floor, he wished he were dead. Then he remembered he already was.

Saunders didn't know it but, twelve miles below, on the Saturnian moon of Mimas, Flight Co-ordinator George McIntyre was about to solve all his problems.

TWO

George McIntyre sat in the Salvador Dali Coffee Lounge of the Mimas Hilton, and stared at a painting of melting clocks while he waited for the tall, immaculately-dressed mechanoid to return with his double Bloody Mary, no ice. He couldn't stand Bloody Mary without ice, but he didn't want his shaking hand to set the cubes clanking around in the glass, advertising his nervousness when his visitors arrived.

Five minutes later they did arrive, and McIntyre wished they hadn't. When he turned and caught sight of them, the heat left his body as quickly as people leave a Broadway first night party when the bad reviews come in.

There were three of them. Big men. They each had the kind of build that looks stupid in a suit. Shoulders tiered from the neck. Thighs like rolls of carpet. Biceps and triceps screaming to be released from the fetters of the finely-tailored lounge suits. The kind of bodies that only look right and natural in posing pouches. In suits, no matter how expensive – and these were expensive – they looked like kids who'd been forced into their Sunday best, all starched and itching. McIntyre couldn't shake the feeling that they were yearning, aching to get nude and start oiling-up.

They didn't say 'hello' and sat down at his table. One of them took up both spaces on the pink sofa, while the other two drew up chairs from a nearby table and squeezed into them. The armrests were forced out into a tired Vee, to the accompaniment of an uneasy creaking sound.

McIntyre just sat there, smiling. He felt as if he was sitting in the middle of a huge barrel of sweating muscle. He was convinced that if he shook hands with any of the three, he would immediately die from an overdose of steroid poisoning.

He wondered, though not too hard, why one of them was carrying a pair of industrial bolt clippers.

The tall, immaculately-dressed mechanoid came up and served McIntyre his Bloody Mary. All three of the men ordered decaff coffee. While they waited for it to arrive, they chatted with McIntyre. Small talk: difficulties parking; the decor; the irritating muzak.

When the coffee came, McIntyre pretended not to notice that they couldn't get their fingers through the cup handles.

The man on the sofa lifted up a briefcase and fiddled clumsily with the lock. For a moment McIntyre found himself feeling sorry for the man — everything was too small for him: the briefcase, the coffee cup, the suit. Then he remembered the bolt clippers, and stopped feeling sorry for the man and started feeling sorry for himself again. The case eventually sprang open and the man took out a fold-out, three-page document and handed it to McIntyre with a pen.

McIntyre explained, apologetically, that it was impossible for him to sign the document.

The three men were upset.

George McIntyre left the Salvador Dali Coffee Lounge of the Mimas Hilton, carrying his nose in a Mimas Hilton Coffee Lounge napkin.

THREE

The four astros paid the fare, leaving the smallest of small tips, and staggered through the jabbering crowd and up the steps into the Los Americanos Casino.

Lister flicked on the 'For Hire' sign, and decided to take the hopper down Central and back towards Mimas docks. He slipped the gear into jump, and braced himself. The hopper leapt into the air, and landed with a spine-juddering crunch two hundred yards down Eastern Avenue. The hopper's rear legs retracted into the engine housing, then hammered into the ground, propelling him another two hundred yards. As it smacked into the tarmacadamed three-lane highway, Lister's neck was forced into the hollow at the base of his skull, further aggravating an already angry headache. The hopper's suspension was completely shot to hell.

Lister began to wish he'd never stolen it.

Hoppers had been introduced to Mimas thirty years previously, to combat the ludicrous congestion which had blocked the small moon's road system so badly that an average Mimian traffic jam could last anything up to three weeks. People had been known to die of starvation in particularly bad ones. Hoppers, which could leapfrog over obstructions, and spend most of their time in the air, helped ease the problem. True, there were a fair number of mid-air collisions, and there was always the possibility of being landed on by a drunk-driven hopper, but, by and large, you reached your destination in the same season you set off.

Lister watched with envy as another hopper overtook him with the easy grace of a frolicking deer. The next landing was the worst. The hopper hit a metal drain cover with such violence that Lister bit his cigarette in half, and the glowing tip fell between his thighs and rolled under the seat of his pants. Frantically, he arched his body out of the seat and tried to sweep the butt onto the floor as the hopper leapt madly down the busy highway, like a sick metallic kangaroo.

Something was burning.

It smelled like hair. And since he was the only thing in the hopper that had hair, it was fairly safe to assume some part of him was on fire. Some part of him that had hair. He liked all the parts of him that had hair. They were his favourite bits.

His eyes searched desperately for a place to park. Forget it.

In London people parked wherever it was possible. In Paris people parked even where it *wasn't* possible. On Mimas people parked on *top* of the people who'd parked where it wasn't possible. Stacks of hoppers, three, sometimes four high, lined the avenue on both sides.

A typical Saturday night on Mimas.

The thick air hung heavy with the smells and noises of a hundred mingling cultures. The trotters, Mimian slang for 'pavements', were obscured by giant serpents of human flesh as people wrested their way past the blinking neons of casinos and restaurants, the on-off glare of bars and clubs; shouting, screaming, laughing, vomiting. Astros and miners on planet leave going wallet-bulging crazy, desperate for a good time after months of incarceration in the giant space freighters that now hung over the moon's shuttle port.

The Earth had long been purged of all its valuable mineral resources. Humankind had emptied its home planet like an enema, then turned its rapacious appetite to the rest of the solar system. The Spanish-owned Saturnian satellite of Mimas was a supply centre and stop-off point for the thousands of mining vessels which plundered the smaller planets and the larger moons and asteroids.

Smoke began to plume from between Lister's legs.

Still nowhere to park.

Traffic blared and leapfrogged over him as he skewed across lanes, fighting to keep control.

In desperation he grabbed the thermos flask lying on the passenger seat, struggled with the unfamiliar cap, and poured the contents into his smouldering lap.

A hiss signalled the end of the cigarette. There was a second of delicious relief.

Then he smelled coffee. Hot coffee. Piping-hot coffee . . . Piping-hot coffee that covered his loins. The pain had already hit him by the time he poured the bottle of upholstery cleaner he found in the glove compartment over his thighs.

The hopper, now madly out of control, caromed off the Mutual Life Assurance building, taking a large chunk out of the neon sign before Lister wrestled it back under control, and, still whimpering in pain, headed towards the docks.

The man in the navy-blue officer's coat and the blatantly false moustache flagged down Lister's hopper and got in.

'A hundred-and-fifty-second and third,' he said curtly, and pressed the tash, which was hanging down on the right-hand side, back into place.

'Going to a brothel?' asked Lister amiably.

'Absolutely not,' said the man in the blue officer's coat; 'I'm an officer in the Space Corps' — he tapped the gold bars on his lapel — 'and I do not frequent brothels.'

'I just thought, what with hundred-and-fifty-second and third being slap bang in the middle of the red light area . . .'

'Well, you're not paid to think. You're paid to drive.'

Lister flicked on the 'Hired' sign, slipped the hopper into jump and bounced off to the district the locals affectionately called 'Shag Town'.

On the first landing, the officer's moustache was jolted almost clear of his face.

'What the smeg's wrong with the suspen—' his head disappeared into the soft felting of the cab's roof '—sion . . .!?' He bounced back down into the seat.

'It's the roads,' Lister lied.

They stopped at a blue light. At right angles to them, thirty hoppers sprang forward like a herd of erratic gazelles pursued by a pack of wolves.

'What's it like?'

'What's what like?' said the man, feeling his jaw, convinced a tooth had been loosened in the last landing.

'Being in the Space Corps? Being an astro? I was sort of thinking of signing up.'

'Were you really?' Contempt.

'D'you need any qualifications?'

'Well, not exactly. But they don't just accept any old body, I doubt whether you'd get in.'

Lister felt for the fare-enhancer button he'd found concealed under the dashboard of the taxi, and added a few dollarpounds to the fare. The lights changed and they lurched off, conversation impossible.

Lister had been trying to get off Mimas for nearly six months now. How he'd got there was still something of a mystery.

The last thing he really remembered with any decent clarity was celebrating his birthday back on Earth. He, and six of his very closest friends, decided to usher in his twenty-fifth year by going on a Monopoly board pub-crawl around London. They'd hitched a ride in a frozen-meat truck from Liverpool, and arrived at lunchtime in the Old Kent Road. A drink at each of the squares was the plan. They started with hot toddies to revive them from the ride. In Whitechapel they had pina coladas. King's Cross station, double vodkas. In Euston Road, pints of Guinness. The Angel Islington, mezcals. Pentonville Road, bitter laced with rum and black-currant. And so they continued around the board. By the time they'd got to Oxford Street, only four of them remained. And only two of the four still had the power of speech.

His last real memory was of telling the others he was going to buy a Monopoly board, because no one could remember what the next square was, and stepping out into the cold night air clutching two-thirds of a bottle of saké.

There was a vague, very vague, poorly-lit memory of an advert on the back of a cab seat; something about cheap space travel on Virgin's new batch of demi-light-speed zippers. Something about Saturn being in the heart of the solar system, and businesses were uprooting all the time. Something about it being nearer than you think, at half the speed of light. Something about two hours and ten minutes. And then a thick, black, gunky fog.

He'd woken up slumped across a table in a McDonald's burger bar on Mimas, wearing a lady's pink crimplene hat and a pair of yellow fishing waders, with no money and a passport in the name of 'Emily Berkenstein'. What was more, he had a worrying rash.

He was broke, diseased and 793 million miles from Liverpool.

When Lister got drunk, he really got *drrrrr-unk*.

He brought the hopper to a crunching halt on the corner of hundred-and-fifty-second and third, outside a garish neon sign promising 'Girls, Girls, Girls' and 'Sex, Sex, Sex'.

'I understand,' said the man in the navy-blue officer's coat, surreptitiously re-gluing his moustache, 'there are some excellent restaurants in this area, offering authentic Mimian cuisine.'

'Look,' said Lister as he short-changed the officer, 'd'you want me to pick you up?' He really didn't feel like cruising around in the bone-juddering hopper for another fare. 'I don't mind waiting.'

The officer glanced down the street at the various pimpy types with poorly-concealed weaponry under their coats.

'Fine. Wait round the corner.'

'How long will you be?'

'Well, I'm led to believe the Mimian bladderfish is particularly exquisite, and I would be insane if I didn't at least try the legendary inky squid soup. Plus, of course, pudding, brandy and cigars. Say . . . ten minutes? Call it twenty to be on the safe side.'

Lister took the hopper round the corner, and saw his fare stride purposefully towards a Mimian restaurant, pause outside, studying the menu, then turn and walk straight into the building with the neon sign boasting 'Girls, Girls, Girls' and 'Sex, Sex, Sex.'

Lister locked the door of the hopper. He wasn't totally crazy about this area, safety-wise. He poured what remained of the coffee into the flask lid, and lit a cigarette. What could be nicer, he thought, than smoking Spanish tobacco and drinking real Spanish coffee? Except, possibly, having your whole body vigorously rubbed by a man with a cheese grater.

He was sick of this armpit of a moon.

He'd spent the last six months trying to get the eight hundred dollarpounds he needed to buy a shuttle ticket home. So far he'd saved fifty-three. And he was probably going to blow that tonight.

Making money on Mimas wasn't easy. For a start you needed a work permit, and Lister didn't have a work permit because, officially, he didn't exist. Officially, Lister wasn't here. Officially, he was a space bag lady called Emily Berkenstein. Hence his problem. Which he attempted to solve by stealing taxi hoppers.

Each evening, or at least each evening he felt in the mood, which turned out to be about one evening in four, he'd hang around taxi hopper ranks and wait for the drivers to converge for warmth and conversation in a single cab. When he was convinced it was safe, he'd steal the rear-most hopper and bounce around the seedier districts of the colony, where few taxi cabs and absolutely no police ever went, and pocket the night's takings before abandoning the hopper at a busy rank back at Mimas Central.

If he'd set about his hopper scam in a slightly more business-like way, the chances are he'd have been off Mimas within a month. Unfortunately, he found Mimas so deeply depressing – quite the most hideous place he'd ever been; worse, even than Wolverhampton – that quite regularly he felt compelled to hit the bars and drinking clubs, and blow every single pennycent he'd saved. In some half-assed, subconscious way, he felt, if only he could get drunk enough he was sure to wake up back outside the Marie Lloyd public house, off Regent Street in London, trying to hail a cab to get a Monopoly board.

Sadly, the price of alcohol on Mimas was so outrageously prohibitive, he could only ever buy enough Mimian sangria to get him in the mood to start drinking seriously, before his money ran out and he'd have to slope back to the shuttle port, where he'd hire a left-luggage locker, and sleep in it.

'Life,' thought Lister, 'sucks.'

Outside the hopper two pimps were having a minor disagreement about a girl named Sandra. It was brief and, for the most part, friendly. It ended when the severed ear of the taller pimp landed with a soft, wet plop on the hopper's windscreen.

Lister double-checked the door locks, and suddenly found it important to read the *A to Z* of Mimas with fierce concentration. He was only half-aware of the hopper rocking gently from side to side as the two men rolled on its bonnet.

Suddenly there was another soft, wet plop, and a second, slightly smaller, ear joined the first on his windscreen.

What the hell's happening? thought Lister. *It's raining ears on my windscreen.* He turned on the wipers, and used his window wash. When the windscreen cleared, the ears had gone, and so had the pimps.

Saturday nights on Mimas were wild. So wild, in fact, the Mimians had instigated an eight-day calendar, so that everybody could have two Sundays to recover from Saturday night. Sunday one and Sunday two, then back to work on Monday.

Lister looked at the hopper clock. Forty minutes since the man in the blue officer's coat had gone for his 'meal'. He slipped his taxi-driver's night stick up the arm of his jacket, stepped over the body of a dead, one-eared pimp, and dashed across the trotter towards the building with the 'Girls, Girls, Girls' sign.

FOUR

Denis and Josie were lovers. Not that they actually *made* love. Not any more. They hadn't made love for the last four years; neither of them had been capable of it. Denis was into Bliss, and Josie was a Game head.

Denis huddled in the shop doorway, tugging the remnants of his plastic mackintosh around his knees for warmth, his hangdog eyes searching the busy Mimian street for a 'roll'. Even though it was cold, he was sweating. His stomach had bunched itself into a fist and was trying to punch its way out of his body. He hadn't eaten for two days; his last meal had been a slice of pizza he'd stolen off a drunken astro. But it was a different kind of hunger that was gnawing at him now. He took out a long-empty polythene bag, and licked pathetically at its already well-licked insides. Denis had a second-class degree in Biochemistry. Though, if you asked him now, he probably couldn't even spell Biochemistry.

Josie was sitting by his side, laughing. She'd been laughing for nearly an hour. Her long, once-blonde hair was matted into a series of whips which lashed at her pale, grimy face as she tossed her head, giggling idiotically. Of the two, she was the really smart one. Josie had a first-class degree in Pure Mathematics. Only, right now she couldn't even have counted her legs.

They'd met at the New Zodiac Festival six years earlier, when the Earth's polar star had changed and the entire zodiac had to be realigned. Everybody shifted one star sign forward.

Josie had moved from Libra to Scorpio, and Denis had changed from Sagittarius to Capricorn. It was a turning-point in both their lives: they both felt so much happier with their new star signs and, along with the other five thousand-or-so space beatniks who'd gathered for the four-day festival in the Sea of Tranquillity, they'd taken many, many drugs, and talked about how profoundly the shifting constellations had changed them, and how maybe the druids were the only dudes who'd ever really got it right.

Now they were on their way to Neptune, for Pluto's solstice, when Pluto took over from Neptune as the outermost planet of the solar system. They'd been travelling for five years, and so far they'd only managed to bum their way up to Saturn. Still, they weren't in a particular hurry – the solstice wasn't going to happen for another fifty years.

So Denis scanned the street for a roll while Josie sat beside him, laughing. Across her brow gleamed the metal band of a Game head. Underneath it, needle-thin electrodes punctured the skull and burrowed into her frontal lobes and hypo-thalamus.

The Game started out actually as a game. It was intended to be the zenith of computer game technology. Tiny com-puter chips in the electrodes transmitted signals directly to the brain. No screens, no joysticks – you were really there, wherever you wanted to be. Inside your head, your fantasies were fulfilled. The Game had been marketed as 'Better Than Life'. It was only a month after its release that people realized it was addictive. 'Better Than Life' was withdrawn from the market, but illicit electronic labs began to make copies.

It was the ultimate hallucinogen, with only one real major drawback.

It killed you.

Once you entered 'Better Than Life', once you put on the headband and the needles wormed into your mind, it was almost impossible to get out.

This was partly because you weren't even aware you were in 'Better Than Life' in the first place. The Game protected itself, hid itself from your memory. Your conscious mind was totally subverted, while your body slowly withered and died. At first, well-meaning friends tried to rescue Game heads by yanking the headset out of the skull, but this always resulted in instant death from shock. The only way out of the Game was to want to leave it. But no one ever wanted to leave.

Most Game heads, unable to look after themselves, died very quickly. But Josie had Denis. And Denis at least shared his food with her, and kept her alive. When Josie first bought the headset from a South African Game dealer on Callisto, she'd urged Denis to get a set too. She wanted to try 'multi-using', when two or more headsets were connected together, so the users could share the same fantasy.

But Denis was into Bliss.

Bliss was a unique designer drug. Unique for two reasons. The first was that you could get addicted to Bliss just by looking at it. Which made it very hard for the police to carry out drug busts. The second was its effect. It made you believe you were God. It made you feel as if you were all-seeing, all-knowing, eternal and omnipotent. Which was laughable, really, because when you were on Bliss you couldn't even lace your shoes. The Bliss high lasted fifteen minutes; after coming down, the resulting depression lasted twenty-five years. Few people could live with it, so they had to take another belt.

Denis took off his boot, unrolled a second polythene bag, which contained a teaspoonful of the soil-coloured substance, and toyed with it pensively. He always saved a final belt for when he needed to roll someone for money. Which is what he was going to do right now.

Lister should have known better. He'd been on Mimas long

enough to know not to turn round when he heard the voice. He should have put his head down and run. But he didn't. And by the time he worked out what was happening, it was too late.

'Stop, my son!' the voice bellowed, and Lister twisted to see the Bliss freak in the plastic mackintosh swaggering towards him in a Mysterious Way.

'Dost thou knoweth who I am?'

Lister's eyes darted from side to side, looking for an exit, but the Bliss freak edged him into a doorway, and there was nowhere to go.

'Dost thou knoweth who I am?' he repeated.

Yes, thought Lister, *you're a smegging Bliss freak.*

'Yes,' he said aloud, 'you're God, right?'

Denis beamed and nodded sagely. The mortal had recognized Him. Not everybody did.

'That's right. I am God. And I have cometh to thee for a mighty purpose. I need some of your mortal money.'

Lister nodded. 'Look, I'm completely strapped, man. I've got absolutely nothing on me. Not a bean.'

The Bliss freak sighed heavily, trying to contain His wrath. 'Would you like Me to call down a mighty plague, and lay waste this entire world?'

'No.' Lister shook his head.

'Would you like to be turned into a pillar of salt?'

'No.' Lister shook his head again.

'Then give Me some money.'

'Look, I've told you. I'm broke.'

The Bliss freak stuck his right hand into the pocket of his ragged raincoat. 'I've got something in here that can hurt you.'

Lister eyed him up and down. He wasn't that big, actually. And what did he have in his raincoat pocket that could hurt him? A lightning bolt? He decided to stand his ground.

'I don't believe you,' he said, smiling pleasantly.

The Bliss freak took his hand out of his pocket and showed Lister what he had in there that could hurt him.

It was his fist.

He swung it round, hitting Lister on the side of his face. The punch had no strength, but it took Lister by surprise. He banged his head against the edge of the doorframe, and went down.

When he came to, barely thirty seconds later, his fifty-three dollarpounds had gone, and so had God.

FIVE

Lister made his way shakily down the brothel's dusky staircase and stepped onto the red, thick-pile carpet of the main reception area. Plastic palm trees encircled a vast, artificial, heart-shaped lagoon in pink tile. Phallus-shaped diving boards cast frightening shadows onto the softly gurgling water, while Chinese chimes, bedecked with glass erotica, tinkled in the strawberry-scented breeze of the air conditioner. A black, fake marble staircase led up to a mezzanine level, where twenty-odd clam-shaped doors marked 'Love Suites' circled the room. Music, which sounded as if all its charm and energy had been surgically removed, trickled out of a number of breast-shaped speakers. Various fat men of various nationalities sat around the lagoon in white towels, sipping fake champagne cocktails.

In front of Lister a small red-haired man, with a porky roll of flesh above his towel-top, was examining a line of girls.

'This one's face . . .'

'Jeanette's face . . .' The Madame followed behind him, taking notes.

'This one's breasts . . .'

'Candy's bosom. An excellent and most popular choice.'

'Legs: I'll have the right one from her, and the left one from her.'

The Madame scribbled furiously.

'Barbie's right . . . Tina's left. And what would sir like, bottom-wise?'

'Uh . . . I think this one.'

'Mandy's derrière.'

The Madame clapped her hands, and two engineers began dismantling the android girls then re-assembling them according to the client's order.

Lister watched, trying to keep his lunch in his stomach, as limbs were changed and buttocks swapped, much to the apparent excitement of the small red-haired man.

The Madame turned to Lister. 'Sorry to keep you waiting, sir. Would you like a pick'n'mix or an off-the-peg?'

'No, I don't want a girl . . .'

'That's absolutely no problem at all, sir – we have some beautiful boy-droids.'

'No, – uh, this is kind of, uh, embarrassing . . .'

'I understand.' She smiled. Before Lister could stop her, the Madame clapped her hands and a flock of android sheep baa-ed their way noisily into the reception area.

'No, look . . . listen . . .'

'Baa.'

'Yes, sir?'

'Baaaaaaaaa.'

'You don't understand . . .'

One of the sheep turned, winked at him coquettishly, and wiggled off, hips swaying provocatively, towards the marble staircase.

'Oh my God, no. I'm looking for someone. I'm supposed to collect him.'

Lister described his fare, and the Madame led him through to a rest room.

The man with the false moustache was sitting in a Jacuzzi, having a heated conversation with a member of staff.

'I want my money back.'

'Absolutely sir. This has never happened before.'

'She nearly pulled the damned thing off.'

'There was a slight circuitry problem . . .'

'She wouldn't stop. It was like being trapped in a milking machine.'

'Well, if sir would care to make another choice, at the expense of the management –'

'Are you insane? It'll be out of commission for at least twelve months! If you hadn't heard my screams . . .' He looked up and saw Lister for the first time. There was an extraordinarily long pause.

'You know,' he continued, pretending he hadn't seen Lister, 'I don't think this is a restaurant at all. I haven't seen so much as a *soupçon* of the spicy bladderfish for which Mimas enjoys such a splendid reputation. I thought it was a bit strange the way you insisted I take off my clothes and wear this skimpy towel. In fact, if you want to know what I think: I don't think this *is* a small bijou eaterie. I think it's a smegging brothel.'

The officer continued his protestations of innocence all the way back to the docks.

The hopper lurched to a halt outside the shuttleport hopper rank. Lister's fare climbed painfully from the cab, paid up, and leaned conspiratorially into Lister's window.

'Look,' said the officer, his moustache still skew-whiff and curling at the edges from the heat of the Turkish bath, 'Space Corps-wise, I'm pretty much a high-flier; and career-wise' – he looked around – 'it might not be such an A1 wonderful idea if this little adventure were to go any further.'

Lister held out his hand, and the man pressed one dollarpound into his palm and winked.

'Go on,' he said, 'enjoy yourself on me.'

Lister let him limp up to the automatic doors in the docking port before he leaned out of the window and shouted. 'Hey, whoremonger!'

The man raced back. 'Keep your voice down, for mercy's sake – people can hear.'

'You made a mistake. Instead of a hundred dollarpound tip, you've only given me a one dollarpound tip.'

'Right,' said the officer, loosening the buckle on his money belt and extracting a brown leather purse, 'it's a dirty world, and I suppose I'm going to have a pay the toll.' He handed over a stale-smelling note.

'You're very kind.' Lister took the note and stuck it behind the upturned earmuffs of his leather deerstalker. 'Very kind.'

'Just provided we understand: this is the end of the matter.'

'Sure.'

'Don't try coming back for more. Don't cross me, OK?'

'Sure.'

'Nobody crosses Christopher Todhunter and gets away with it.'

He closed his purse, which was monogrammed: 'Arnold J. Rimmer, BSc, SSc', and walked back across the forecourt.

Lister leaned out of the window. 'See you, Rimmer.'

'Yeah. 'Bye,' said Rimmer, absently.

SIX

George McIntyre placed the antique Smith and Wesson in his mouth and pulled the trigger. His last thought was: *I bet this doesn't work.* But he was wrong.

The bullet passed through the back of his head, killing him instantly, before it sailed through his rubber plant and ended its brief but eventful journey in the wall of his office.

The rubber plant was surprised. If the rubber plant could have spoken, it wouldn't have said anything. That's how surprised the rubber plant was. Over the last few weeks it had witnessed the gradual deterioration of McIntyre's mental health, but if the rubber plant had had a name it would have said: 'George McIntyre is not the kind of guy to commit suicide, or my name's not . . .' – whatever its name would have been, had it had one.

Three medical orderlies duly arrived, followed by two doctors, the Captain, the Morale Officer, and the ship's Head of Security. They put McIntyre's body on a stretcher and took him away.

Eight people in all passed through McIntyre's room, and not one of them, the rubber plant reflected rather bitterly, had expressed the slightest interest in the gaping bullet hole which went straight through the middle of his favourite leaf. His biggest and greenest leaf. The only leaf he was truly one hundred per cent happy with.

The humans muttered darkly about why McIntyre would

have done such a thing. The rubber plant knew, but it wouldn't have told them, even if it could have.

Saunders lay on the brown leather couch in the medical unit. Or so it appeared to the naked eye. In actuality, he was suspended half a millimetre or so above it. The hologramatic illusion of Saunders' body was provided by a light bee. The light bee, a minute projection device the size of a pin head, hovered in the middle of his body receiving data from the Hologram Simulation Suite, which it then transmitted into a 3-D form.

The effect was so convincing, so real, that all holograms bore a two-inch high, metallic-looking 'H' on their foreheads, so they could never be mistaken for living people. The stigma of the Dead. Not the mark of Cain, the killer, but the mark of Abel, the slain.

And so Saunders lay suspended an infinitesimal distance above the brown leather couch in the medical unit, trying to fend off a vision of his wife's seduction of the entire offensive line of the London Jets' Zero-Gee football team.

'There was a Being,' the metaphysical psychiatrist was saying, 'and this Being was called "Frank Saunders". Now, that Being died.'

'Yes,' said Saunders, 'he was hit on the head by a four thousand kilogram demolition ball. He couldn't be deader.'

The good doctor shifted in his seat, re-crossed his thin legs, and tugged thoughtfully on his long nose. 'Frank,' he said eventually, 'let me ask you a question. Do you believe man has an eternal soul?'

'I don't know,' Saunders said, wide-eyed with exasperation. 'I'm from Sidcup. I'm an engineer.'

'I do, Frank.'

'Do you?'

'Yes, I do. And I believe, as we speak, Frank, your eternal soul has passed on to the next plane of existence, where it's very happy.'

'The point is,' Saunders said, 'if you have an eternal soul, then there's got to be something badly wrong when it's having a lot more fun than you.'

'Look,' the metaphysical psychiatrist continued unabashed; 'you are *not* the Being called Frank Saunders. The Being called Frank Saunders no longer exists in this dimension.'

'So, who's lying on this brown leather couch talking to you, then?'

'You, Frank, are a simulation of Frank Saunders. You act in the way the computer estimates Frank Saunders would probably have acted. You are a simulation of a *possible* Frank Saunders, or, rather more accurately, a *probable* Frank Saunders.' He said this very slowly, as if he were talking to a small baby who'd splattered mashed apple and apricot dessert over the jacket of his father's new suit.

So Saunders was a computer simulation of a probability of a possible person. He didn't *feel* like a computer simulation of a probability of a possible person. He also didn't feel like listening to another philosophical discussion about the nature of Reality.

What he *did* feel like doing was taking a small ball-peen hammer and tapping it several times on top of the balding pate of the metaphysical psychiatrist who was now twittering on about tables – in particular, tables which had a quality of 'tableness'. And then, when Saunders was completely lost, the balding counsellor asked him if he was familiar with 'The Cartesian Principle'.

'Yes,' Saunders nodded. 'Didn't they get to number five with *Baby, I want your Love Thing*?'

'No, Frank. The Cartesian Principle is: "I think, therefore I am." And although you're not thinking, the computer is just making you think you're thinking; nevertheless, you think you're thinking, therefore you possibly are.'

'I possibly are?'

'Yes, Frank.' The psychiatrist smiled, believing Saunders had grasped the concept at last.

For a short time Saunders listened to the relentless clicking of the clock in the corner.

'I possibly are what?'

'You possibly *are!*'

'Ah! I possibly are!'

'Yes!' The Counsellor beamed.

'Well, thank you for all your help.' Saunders got up and made his way to the exit hatch. 'If I have any other little difficulties, any other little problems I don't understand, rest assured I'll be round in a shot.'

'I really have been of help?'

'None at all.' Saunders smiled for the first time in two weeks. 'You're a useless big-nosed goit.'

As Saunders turned to go, Weiner raced through his holo-gramatic body, and into the medical unit.

'Sorry, Frank,' she said, turning to Saunders.

'Doesn't matter. It's not as if I *am* – I only possibly are, anyway.'

Weiner crossed into the room, her face flushed from run-ning.

'I've got some bad news, Frank. You'd better sit down.'

Saunders was a little bemused as to what could possibly constitute bad news for a dead man.

As Weiner relayed the news of McIntyre's suicide, the consequences began to dawn on Saunders. McIntyre was a flight co-ordinator. He outranked Saunders. Hologram sim-ulation of a full human personality took up forty per cent of the computer's run-time, and burned up enough energy per second to illuminate Paris for three years, which was why *Red Dwarf* was only able to sustain one hologram at a time. With his superior rank, McIntyre would take precedence over Saunders and become the ship hologram.

'So,' he said, slowly, 'I'm going to be turned off.'

'Maybe not,' said the psychiatrist. 'He committed suicide. Maybe he's unstable; not suitable for revival.'

'Of course he is,' Saunders said firmly. 'I'm going to be turned off. I'm going to die for a second time in a fortnight.' He gave the air a celebratory uppercut and danced a little jig of joy. 'Smegging great!'

SEVEN

'Surname?'

'David.'

'First name?'

'I told you: David.'

'Your name's David David?'

'No, it's David Lister.'

Caldicott sighed and reached for the Tipp-Ex.

Lister gazed out onto the busy Mimian street and tried to read the sign on the window: 'ERTNEC TNEM-TIURCER NOITAROPROC GNINIM RETIPUJ'.

On a poster on the wall of the newly-painted office, two crisply uniformed officers, male and female, linked arms and smilingly invited all and sundry to 'Join the Corps and see Space'.

Caldicott Tipp-Exed out 'David' from the surname box on the recruitment form and, in his meticulously neat handwriting, replaced it with 'Lister'.

'Date of birth?'

'Unknown.'

'What d'you mean, unknown?'

'I was found.'

'In what way "found"?'

'In a pub. Under the pool table.' Lister paused. 'In a cardboard box.'

Caldicott eyed him dubiously. Caldicott spent his entire

working day sitting in his immaculate white uniform in the window of the recruitment centre, projecting the Space Corps' corporate image. Which was white and brave, strong and smiling. Once the suckers had signed up, they'd learn the truth soon enough. In the meantime, it was his job to be white and brave, strong and smiling.

He looked at the object sitting opposite him, presently working some unspeakable substances from the tracks on the soles of his boots with one of Caldicott's pencils. Four or five gangly, matted plaits dangled from under the fur-rimmed leather deerstalker atop a podgy face built for a perpetual smile. Short, fat fingers, the nails blotched white from zinc deficiency, scratched at the gap between the top of green, multi-stained combat trousers and the bottom of a T-shirt, whose original colour was long lost in the mists of time. He looked like a casualty in a catering war: as if all the world's chefs had had a gigantic food fight, and somehow he'd got caught in the middle. If his daughter had brought home this specimen, Caldicott reflected, he would have shot them both without a second's reflection.

'Do you know when you were found?' He smiled whitely.

'Some time in November. 'Fifty-five.'

'Well, I need a date of birth for the form. When do you celebrate your birthday?'

'Most of the time, actually.'

'I'll put 1st November, 2155.'

'Not November. I was about six weeks old then. It was probably some time in October.'

Caldicott reached for the Tipp-Ex again.

'How about 14th October?'

'Brutal.'

'Why do you want to join the Space Corps?'

Lister thought for a moment. 'I want,' he said, 'to visit strange new worlds, to seek out new life and new civilizations. To boldly go where no person has gone before.'

Caldicott smiled wanly and wrote: 'Possible Attitude Problem' in the comments box.

'Qualifications?'

'Technical Drawing.'

'What level?'

'What d'you mean?'

'Master's degree, perhaps?' said Caldicott, almost imperceptibly raising his left eyebrow. 'Ph.D., maybe?'

'GCSE.'

Caldicott wrote '1 GCSE, Technical Drawing'.

'It doesn't really count, though, that, does it?' Lister picked at a flap of rubber hanging from the sole of his boot.

'Why not?'

'I failed.'

Caldicott took out the Tipp-Ex again and obliterated the word 'Possible'.

'If you'd just like to read through this, and sign where I've indicated.' Caldicott pushed over the application papers, picked up the phone and stabbed in a ten-digit number.

Lister cast his eyes over the conditions of employment. He was signing up for five years. Five long years. When he got out, he'd be pushing thirty. An old man.

Ha! Want to bet?

He wondered why he hadn't thought of this before. Join the Space Corps, get on an Earth-bound ship, and as soon as he got home: thank you, goodnight. Lister, David, AWOL.

He signed and pocketed the pen, including its metal chain and holder.

'OK,' said Caldicott, putting down the phone, 'the situation is this: there are fourteen ships in dock, but no vacancies for anyone with your . . . abilities.'

'What are my abilities?'

'You haven't got any. You'll have to enter at third technician level.'

'Technician?' repeated Lister, impressed.

'That's right,' said Caldicott, smiling.

A third technician's duties basically consisted of making sure the vending machines didn't run out of chicken soup, mopping floors, and a thousand-and-one other tasks considered too menial for the service droids. Caldicott didn't feel this was absolutely the best time to put Lister in the picture.

'Tech-nishern,' said Lister, putting on a pseudo-swanky voice. He glanced up at the white uniformed officer with the Burt Lancaster smile in the poster. 'I'm a bleeding technishern, don't yew know.'

'As soon as something crops up, we'll let you know. Leave your address.'

'Address?' Lister wondered what to put.

He settled on: 'Luggage locker 4179, Mimas Central Shuttle Station.'

EIGHT

'Shuttle Flight JMC159 for *White Giant* now boarding at gate number five,' the tannoy announced, and proceeded to make the same announcement in Esperanto, German and three different dialects of Chinese.

A group of miners stubbed out their cigarettes and finished their beers, then reluctantly swung their kit-bags over their shoulders before joining a group of white-suited officers and some grey-suited technicians in the queue to gate five.

Two Shore Patrol officers strode through the milling crowds, casually swinging their argument-settlers. People pretended not to look at them. You didn't mess with the Shore Patrol. Not unless you wanted your skull rearranged to resemble a relief map of Mars, canals and all.

'This has got to be a joke.'

'This is the address we were given,' said the blonde.

They stopped at the huge bank of luggage lockers and looked around, searching for number 4179. The dark-haired one banged on the door.

'This has got to be a joke,' she repeated.

Lister was awakened from a dream about a pickle sandwich that spoke fluent Italian by the deafening metallic clanging, as Shore Patrolwoman Henderson beat the luggage locker door with her steel truncheon.

'It's a joke. I'm telling you.'

'Hang on,' called Lister. 'Let me get dressed.' In the

confined space of the locker, which was designed to accommodate two smallish suitcases, he groped around in the blackness, located his clothes, and pulled on his coffee-and-upholstery polish-stained trousers. 'Who is it?'

'Shore Patrol. We're looking for a guy called "Lister".'

'I'll see if he's in,' called out Lister, stalling for time. 'Uh . . . why d'you want him?'

'He's been assigned. They've found him a ship.'

The door opened and Lister jumped the six feet down to the ground. He cupped his chin in one hand, placed the other on the back of his neck and snapped his head to one side, to the accompaniment of a series of stomach-churning cracks.

'Your papers have come through,' said Henderson, 'and –'

'Wait a minute,' said Lister; 'I can't see yet. Give me a minute.'

He blinked a few times and rubbed his eyes. Slowly, the two Shore Patrolwomen came into focus.

'Hi,' said Lister. 'I'd invite you in, but it's a bit of a mess. It's more of a bachelor luggage-locker than –'

'How long have you been sleeping in there?' Henderson interrupted.

'Since my second night on Mimas. I tried sleeping on a park bench, but I woke up in the middle of the night completely naked, and this old Chinese guy was licking my foot. So, compared with that, this is the Mimas Hilton.'

'No work permit, right?'

'I have, actually, but it belongs to a woman called Emily Berkenstein. It's a long story.'

'Get your stuff together.'

'I've got my stuff together.'

'Where is it?'

'In my pocket.'

They walked back across the shuttle lounge towards the departure gates.

'We've got to deliver you to gate nine.'

'Time for breakfast?'

'If you make it quick.'

Lister peeled off from his escort and, without ever stopping, walked through the Nice'n'Noodly Kwik-Food bar, picking up a half-eaten soya sandwich and a three-quarter finished noodle burger that people with weaker constitutions had left behind.

'You're probably thinking I'm a slob,' said Lister, finishing off a quintuple-thick milkshake and hoovering around the base with the straw. 'But I'm not – I'm just hungry, O K?'

'Hey, it's a real pity you've got to go on this ship, and everything,' said Henderson; 'because, otherwise, you could maybe have taken me out for dinner. You know, a couple of half-eaten egg rolls. Maybe root through a bin for the remnants of a Kentucky Fried Chicken. Then back to your place for half a bottle of paraffin. It could have been so romantic.'

'Well, listen,' said Lister, totally missing the irony, 'I'm not exactly married to this spaceship idea. Why don't we do it? Just promise not to bring your steel truncheon.'

> 'To Ganymede and Titan,
> Yes, sir, I've been around,
> But there ain't no place
> In the whole of Space,
> Like that good ol' toddlin' town . . .
>
> Lunar City Seven,
> You're my idea of heaven.
> Out of ten, you score eleven,
> You good ol' artificial terra-formed
> settlement . . .'

Through the shuttle's tinny sound system Perry N'Kwomo,

the African ballad singer, was crooning one of the many 'easy listening' hits from his best-selling album, *Nice 'n' Nauseating*.

Lister sat in the packed shuttle with the rest of the new recruits on the twenty-five minute jag up to their assigned ship, gazing out from his window seat as Mimas dropped away below him like a bad taste he'd spat into the night.

He thumbed through the shuttle's in-flight magazine, *Up, Up, And Away!* He stared for a brief moment at the blisteringly unpromising contents page: 'Salt – An Epicure's Delight'; 'Classic Wines of Estonia'; and 'Weaving the Traditional Way' were just some of the more fascinating articles. How is it possible, Lister wondered, to fill a hundred-and-twenty-page magazine without actually including anything remotely readable? He tucked it back into the netting of the seat in front of him, and decided to read the plastic card containing the crash-landing instructions for the second time.

The shuttle buzzed slowly through the groups of gargantuan space freighters that bobbed in orbit like a bunch of clumsy balloons.

Aerodynamics was never a consideration in starship design. All the ships were constructed in orbit, designed never to land, never to encounter wind resistance or gravity, and were consequently, a variety of bizarre and outlandish shapes.

For five full minutes the shuttle ran alongside a supply ship called the *Arthur C. Clarke*: a two-mile length of dirty grey steel, orange lights dotting the huge, bulbous cargo hold, out of which sprang a long, thick, tubular nose section, curling and twisting like the stem of an oriental hookah.

Eventually the shuttle reached the cusp of the star freighter's bulb, and turned.

Lister's window was filled with red.

And red.

And red.

He couldn't see where it started and he couldn't see where it finished. But it was big. No, it was *BIG*.

A big, red, red, big clenched fist of metal.

As the shuttle accelerated towards the redness, details slowly emerged through the thick gloom of space. Gradually, Lister made out the thousands of tiny pin-pricks of windows and a tooth floss-thin line of light ringing the ship: the vessel's metro system.

A huge, shadowy carbuncle jutted out a mile or so from the red monster's belly – a small moon, torn out of orbit, had flung itself into the ship's solar plexus and was now embedded in the hull, hanging there like a giant stone leech.

As the shuttle swung out to align itself for docking, the red ship's nose-cone loomed into view – six half-mile steel poles, bound by magnetic cable, as if the fist were clutching a huge shuttlecock. This was the scoop. The scoop sucked hydrogen from the currents of space and converted it into fuel, theoretically making the ship capable of travelling forever.

Lister was aware of the hot whisky breath of the burly astro beside him, who was now leaning over him to share his window.

'The *Dwarf*,' he said in a Danish accent, ripping open another can of Glen Fujiyama.

'The what?' Lister tried not to inhale.

'*Red Dwarf*.'

'How *big* is it?'

'It could eat Copenhagen,' said the Dane, 'and have Helsingør for afters.'

Lister accepted a belt from the whisky can, and they swapped names.

'It's got to be five miles long.'

'Something like that,' said Petersen.

Lister squinted out of the window again. 'And God, is it ugly!'

'Ugly as my mother.' Petersen smiled through bar-brawl broken teeth. 'First trip?'

Lister nodded.

Petersen belched, crumpled up the whisky can, tossed it into the aisle, and fished in his knapsack for another. 'I'd offer you one,' he said apologetically, 'but I have only twelve left. Been on Mimas long?'

'Six months.'

'It's a bit of a dump, right?'

'It's a lot of a dump.'

'Wait till we get to Triton. Triton's OK.'

'Triton?' Lister's brow furrowed. 'We're going to Earth.'

'Sure, we're going to Earth. But first we've got to go to Triton to get the ore to take to Earth.'

Lister closed his eyes. 'Where's Triton?'

'Round Neptune.'

'Oh,' said Lister. 'Neptune. Right.' He took a swig from Petersen's nearly-empty whisky can. 'Where's Neptune?'

'From here?' Petersen took out a calculator. 'I'll tell you exactly.' He punched a lot of numbers into the machine. 'It's two billion, seven hundred and seven million miles away.'

Lister sighed like a burst tyre. 'How long is that going to take?'

'Say, eighteen months,' said Petersen. 'Eighteen months, not counting Customs. And Triton Immigration Control is a son-of-a-bitch. It's worse than New York.'

'Eighteen months?'

'Then twelve months' mining,'

'Twelve months' *mining*?'

'Then two more years to get back to Earth.'

'Four-and-a-half-years?'

'It's an old ship. It only does two hundred thousand miles an hour.'

'Four-and-a-half-years,' Lister repeated like a mantra, 'Four-and-a-half-years.'

He turned and looked out of the window as the shuttle ducked into the trench cut deep into *Red Dwarf*'s back. On either side, buildings flitted past: skyscrapers, tower blocks a hundred storeys high; monoliths of steel and glass. One minute it was as if they were flying through Manhattan; then without warning the architecture changed, and it looked like Moscow; then fluted pillars and elaborate neo-classic arches, and they could have been in New Athens: a tasteless mish-mash of styles from the decades upon decades the vast mining ship had taken to build.

For a tantalizing moment, between a huge mosque-shaped dome and a line of industrial chimneys, the tiny blue light that was Earth winked and flickered invitingly in the glow of the distant Sun, then just as suddenly was gone, as they swooped towards the yawning doors of the docking bay.

'Four-and-a-half-years,' said Lister catatonically.

NINE

Lister pushed through the crowded docking bay, fighting his way to the Intake Clearance Zone, a now moronically drunk Petersen in tow. They'd been stopped at *Red Dwarf* customs and Petersen had been bag-searched. His possessions had comprised a toothbrush, one pair of underpants, three socks and eleven cans of whisky. Informed that he couldn't bring the liquor aboard without paying duty, he had stood in the green channel and downed all eleven cans, one after the other, offering Lister a sip a can.

Now Petersen was walking sideways, his head cocked at a curious angle, singing a lewd Danish folk song, punctuated with appropriate gestures and slobbering leers, as Lister dragged him by his lapel towards the moving walkway.

High above, dominating the ship's shuttle port, was a monitor screen the size of a football pitch, from which a disembodied head was lugubriously dispensing information. The head was a digitalized reproduction of a balding forty-year-old man, with a voice that had a slight East London twang.

'The floor's stopped moving,' said Petersen as they reached the end of the walkway; 'that's a very good thing.'

Lister scanned the various name-cards that *Red Dwarf* induction staff were holding above the heads of the jostling crowd.

'Hi, I'm Chomsky.'

'Chomsky? Pierre, right?' Rogerson ticked his clipboard.

'OK stand there a second. We're still looking for a Burroughs, a Petersen, a Schmidt and a Lister.'

'I'm a Lister,' said Lister.

'I'm going to be sick,' said Petersen. And he was. Exorcist sick.

'Yerrrrrrrrrgh.

'YAAAAAAAAAAAAAAAAAARGHHHHHH.'

A pause. A sigh.

'Yuuuuuuuuuuuuuuuuuuuuuuuuuuuuuuuuuuuuuuuuuuurh.

'Yurgh.' Petersen smacked his lips and wiped his face with the back of his sleeve. 'That's better.'

Two skutters, claw-headed service droids which looked like miniature amputee giraffes on motorized bases, swept into view and cleaned up the mess. Petersen tried to tip them.

'We're still looking for a Burroughs and a Schmidt,' Rogerson said, trying to disguise his disgust.

'What's that thing?' asked Lister, pointing up to the disembodied head on the monitor screen.

'Holly, the ship's computer. He's got an IQ of six thousand. You want to ask him a question?'

'Like what?'

'Like anything at all.' Rogerson called up to the ceiling; 'Hey, Holly – this is Lister . . .'

The huge eyes rolled down in their direction. 'I know. Lister, David. Date of birth, 14th October, 2155. Qualifications: GCSE, Technical Drawing, failed. Rank: Technician, Third Class. Ambitions: to visit strange new worlds, to seek out new life and new civilizations: to boldly go where no person has gone before. All right, Dave?' A huge eyelid rolled over the digital eye and winked at Lister.

'Ask him something,' Rogerson urged.

'Who holds the all-time record for three-dimensional yardage in a single Zero–Gee football season?'

'Jim Bexley Speed, London Jets Roof Attack, season '74–

'75. Four thousand, six hundred and thirty-six square yards in the regular season.'

'And what colour tie was he wearing when he was interviewed by Mark Matheson after Megabowl 102?'

'Aquamarine, with a diagonal lemon stripe.'

'Brutal.' Lister grinned.

Chomsky chipped in: 'Who was the Chinese Emperor of the Ming dynasty in 1620?'

'T'ai-ch'ang,' Holly replied immediately; 'also known as Chu Ch'ang-lo Kuang Tsung. Born 1582.'

They all began shouting questions: 'Who was the...?' 'How many...?' 'When did...?' and, one by one, Holly got them right.

Finally Petersen asked a question. 'Why is the room going round and round?'

'Because you're drunk,' said Holly.

'That's *riiiiight!*' Petersen clapped, delighted.

Burroughs and Schmidt finally arrived, and the ten of them were herded onto the *Red Dwarf*'s Northern Line, one of a network of tube trains which criss-crossed the length and breadth of the ship. Spread evenly throughout the carriage were more monitors displaying the genius computer, who was capable of conducting several thousand conversations simultaneously, ranging from what was on the ship's movie channel that night to discussing the melding of quantum mechanics and general relativity.

Some thirty minutes later they boarded the Xpress super lift, which whisked them up to Floor 9,172, where they were met by a ship rover – a three wheel electric buggy-bus – and driven down two miles of corridors towards the sleeping quarter, Area P.

'OK,' said Rogerson, showing Lister into his sleeping quarters. 'Make yourself at home. I'll just go and fix up the other guys.'

Lister looked round the room which was going to be his

home for the next four-and-a-half years. Dull, gunmetal grey walls reflected his mood. Neon strips around the walls simulated the time of day. Dirty yellow at the moment signalled the middle of the afternoon. A dirty orange would signal early evening, and a dirty blue would indicate night.

Two bunk cubicles were carved into recesses in the wall, one above the other. To the right stood a simple pedestal wash basin and mirror, which, when voice-activated, swivelled on its base to reveal an antiquated chemical toilet bearing the legend: 'Now please irradiate your hands'. Lister began to wish he was in his nice, cosy luggage locker back at Mimas Central.

Behind him was a bank of fitted aluminium wardrobes, and two steps led down to what was laughingly sign-posted 'Lounge Area'. The lounge area was about two metres square, with a three-seater reinforced steel settee, and a tiny coffee table welded to the floor.

Nice, thought Lister. *Very homely*.

The other occupant of the room left very little evidence of his existence. Whatever he did possess was meticulously tidied away. On the wall of his bunk, the lower one, hung a home-made revision timetable in worryingly neat handwriting, and an array of startlingly complex colour codes. Beside it were a number of certificates, neatly framed, and a series of cut-out newspaper headlines, all along the lines of: 'Arnie Does It Best'; 'Arnie Comes Out On Top'; and 'Arnold – A Living Legend'.

Lister scanned the titles in the bookcase built into a recess above the video screen: *Astronavigation and Invisible Number Theory Made Simple*; *Conceptual Foundations of Quantum Mechanics Made Simple*; *Heisenberg's Uncertainty Principle for Beginners*; *An Introduction to the Liar Paradox and the Non-Mechanizability of Mathematics;* and *How to Get More Girls by Hypnosis*.

He opened his bunk-mate's wardrobe and peered in.

Twenty pairs of identical, military blue underpants hung on coat hangers in protective cellophane sheaths, next to seven pairs of pale blue pyjamas, with dry-cleaning tags pinned to the collars. Lister was disturbed to see that the pockets of the pyjamas bore an insignia of rank. Brightly polished boots stared unblinkingly in rows on the floor. A pair of mono-grammed slippers on the shoe-trees stood beside them.

Lister closed the wardrobe, struck a match on the 'No Smoking' sign, lit up, and sat down on the metal settee.

'Nice. Very, very nice.'

Rogerson came back in. 'Oh, David, meet your bunk-mate . . .'

Lister looked up. Behind Rogerson stood a grey-suited technician; tall and rangy, flared nostrils and wide, slightly manic eyes and a hyperactive, constantly jiggling right leg that always seemed to want to be somewhere else. Even without his false moustache, there was no mistaking the 'officer' who'd hired his hopper.

'He's also your shift leader, so he's the guy who'll be showing you the ropes. Lister, this is First Technician –'

'Arnold Rimmer,' said Lister. 'We've already met.'

'No, we haven't,' said Rimmer, smiling too much.

'You're a technician,' said Lister, surprised. 'I thought you said you were an officer.'

'Shut up,' said Rimmer, pumping his hand and smiling even harder.

TEN

On the first morning into space, Lister sat in the lecture theatre, with the other eleven members of Z Shift, in his brand new technician's uniform which made him itch in nineteen different places, while his left arm and his right buttock competed for the title 'Most Painful Appendage', following his twelve inoculation jabs.

The rest of the previous morning and the whole of the afternoon had been a long process of multifarious humiliations: hours standing around in backless surgical gowns (*Why* backless? When did a surgeon ever need to get to your bottom in a hurry?) giving various bodily fluid samples – Petersen had, in fact, delivered rather more bodily fluid samples than was absolutely necessary, and nobody was pleased; IQ tests; genetic fingerprinting; hand-to-eye co-ordination work; centrifugal weightlessness simulation; then, finally, they'd all been marched like a serpent of school children down to the computer decks, where they each had their personalities recorded for storage in the hologram library. Lister had sat in the suite, a metal skull-cap bolted to his head, while his every memory and personality trait had been logged onto a depressingly small computer slug. His entire life; his whole personality copied and duplicated on a piece of computer hardware the size of a suppository. Petersen's recording had crashed three times, with an error-message which read 'Non-Human Lifeform'. In the end, they had to drip-feed him coffee and subject him to several very cold showers before his brain was functioning sufficiently well to be recorded. If, in the highly unlikely circumstance of Petersen achieving the status of 'Indispensable Personnel', and then dying, he would be retrieved as a hologram with the mater and pater of all hangovers.

The lecture theatre hatchway breezed open, and Rimmer clicked up to the podium in boots so brightly polished you could see infinity in them.

The previous evening in the sleeping quarters, no mention had been made of the incident in the brothel. In fact, Rimmer had played the part of a man who'd never met Lister before very credibly indeed. He was, he had declared, not exactly in love with the idea of bunking out with a subordinate, but it was something that they both had to put up with.

'There's just one rule,' he'd maintained, polishing his boots for the third time, 'and that rule is K-I-T. D'you know what K.I.T. stands for?'

'Ken Is a Transvestite?' Lister had offered.

'Keep It Tidy. And if you K.I.T., then we'll G.O.J.F.' He'd left this hanging in the air for effect before translating: 'Get On Just Famously.'

Lister spent the rest of the evening trying to take advantage of the fact that he now had a proper bed, of sorts, for the first time in six months. Though, curiously, he'd discovered he couldn't drop off to sleep until he sat up in bed and wrapped both arms around his knees, luggage locker-style. Meanwhile, Rimmer sat at his slanting architect's desk and whiled away the time until Lights Out reading a book called: *How to Overcome Your Fear of Speaking in Public*.

Rimmer gripped the podium tightly, the inside of his wrists pointing out towards the new intake, a trick which, his book told him, would make his audience trust him, and began his speech to Z Shift.

'My name,' he said, 'is Arnold J. Rimmer. You will call me "sir" or "First Technician". I am your shift leader. This is my very first command, and I don't intend it to be my last. What I do intend is for Z Shift to become the best, the fastest, the tightest, the most efficient Routine Maintenance, Cleaning and Sanitation Unit this ship, or any other ship in the Space Corps, has ever seen.' He paused.

Silence. The book said silence could be as effective as speech, if used judiciously. Use silence, it urged. Rimmer stood there, being silent. Enough silence, he decided. More speech.

'When we do something, we do it fast and we do it right.'

More silence.

Still more silence.

No, this was a dumb place to have silence. It just made him look like he'd forgotten what he was saying.

'This ship is three miles wide, four miles deep, and nearly six miles long. But . . .' he paused again – a most excellent and petite silence, he congratulated himself. Very telling. '. . . if anywhere on it a vending machine so much as runs out of chicken soup, I want a member of Z Shift to be there within four minutes.'

More silence. The best silence yet.

'You used to think your mother was your best friend. Not any more. From now on, your best friend is this . . .' he held aloft a three-foot-long metallic tube, with a vari-twist grip and seven detachable heads. 'It's called a sonic super mop. It washes, it steam-cleans, it mops and it vacuums. And from now on, it never leaves your side. Wherever you go, the SSM goes with you. You work with it, you eat with it, you sleep with it.'

The new members of Z Shift exchanged glances.

Rimmer gave them another shot of silence. It had gone well, he thought. Nice, pointy speech. Some good silences. No! Some *great* silences. And he was especially proud of the macho bit at the end about the sonic super mop, which he'd lifted shamelessly from his favourite movie, *God, I Love This War*.

Lister stood up and snapped a salute. 'Sir, permission to speak, sir!'

Sloppy salute, Rimmer thought. He'd have to teach them all his own salute – the one he'd invented. The one he'd drawn diagrams of and sent off to the Space Ministry, in the hope that it would replace the passé, old-fashioned standard one. It was a great salute, and one day it would make him famous. It went thus: from the standard attention pose, the saluter brought his right arm sharply out in front of him, at a perfect angle with his body. He then twirled his wrist in five circles, to symbolize the five arms of the Space Corps, then snapped his arm back, fingers rigid, to form an equilateral triangle with his forehead; he then straightened the elbow, so the arm was pointing sideways from the body, from which position it was snapped smartly back down to his side. There were also variants: the 'Double-Rimmer', for dress occasions, where the salute was performed with both arms simultaneously, and the 'Half-Rimmer', with only one arm, and only three circles for emergency situations, when there wasn't time to carry out the 'Full-Rimmer'.

'Permission granted,' said Rimmer, returning Lister's salute with a five-loop Full-Rimmer.

'Sir . . .'

'Yes, Lister?'

'Is it possible to get a transfer to another shift, sir?'

'Why?'

'Well, with respect, sir, I think you're mentally unstable.

'Sit down.' Rimmer shook his head. 'There's always one, isn't there? One wag. One clown. One imbecile.'

'Yes, sir,' Lister agreed, 'but he's not usually in charge, sir.' Laughter.

This was a tricky situation. Rebellion, a loss of respect. It had to be stamped on, it had to be crushed. His book on 'Poweramics' was quite clear on that. To crush a minor mutiny, you choose the leader: the toughest, the biggest, the strongest; and you humiliate him. And the rest follow like lambs.

Don't look angry. Smile. Real power, true power, is unspoken – understated.

Rimmer smiled. Slowly they stopped laughing.

Excellent. Time to strike.

Without warning he wheeled round and pointed. 'You! On your feet!'

A man with a face like moon rock hauled his two hundred and fifty pound frame onto its feet. Rimmer climbed down from the podium and slowly, casually, strolled over to face him. He looked up at the small black shark eyes, the bald bullet head, the long, matted nostril hair. He was a good eighteen inches taller than Rimmer. And Rimmer was tall.

'What are you chewing?' Rimmer said, after a suitable amount of silence.

'Tobacco.'

'Tobacco?' A grin.

'Yeah.' Defiance.

Rimmer smiled and nodded, looking around the lecture theatre.

'Well, I hope you brought enough along for all of us.' The others laughed. On Rimmer's side. 'Well?'

'Nope.' Slightly nonplussed.

'Nope, *sir*.' Victory! 'Get rid of it.'

The big man chewed thoughtfully for a few seconds. Then, suddenly, a long plume of brown sputum plopped onto the polished toe-cap of Rimmer's left boot.

Rimmer looked at his left boot, then slowly raised his head.

'Some people's respect I've won already. I can see with you it's going to take a little longer. Now, get on the floor and give me fifty, mister.'

'Ppt,' said the big man, and a second stream of half-chewed tobacco arrived on Rimmer's right boot.

Rimmer rocked back and forth on his heels, nodding his head and still smiling.

'Right. OK,' he said, pleasantly, 'I think that's about everything. Shift dismiss.'

Slowly, Z Shift began to meander out of the lecture theatre.

'Oh, by the way . . .' Rimmer called after the tobacco chewer. As the man half-turned, Rimmer leapt through the air and, with a kamikaze scream, wrapped his arms and legs round the big man's frame, and they crashed into a row of chairs.

As Lister left the theatre, Rimmer was having his head rhythmically beaten against one of the desk tops.

BONK.

'Fine,' Rimmer was saying.

BONK.

'There's nothing wrong . . .'

BONK.

'. . . with your reactions.'

BONK.

'Just checking.'

BONK.

'So you like chewing tobacco, eh?'

BONK.

'Well, that's absolutely fine and dandy.'

BONK.

'Perhaps you'd like me to run down to Supplies and buy you some more.'

BONK.

'I think I'm going to lose consciousness now.'

BONK.

BONK.

BONK.

ELEVEN

Everyone agreed it was a splendid funeral, but no one enjoyed it more than the deceased himself.

'I can't tell you how great it is, being dead,' he told everyone who would listen. 'It's solved all my problems.'

Every off-duty member of the eleven thousand, one hundred-and-sixty-nine-strong crew had packed into the vast ship canteen.

McIntyre sat at the top table, a huge coffin-shaped cake containing his own effigy in marzipan before him, and listened, his ego aglow, while his fellow officers sang his praises.

Saunders, much to his own personal delight, had finally been turned off, and although initially there had been some concern about hologramatically reviving a man who had killed himself, those doubts were allayed when the reasons for McIntyre's suicide were discovered.

McIntyre rose to the sound of tumultuous applause, and fingered the 'H' emblazoned on his hologramatic forehead, as over eight thousand people stamped on the floor and banged wine glasses with forks and spoons.

'Well, first I want to thank the Captain for the beautiful eulogy – uh, it was very flattering and deeply moving, and it was well worth all that time I spent writing it.'

A huge laugh echoed round the canteen, and McIntyre smiled happily.

'On a serious note, I know there's a rumour going round

that I committed suicide. I'd like to try and explain why I did it . . .'

McIntyre started to talk about his gambling debts. Debts he'd incurred during his ship leave in bars on Phoebe, Dione and Rhea playing 'Toot'.

'Toot' was a banned bloodsport, involving a fight to the death between two specially-bred Venusian fighting snails. The ferocious gastropods, with hand-sharpened horns, would meet in a six-foot square pit, and bets would be taken on the eventual victor. 'Eventual' was the word; a single butt from a Venusian fighting snail could take upwards of three hours to deliver, and the whole combat often took days. Meanwhile, the baying spectators got drunker and drunker, placing bets of wilder and wilder proportions. You could lose a lot of money playing 'Toot'. And McIntyre had. McIntyre admitted it was a cruel and pointless sport, which said much about man's inhumanity to just about everything to which he could be inhuman. But the buzz from watching two killer snails charging about slowly in the concrete pit; the roaring of the crowd as one snail drew blood, and the other retreated into its shell for hours on end . . . well, you had to be there to believe it.

Before he knew it, McIntyre had debts amounting to almost five times his annual salary. In desperation to pay off the Ganymedian Mafia who ran the snail pits, he'd taken a massive loan from the Golden Assurance Friendly and Caring Loan Society, which, as it turned out, was also run by the Ganymedian Mafia. He didn't know it when he signed, but they charged an annual percentage rate (APR) of nine thousand eight hundred per cent.

The clause in the contract which specified this took the term 'small print' into a whole new dimension.

The clause was concealed in a microdot, occupying the dot of the 'i' on page three of the loan agreement, in the phrase: 'Welcome, you are now a member of the Golden Assurance family.'

Startled to discover his first monthly instalment was some seven times more than the original loan, he gambled what was left, and lost that, too.

McIntyre wrote to the Society, explaining the situation, and a number of increasingly anxious letters were exchanged during *Red Dwarf*'s tour of the Saturnian satellites. Eventually, McIntyre agreed to meet a representative from the company's head office when the ship docked over Mimas, to discuss a repayment plan.

Duly, on the first evening in orbit round Mimas, McIntyre donned his dress uniform and went to the coffee lounge of the Mimas Hilton, where he met three gentlemen, representatives of the Golden Assurance Friendly and Caring Loan Society who arrived in Mimas's one and only five star hotel brandishing a pair of industrial cable clippers.

There, before the eyes of hotel guests casually taking coffee and scones with clotted cream, McIntyre was force-fed his own nose.

He needed little further persuasion before deciding to try a new repayment plan, and finally plumped for the Golden Assurance Friendly and Caring Loan Society's Pay-By-This-Evening-And-Don't-Get-Murdered Super Discount Scheme.

Half-crazed with fear, he staggered back to his office aboard *Red Dwarf*, briefly explained his predicament to his rubber plant, and killed himself.

The beauty part of this scheme was of course that, as a hologram, he was now safe from reprisals. He could continue his life, dead and untroubled. Which is why he was telling everyone who would listen how great it was to be dead, and how it had solved all his problems.

McIntyre finished his speech by thanking everyone for their understanding, and kind words, and concluded by paraphrasing Mark Twain. 'Rumours of my death,' he said, 'have been greatly understated.' Out of the eight thousand assembled, only five people got this joke, and none of them laughed. McIntyre didn't even understand it himself; he'd been told to say it by the ship's metaphysical psychiatrist who assured him it would get a 'big laugh'.

After the toast, the Captain, a short, dumpy American woman who'd had the misfortune to be born with the surname 'Kirk', made a short yet very boring speech welcoming the new intake aboard and outlining the schedule for the jag to and from Triton, before sitting down and thus signalling the beginning of McIntyre's death disco.

The huge sound system vibrated and shook as it pumped out a Hip-hop-a-Billy reggae number from a band which had been red hot for two weeks, five years previously.

Two thousand crew members stood on the dance floor, swaying and sweating, while the rest sat around tables, drinking and sweating.

Though they'd been aboard less than two days, all the low-lifes, ne'er-do-wells and slobs in general had somehow found each other, kindred spirits, and were sitting around in noisy, moronic pockets having drinking competitions. Equally, all the ambitious career-types had somehow been sucked together, and were drinking low alcohol white wine, or slimline mineral water, and talking intensely about work.

Except for Phil.

For some reason, Phil Burroughs had accidentally got himself attached to Lister's group. Phil was a serious-minded academy undergrad on a two-year attachment. It would be a full twenty-four hours before he realized he had joined the wrong group, and had absolutely nothing in common with any of the people with whom he was presently sharing his evening. In the meantime, Petersen was pouring a pint of beer into his jacket pocket.

'That's my beer! What the hell are you doing?' screamed Phil.

'It's just my way,' Petersen beamed charmingly, 'of saying it's your round, pal.'

Phil got up and staggered to the bar. Although there were only five of them at the table, Lister, Petersen, Chen, Selby and himself, he'd been told to order twenty pints of beer. For some reason he couldn't understand, every round consisted of four pints each. 'Saves on shoe leather,' Petersen had pointed out. It didn't seem to matter whether or not you wanted them, either. Each round Phil had requested a low alcohol white wine, and each round he'd been delivered four pints of foaming Japanese lager. He knew for a fact Chen and Petersen were filching at least two of his four pints, but that was absolutely fine with him; his top limit was three pints a night, and he'd had seven already.

Three identical barmen asked for his order. He asked for twenty pints, laid his head in a beery pool on the bar, and promptly fell asleep.

Back at the table, Lister finished his story about how he'd been shanghaied aboard. He'd embellished it only slightly. In his version, for instance, both the Shore Patrolwomen had seduced him in a Photo–U–Kwik booth, and that's why he had that slightly shocked expression on his passport photograph.

Petersen took his turn. He'd arrived on Mimas on a nuclear waste dump ship called *Pax Vert*, which had ejected its putrid load on the Saturnian moon of Tethys, and was now returning to Earth. He was trying to work his passage across the solar system to Triton, where he'd bought a house. As he explained, since Triton was on the very edge of the solar system, being over two-and-a-half billion miles away from Earth, house prices there were really reasonable. For just two thousand dollarpounds, Petersen had bought a twenty-five bedroom home dome, with twelve en-suite bathrooms and a zero-gee squash court.

'At first I thought there was something wrong with it,' he

said, showing Lister a sketch he'd been sent by the estate agent, 'but look, it's beautiful.'

'They didn't send you a photograph?' said Lister, his eyes narrowing.

'No, you can't photograph in a methane atmosphere.'

'You're telling me they haven't installed an oxygen atmosphere yet?'

'No. I'll have to wander around my house in a spacesuit. But that's why it's so cheap!' He quickly downed two pints. 'You ought to move there. There's a plot of about two thousand miles right next door to me. I'm telling you – it's a great investment. Ten, twelve years, they have plans to install oxygen. Can you imagine what will happen to house prices once the atmosphere's breathable? They'll rocket, baby!'

Lister looked at him. Was he *serious*? Yes, he was.

'No, listen,' Petersen continued. 'Do you know Triton is the only moon in the whole solar system which rotates in the opposite direction to the planet it's orbiting?' Petersen demonstrated the scientific principle by rotating his head and swooshing his beer glass around it the other way. Thin, fizzy lager cascaded onto the already sodden table.

'Maybe,' said Lister, who was seriously beginning to wonder whether Petersen was brain-damaged, 'but that's no reason to buy a house there.'

'True,' agreed Petersen, 'but if ever you have guests, it's a nice talking point.'

The music changed; a Johnny Cologne number: *Press Your Lumps Against Mine*. It was smooch time.

There was a loud scraping of chairs as people stood up and guided their partners onto the already packed dance floor. A huge, multi-limbed beast rippled, ebbing and flowing, contracting and expanding to the gentle sway of the music.

Lister suddenly found himself alone at the table, the others lost in the undulating, pulsating mass of smooching bodies. He squinted drunkenly around the vast disco. So many people. People dancing, people touching, people laughing, people talking, people kissing.

So many people.

In just over seven months, every one of them would be dead.

TWELVE

Five months later, Lister stared out of the sleeping quarters' viewport window and saw nothing. Just a few, very distant stars, and an awful lot of black. It was pretty much the same view he'd had for the past twenty-one weeks. At first he'd found it awe-inspiring. Then, slowly, that had given way to just plain dull. Then very dull. Then deeply dull. And now it was something below deeply dull, and even below deeply, hideously dull; a word for which had yet to be devised. It was, he thought, even more mind-numbingly, deeply, hideously dull than an all-nighter at the Scala, watching a twelve-hour season of back-to-back Peter Greenaway movies.

If you went to the British Library and changed every word in every single book to the word 'dull', and then read out all the books in a boring monotone, you would come pretty close to describing Lister's life on board *Red Dwarf*.

He looked at his watch. 19.50, ship time. He was waiting for Petersen to show up, and they were going to go down to the Copacabana Hawaiian Cocktail Bar to spend the evening exacly in the same way they'd spent one hundred and thirty-three of the last one hundred and forty-seven evenings: drinking hugely elaborate San Francisco Earthquakes from plastic coconuts, with Chen and Selby, and failing to meet any interesting women. Or, more to the point, any interesting women who were interested in them.

Dull and gruesomely monotonous as his social life was, Lister knew for a fact it was at least four hundred and seventy-four times more interesting than his working life on Z Shift under Rimmer.

Rimmer was sitting at his slanting architect's desk, under the pink glow of his study lamp, with a tray of watercolours, making out a revision timetable in preparation for his astronavigation exam.

In all, he'd taken the exam eleven times. Nine times, he'd got an 'F' for fail, and on two occasions he'd got an 'X' for unclassified.

But he persevered. Each night he persevered, under the pink glow. Each night he nibbled away at his skyscraper-high stack of files which stored his loose-leaf revision notes. He nibbled away, trying to digest little morsels of knowledge. Little morsels that stuck in his gullet, that wouldn't go down. It was like trying to eat wads of cotton wool. But he persevered. Rimmer wanted to become an officer. He ached for it. He yearned for it. It wasn't the *most* important thing in his life. It *was* his life.

Given the opportunity, he would gladly have had his eyes scooped out if it meant he could become an officer. He would happily have inserted two red hot needles simultaneously through both his ears so they met in the middle of his brain, and tap-danced the title song from *42nd Street* barefoot on a bed of molten lava while giving oral sex to a male orang-utan with dubious personal hygiene, if only it meant attaining that single, elusive golden bar of an Astronavigation Officer, Fourth Class.

But he had to do something much more demanding, much more impossible, and much more unpleasant. He had to pass the astronavigation exam.

Born on Io, one of Jupiter's moons, thirty-one years earlier, he was the youngest of four brothers. Frank was a gnat's wing away from becoming the youngest captain in the Space Corps. John was the youngest captain in the Space Corps. Howard had graduated third in his class at the academy and was now a test pilot for the new generation of demi-light speed Zippers at Houston, Earth.

'My boys,' his mother would say, 'my clever, clever boys. Johnny the Captain, Frankie the First Officer, Howie the Test Pilot, and Arnold . . . Arnold, the chicken soup machine cleaner. If you could sue sperm, I'd sue the sperm that made you.'

'I'll do it, Mother. One day, I will become an officer.'

'And on that day,' his mother would say, 'Satan will be going to work in a snow plough.'

If Rimmer hadn't been such a dedicated anal retentive, he would have realized the simple truth: he wasn't cut out for Space.

He wasn't cut out for it.

He would have realized he wasn't the slightest bit interested in astronavigation. Or quantum mechanics. Or any of the things he needed to be interested in to pass the exams and become an officer.

Three times he'd failed the entrance exam to the Academy. And so, one night after reading the life story of Horatio Nelson, he'd signed up with a merchant vessel as a lowly Third Technician, with the object of quickly working his way through the ranks and sitting the astronavigation exam independently, and thereby earning his commission: the glimmering gold bar of officerhood.

That had been six years ago. Six long years on Red Dwarf, during which he'd leapt from being a lowly Third Technician to being a lowly First Technician. In the meantime, his brothers went for ever onward, up the ziggurat of command. Their success filled him with such bitterness, such bile, that even a Christmas card from one of them – just the reminder that they were alive, and successful – would reduce him to tears of jealousy.

And now he sat there, under the pink glow of his student's table lamp ('Reduces eye-strain! Promotes concentration! Aids retention!' was the lamp manufacturer's proud boast), preparing to sit the astronavigation exam for the thirteenth time.

He found the process of revising so gruellingly unpleasant, so galling, so noxious, that, like most people faced with tasks they find hateful, he devised more and more elaborate ways of not doing it in a 'doing it' kind of way.

In fact, it was now possible for Rimmer to revise solidly for three months and not learn anything at all.

The first week of study, he would always devote to the construction of a revision timetable. At school Rimmer was always at his happiest colouring in geography maps: under his loving hand, the ice-fields of Europa would be shaded a delicate blue, the subterranean silica deposits of Ganymede would be rendered, centimetre by painstaking centimetre, a bright and powerful yellow, and the regions of frozen methane on Pluto slowly became a luscious, inviting green. Up until the age of thirteen, he was constantly head of the class in geography. After this point, it became necessary to know and understand the subject, and Rimmer's marks plunged to the murky depths of 'F' for fail.

He brought his love of cartography to the making of revision timetables. Weeks of patient effort would be spent planning, designing and creating a revision schedule which, when finished, were minor works of art.

Every hour of every day was subdivided into different study periods, each labelled in his lovely, tiny copperplate hand; then painted over in watercolours, a different colour for each subject, the colours gradually becoming bolder and more urgent shades as the exam time approached. The effect was as if a myriad tiny rainbows had splintered and sprinkled across the poster-sized sheet of creamwove card.

The only problem was this: because the timetables often took seven or eight weeks, and sometimes more, to complete, by the time Rimmer had finished them the exam was almost on him. He'd then have to cram three months of astronavigation revision into a single week. Gripped by an almost deranging panic, he'd then decide to sacrifice the first two days of that final week to the making of another timetable. This time for someone who had to pack three months of revision into five days.

Because five days now had to accommodate three months' work, the first thing that had to go was sleep. To prepare for an unrelenting twenty-four hours a day sleep-free schedule, Rimmer would spend the whole of the first remaining day in bed – to be extra, ultra fresh, so he would be able to squeeze three whole months of revision into four short days.

Within an hour of getting up the next morning, he would feel inexplicably exhausted, and start early on his supply of Go-Double-Plus caffeine tablets. By lunchtime he'd overdose, and have to make the journey down to the ship's medical unit for a sedative to help him calm down. The sedative usually sent him off to sleep, and he'd wake up the following morning with only three days left, and an anxiety that was so crippling he could scarcely move. A month of revision to be crammed into each day.

At this point he would start smoking. A lifelong non-smoker, he'd become a forty-a-day man. He'd spend the whole day pacing up and down his room, smoking three or four cigarettes at a time, stopping occasionally to stare at the titles in his bookcase, not knowing which one to read first, and popping twice the recommended dosage of dog-worming tablets, which he erroneously believed to contain amphetamine.

Realizing he was getting nowhere, he'd try to get rid of his soul-bending tension by treating himself to an evening in one of *Red Dwarf*'s quieter bars. There he would sit, in the plastic oak-beamed 'Happy Astro' pub, nursing a small beer, grimly trying to be light-hearted and totally relaxed. Two small beers and three hours of stomach-knotting relaxation later, he would go back to his bunk and spend half the night awake, praying to a God he didn't believe in for a miracle that couldn't happen.

Two days to go, and ravaged by the combination of anxiety, nicotine, caffeine tablets, alcohol he wasn't used to, dog-worming pills, and overall exhaustion, he would sleep in till mid-afternoon.

After a long scream, he would rationalize that the day was a total write-off, and the rest of the afternoon would be spent shopping for the three best alarm clocks money could buy. This would often take five or six hours, and he would arrive back at his sleeping quarters exhausted, but knowing he was fully prepared for the final day's revision before his exam.

Waking at four-thirty in the morning, after exercising, showering and breakfasting, he would sit down to prepare a final, final revision timetable, which would condense three months of revision into twelve short hours. This done, he would give up and go back to bed. Maybe he didn't know a single thing about astronavigation, but at least he'd be fresh for the exam the next day.

Which is why Rimmer failed exams.

Which is why he'd received nine 'F's for fail and two 'X's for unclassified. The first 'X' he'd achieved when he'd actually managed to get hold of some real amphetamines, gone into spasm and collapsed two minutes into the exam; and the second when anxiety got so much the better of him his subconscious forced him to deny his own existence, and he had written 'I am a fish' five hundred times on every single answer sheet. He'd even gone out for extra paper. What was more shocking than anything was that he'd thought he'd done quite well.

Well, this time it was going to be different, he thought, as he sat carefully colouring all the quantum mechanics revision periods in diagonal lines of Prussian blue on a yellow ochre background, while Lister stared out of the viewport window.

Petersen clumped noisily into the room and did his trational parody of the full Double-Rimmer salute, which ended with him slapping his face several times and throwing himself onto the floor. The first time Lister had seen it, it was funny. This was the two hundred and fifty-second time, and it was beginning to lose its appeal.

Lister and Petersen then went down to the Copacabana Hawaiian Cocktail Bar for the hundred and thirty-fourth time. Only, this time Lister did something incredibly stupid.

He fell in love.

Hopelessly and helplessly in love.

THIRTEEN

Third Console Officer Kristine Kochanski had a face. That was the first thing Lister noticed about her. It wasn't a beautiful face. But it was a nice face. It wasn't a face that could launch a thousand ships. Maybe two ships and a small yacht. That was, until she smiled. When she smiled, her eyes lit up like a pinball machine when you win a bonus game. And she smiled a lot.

Lister could perhaps have survived the smile. But it was when he found the smile was attached to a sense of humour that he became irretrievably lost.

They were both standing at the bar, queuing to get a drink, and Lister was looking at her in a not-looking-at-her kind of way: in the bar mirror, in the reflection in his beer glass, over his shoulder, pretending to look at Petersen, at the ceiling just above her head, and occasionally, because it was permitted, directly at her. His heart sank when a tanned, white-uniformed officer, who obviously knew her, came up and touched her on the shoulder. Touched her on the shoulder – just like she was some kind of ordinary person. It really made Lister mad.

The tanned, white-uniformed officer noticed a book sticking out of her black jacket pocket. Lister had noticed it too. It was called *Learn Japanese*, by Dr P. Brewis.

'"Learn Japanese"?' the officer snorted. 'Talk about pretentious!'

What she said next tipped Lister over the edge.

'Pretentious?' she placed her palm on her chest, 'Watashi?'

Lister didn't know any Japanese but he guessed, rightly, that it was an adaptation of the 'Pretentious? Moi?' joke.

The officer just looked at her blankly.

She got her drinks and went back to her seat, while Lister was still trying to think of something to say which would start a conversation.

For the next hour Petersen droned on about the supply station at the Uranian moon, Miranda, where *Red Dwarf* was due to stop off for supplies in seven weeks. It was to be their only shore leave between Saturn and Triton, and Petersen was telling him what a great time they were going to have. But Lister wasn't listening. He was looking across the crowded cocktail bar, trying to calculate the amount of drink left in the glasses of the girl with the pinball smile and her female companion, so he could be at the bar just as she arrived, and casually offer to buy her a drink.

Who was he kidding? How do you casually offer to buy someone a drink, without making it sound like 'I want you to have my babies'? If he hadn't been crazy about her, it wouldn't have been a problem. Lister never had any trouble asking women for a date, provided he wasn't too keen on them. When he was, which didn't happen too often, he had all the charm, wit, and self-possession of an Alsatian dog after a head-swap operation.

She got up to go to the bar. Lister got up, too. They exchanged smiles, ordered drinks and went back to their separate tables.

Damn. Smeg. Blew it.

She got up again.

'My round,' said Petersen, rising. Lister thrust him back in his chair and went to the bar. They exchanged smiles and 'Hi's this time, ordered their drinks, and went back to their separate tables.

Damn. Smeg. Blew it again.

She'd hardly sat down before she was getting up again. The two girls' glasses were full.

She's going for peanuts, thought Lister.

'You want some peanuts?' he asked Petersen.

'No, thanks.'

'I'll go and get some.'

They stood at the bar again. They exchanged smiles again. Then she introduced herself and asked him out for a date.

And so it began.

Lister became a walking cliché. His senses were heightened, so even the foul, recycled air of the ship tasted crisp and spring-like. He went off his food. He stopped drinking. Pop lyrics started to mean something to him. Magically, he became better-looking; he'd heard that this happened, but he'd never really believed it. He got out of bed before his alarm clock went off – unheard of. He started to marvel at the view out of the viewport window.

And his face acquired three new expressions. Three expressions which he'd stolen from her. Three expressions which, on her, he found adorable. He wasn't aware of even copying them, and he certainly wasn't aware how stupid he looked when he pulled them. And even if he had been aware, he wouldn't have cared. Because Third Console Officer, Kristine Kochanski, a.k.a. 'Babes', a.k.a. 'Ange' (short for Angel), a.k.a. 'Krissie', a.k.a. 'K.K.', 'Sweetpea', and a host of others too nauseating to recount, was madly, electrically in love with him.

Lister's all-time favourite movie was Frank Capra's *It's A Wonderful Life*, and, just to make things totally perfect, it happened to be Kochanski's too. They sat in bed – Kochanski's bunk-mate, Barbara, had been chased away to the ship's cinema yet again – eating hot dogs doused in mustard, and watching, for the third consecutive night, *It's A Wonderful Life* on the sleeping quarters' vid-screen.

Suddenly, in the middle of the scene where Jimmy Stewart's father dies, Lister found himself for the first time in his life talking about his own father's death.

It wasn't, of course, his real father, but he was only six at the time and he didn't know then that he'd been adopted. It had been a gloriously hot day in mid-summer, and the six-year-old Lister was given toys and presents by everyone. It was better than Christmas. He remembered wishing at the time that a few more people would die, so he could complete his Lego set.

She held his hand and listened.

'My grandmother tried to explain. She said he'd gone away, and he wasn't coming back. So I wanted to know where, and she told me he was very happy, and he'd gone to the same place as my goldfish.' Lister toyed absently with his plaited locks. 'I thought they'd flushed him down the bog. I used to stand with my head down the loo, and talk to him. I thought he was just round the U-bend. In the end, they had to take me to a child psychologist, because they found me with my head down the pan, reading him the football scores.'

This had never stuck Lister as being funny. But when Kochanski started roaring with laughter, he started laughing too. It was like a geyser going off. Something was exorcized. And as they lay in the crumb-laden sheets, wrapped in each other's arms, giggling like idiots – and even though they'd only been dating for three-and-a-half short weeks – Lister knew more certainly than he'd ever known anything in his life before that they'd be together, forever.

FOURTEEN

Seven months out into space, while Rimmer sat at his slanting architect's desk under the pink glow of his study lamp, Lister stared out of the sleeping quarters' viewport window, longing to be bored again.

He'd been not going out with Kochanski now for three weeks.

The whole affair, the glorious 'forever' he'd imagined, had lasted just over a month. Then one evening in her sleeping quarters, as Lister arrived to take her to a movie, she'd told him she wanted to break it off. He'd laughed. He thought it was a joke. But it wasn't.

She'd been seeing 'Tom' (or was it 'Tim'?), a Flight Navigation Officer, for almost two years. Tom or Tim (it may have been Tony) had left her for a fling with some brunette in Catering. And Lister had been a rebound thing. She hadn't realized it at first, but when Tom, Tim, Tony or Terry, or whatever the smeg he was called, had turned up at her door, having dumped the brunette in Catering, she'd gone scurrying back.

There were tears, there were apologies, and pathetic clichéd platitudes: they could still be friends; if he met Trevor, he'd really like him; she wished she were two people, so she could love both of them; ad nauseum.

She'd returned the blue jumper he'd left. She'd returned his DAT tapes, and offered to give back the necklace he'd bought her, which, of course, he'd declined.

And that was that.

Except it wasn't. Because now she was everywhere. Everything he did, he did *without* her. Everywhere he went, he went *without* her. When he went shopping, he didn't go shopping, he went shopping without Kochanski. When he went to the bar, he didn't go to the bar, he went to the bar without Kochanski. She'd infected every part of his life. His mental map of the ship now judged all distances in relation to her sleeping quarters, or the Drive Room, where she worked. He wasn't walking on such-and-such a corridor, he was walking on such-and-such a corridor which was *n* floors above or *n* floors below where she was at that precise moment.

So he lay on his bunk, staring out of the viewport window, longing for the anaesthetic of the stupifying monotony which he used to feel two short months earlier.

His only relief from the Kochanski blues had been three days' planet leave on the alcohol-dry Uranian moon, Miranda, when *Red Dwarf* had docked for supplies. Three days drinking cola and playing video machines with Petersen. Petersen, who'd got drunk every night of his life since he was twelve, was so thrilled with the benefits of being sober, he'd gone teetotal overnight. So their excursions down to the Copacabana were a thing of the past, denying Lister his one last refuge.

He sighed like a senile dog and looked down at Rimmer, hard at work.

'Do you fancy going for a drink?' he asked, knowing the answer would be 'No' even before he'd finished saying the word 'Do'.

'No,' said Rimmer, without looking up.

'That's a surprise.'

'As it happens, I am going out tonight. Just not with you.'

'What about your revision?'

Rimmer had decided to change.

His latest three-month revision timetable had been constructed within two hours. And four hours a day, come what may, he read his course books, made notes, and revised in a sensible way. And revising in a sensible way obviously meant an adequate provision for leisure time.

'Well, where are you going, then?'

'Out.'

'Where?'

Rimmer ignored him. He was going to spend the evening not getting any older. He was going to spend it in a stasis booth.

Red Dwarf, like most of the older ships, was equipped with stasis booths for interstellar travel. A hundred years earlier, travelling to other star systems had been considered economically and philosophically interesting. But not any more.

To travel the vast distances involved, even with craft which could achieve demi-lightspeed, took decades. Necessity being the mother of invention, the stasis booth was duly invented. Basically, it was a fool-proof form of suspended animation, but instead of freezing the body cryogenically, and having all the attendant revival problems, the stasis booth simply froze time.

Once activated, the booth created a static field of Time; in the same way X-rays can't penetrate lead, Time couldn't penetrate a stasis field. An object caught within the field became a non-event mass with a quantum probability of zero.

In other words, the object remained in exactly the same state, at exactly the same age, until it was released. Most of the important groundwork for Time-freezing and stasis theory had been done by Einstein in the 1950s. Unfortunately, just as he was on the verge of a breakthrough, he started dating Marilyn Monroe, and basically lost interest in the project. Even after their short affair was over, he found it difficult to concentrate on quantum theory, and spent much of the rest of his life taking cold showers.

His notes on the theory were later discovered and developed – and the stasis booth was born.

For a period, ships full of astros in stasis booths were hurled out of our solar system, and interstellar travel enjoyed its golden age. The big hope, of course, was that they'd contact intelligent life.

They didn't.

Not even a moderately intelligent plant. Not even a stupid plant.

Nothing.

And it was surmised correctly, although it wasn't confirmed for a further two thousand years, that Mankind was completely and totally and inexplicably alone.

In all of the universe.

In all of the universe, the planet Earth was the only planet with any life forms.

That's all there was.

Interstellar travel was abandoned as a total waste of time. And the returning stellarnauts tried to reintegrate into society and cope with the fact that many of them were now fifty years younger than their own children. This led to curious generation gap problems, of which the greetings cards industry took full advantage.

Rimmer had a keycard to one of *Red Dwarf*'s stasis booths, which he used whenever he could.

While morons like Lister and Petersen were urinating their lives down the gutter in the Copacabana Hawaiian Cocktail Bar, he was in a stasis booth, not existing, not getting any older.

It made great good sense to Rimmer. Take tonight. There was nothing he particularly wanted to do. He'd achieved all the aims on his daily goal list, and under normal circumstances he'd just lounge around, doing not very much, and eventually go to bed. As it was, when they took to their bunks that night, Rimmer would be three hours less older than Lister. Because he wouldn't have lived those three hours: he'd have saved them. Saved them for when he really needed them.

True, technically, he wouldn't be living.

But he didn't particularly want to live tonight. He wasn't in the mood.

It was just like a bank, only, instead of saving up money, he was saving up time. He'd been doing it, on and off, for about five years, and in this way he used up most of his free leisure time. Most Sundays were spent boothing. And then, usually, three evenings a week, for three hours or so. And obviously, if there were any bank holidays, he'd take full advantage of the facility not to exist, and pinch back a few hours from Father Time.

In just five years he'd saved three hundred and sixty-nine full days. Over a full Earth year. In five years, he'd only lived for four. Although his birth certificate said he was thirty-one, technically he was still only thirty.

Occasionally Rimmer reflected that his boothing could possibly be the reason why he didn't have any friends, but, as he pointed out to himself, if having friends meant having to hang around and get older with them, then he wasn't sure he wanted any. Especially since the perks were so astonishing. He often looked in the full-length mirror, when Lister wasn't there, and reflected that, although he was thirty-one, he still had the body of a thirty-year-old. If he could maintain this routine, by the time his birth certificate said he was ninety he'd actually only be a very sprightly seventy-eight-year-old. Pretty a-smegging-mazing, eh?

Lister slumped off to try and persuade Peterson to go for a drink. Rimmer watched him go, then showered and changed, treated himself to a little aftershave, and went off to spend the very last evening of his life not existing.

FIFTEEN

On the very last morning of his life, Rimmer strode into the lecture theatre to give Z Shift their work schedule for the day.

'OK, men,' he said as always, 'Listen up.'

As always the whole of Z Shift inclined their heads to one side and pointed their ears at the ceiling. But, as always, Rimmer missed this as he turned his back to pull down the blackboard he'd prepared the day before. As always his schedule wasn't there. What was there was a crudely-drawn cartoon of a man making love to a kangaroo, wearing hugely exaggerated footwear covered in brown spit, and underneath, in the same crude hand, 'Old Tobacco Boots goes down under!'

Nobody laughed. Rimmer looked round at a sea of blank faces. He'd long since given up referring to the blackboard insults.

'OK,' he said, consulting his notes, 'Today's schedule. Turner, Wilkinson: we've had a number of reports that machine 15455 is dispensing blackcurrant juice instead of chicken soup. While you're down there, Corridor 14: alpha 12 needs new Crunchie bars. Thereafter, I want you to go down to the reference library and hygienize all the headsets in the language lab. Saxon and Burroughs: continue painting the engineers' mess. And I want that finished today. McHullock, Schmidt, Palmer: as yesterday. Burd, Dooley, Pixon: laundrettes on East alpha 555 report no less than twenty-four driers out of commission. I want them up and drying by nightfall. Also, there's an unconfirmed rumour that the cigar machine in the officers' club is nearly empty. Now, it may be nothing, but just in case: for pity's sake, stay by a phone.'

A paper dart whistled past his head.

'OK, roll out. Lister, you're with me today.'

The men began to shuffle out.

'Why me?' Lister moaned.

'Because it's your turn.'

As always, just before the first man reached the door, Rimmer called out his team chant, which he hoped would catch on.

'Hey, and remember: "We are tough, and we are mean – Rimmer's Z Shift gets things clean".'

Z Shift shuffled out silently.

Two of the three worst things that ever happened to Rimmer happened to Rimmer on this day.

The worst thing that ever happened was, of course, his death. But that was a clear twelve hours away.

The second worst thing that ever happened had happened thirteen months earlier and it was so horrible his subconscious had created a new sub-department to hide it from his waking thoughts. It involved a bowl of soup.

The third worst thing that ever happened to Rimmer happened to Rimmer shortly after ten o'clock, as he and Lister made their way towards Corridor 1: gamma 755, to check, just to put Rimmer's mind at ease, that there was enough shower gel in the women's wash-room.

At first it was Lister who had a horrible thing happen to him, as he pushed his squeaky four-wheel hygiene truck along the steel mesh floor. First Technician Petrovitch rounded the corner.

Rimmer didn't like Petrovitch. Petrovitch, three years his junior, was his equal in rank, and leader of A Shift – the best shift. A Shift got all the plum jobs, the serious, technical work, repairing porous circuits, and, if that weren't bad enough, Petrovitch had taken and passed the astronavigation exam the exact same time Rimmer had made his claims to fishhood, and was now merely waiting for his orders to be processed before he got his gold bar and took up the rank of Astronavigation Officer, Fourth Class. Also, he was good-looking, popular, charming and amiable. All in all, as far as Rimmer could see, there wasn't a single thing *to* like about Petrovitch.

There'd been a wild rumour some months back that Petro-vitch was a drug dealer. And Rimmer did whatever he could to spread it. He didn't know whether it was true, but, God, he hoped it was. Whenever he was feeling low, he entertained himself with visions of Petrovitch having his badges of rank ripped from his uniform, and being led away in manacles. Still, there was no evidence that it was true, so all Rimmer could do was keep spreading those malicious rumours, and hoping.

'What the smeg is wrong with your bleepers? I've been trying to get hold of you for an hour,' said Petrovitch. 'Lister, the Captain wants to see you.'

Rimmer looked dumbfounded. Why should the Captain want to see Lister? In the ordinary course of things, Lister, being a lowly Third Technician, should go the whole trip without ever meeting the Captain.

Unless, thought Rimmer, brightening, *he's in very, very deep smegola indeed*. And by the slightly sick look of Lister's smile, Rimmer confidently surmised the very same thought had occurred to him.

'Why does she want to see *me*?'

'I think you know why,' said Petrovitch, his usual geniality completely absent.

Lister dragged himself off towards the Xpress lift.

'Oh dear,' said Rimmer, breezily. 'Oh dear, oh dear, oh

dear.' He tutted and shook his head. 'Dearie me. Dearie, dearie, dearie me '

Petrovitch didn't smile; he made to follow Lister, but then stopped and turned. 'What are you doing with Lister, anyway? It's five past ten.'

'So?' said Rimmer.

'I thought you were taking the astronavigation exam.'

'That's November the twenty-seventh, you square-jawed chump,' said Rimmer, with naked contempt.

'No, it's October the twenty-seventh.'

'I think, Petrovitch, I know when my own exam is, thank you so very, very much.'

'My bunk-mate is taking it today.'

'Hollerbach?'

'Yeah. He went up at ten.'

Rimmer's smile remained exactly where it was, while the rest of his face sagged like a bloodhound's. He looked at his watch. 10.07. He tapped it a couple of times, and walked off without saying anything.

Rimmer arrived, breathless, back at the sleeping quarters. He skidded to a halt in front of his timetable. His eyes scanned the chart for an error. He couldn't find one. He couldn't find one for a whole two minutes. Then he froze. In his haste not to dwell on the construction of the chart, somehow he'd included two Septembers.

'August, September, September, October, November', ran the new Rimmerian calendar.

How could I have included September twice, and not noticed? thought Rimmer, sucking on his fist. *This is what happens when you spend most of your social life not existing.*

He looked at his watch. 10.35. He'd missed thirty-five minutes of a three-hour exam.

A strange calmness overtook him.

Well, he could still get to the exam by, say, 10.45.

If he kept his answers short and pertinent, it was still more than possible to pass. So far, so good. What would be slightly trickier was cramming a whole month's revision into minus thirty-five minutes. Thirty-five minutes was hard enough, but minus thirty-five minutes – well, you'd have to be Dr Who.

As always at crisis times in his life, Rimmer asked himself the question: 'What would Napoleon do?'

Something French, he thought. *Probably munch on a croissant, and decide to invade Russia. Not really relevant*, he decided, *in this particular scenario. What, then . . . what, then?*

The seconds ticked away. Then it came to him. He knew exactly what he must do.

Cheat.

Rimmer took out a black felt tip pen, stripped off his shirt and trousers, and began work. He had, he estimated, twenty minutes to copy as much of his textbooks onto his body as humanly possible.

SIXTEEN

Lister had never been up to the Drive Room before.

It was enormous.

Hundreds of people scurried along the network of gantries stretching above him. Banks of programmers in white officers' uniforms clacked away at computer keyboards, in front of multi-coloured flashing screens arranged in a series of horseshoe shapes around the massive chamber. Skutters, the small service droids with three-fingered clawed heads, joined to their motorized bases by triple-jointed necks, whizzed between the various computer terminals, transporting sheets of data.

Occasionally a voice could be heard above the unrelenting jabber of hundreds of people talking at once.

'Stop-start 0A3! Stop-start 0A3! Thank you! At *last*! Stop-start 0A4! Is anybody *listening* to me?!'

Lister followed Petrovitch as he zigzagged through a maze of towering columns of identical hard disc drives and people pushed past them, desperate to get back to wherever they had to get back to.

Up above them, Holly's bald-headed digitalized face dominated the whole of the ceiling, patiently answering questions and solving quandaries, while dispensing relevant data updates from other areas of the ship.

Through the computer hardware Lister caught sight of Kochanski, expertly clicking away at a computer keyboard, happily going about her business, just as if nothing had happened. Lister didn't exactly expect her to be sobbing guiltily onto her keyboard. But smiling? Actively smiling? It was obscene. Lister remembered reading in one of Rimmer's *Strange Science* mags that an Earth biochemist claimed he'd isolated the virus which caused Love. According to him, it was an infectious germ which was particularly virulent for the first few weeks, but then, gradually, the body recovered.

Looking at Kochanski merrily tippy-tapping away, Lister was inclined to believe the biochemist had a point. She'd shrugged him off like a bout of dysentery. She'd recovered from him like he was a dose of 'flu. She was fine and dandy. Back to normal.

They climbed the gantry steps to the Admin level, where glass-fronted offices wound round the entire chamber, like the private boxes which skirted the London Jets Zero-Gee football stadium.

Five minutes later they arrived outside the Captain's office. Petrovitch knocked, and they went in.

'Lister, sir,' said Petrovitch, and left.

The office looked like it had been newly-burgled and freshly-bombed. The Captain was mumbling into a phone buried beneath gigantic reams of computer print-out, surrounded by open ledgers and piles of memoranda.

Lister shifted uncomfortably and waited for her to finish her call.

'Well, you see he does exactly that,' finished the Captain, and before the phone had even hit its holder, and without looking up, she said: 'Where's the cat?'

'What?' said Lister.

'Where's the cat?' repeated the Captain.

'What cat?'

'I'm going to ask you one last time,' she said, finally looking up: 'Where is the cat?'

'Let me get this straight,' said Lister. 'You think I know something about a cat, right?'

'Don't be smart.' The Captain was actually smiling with anger. 'Where is it?'

'I don't know what you're talking about.'

'Lister, not only are you so stupid you bring an unquarantined animal aboard. Not only that,' she paused, 'you have your photograph taken with the cat, and send it to be processed in the developing lab. So, let's make this the last chorus. Where's the cat?'

'What cat?'

'This one,' she shouted, pushing a photograph into Lister's face. 'This goddam cat!'

Lister looked at the photograph of himself sitting in what were unmistakably his sleeping quarters, holding what was unmistakably a small black cat.

'Oh, *that* cat.'

'Where'd you get it? Mimas?'

'Miranda. When we stopped for supplies.'

'Don't you realize it could be carrying anything? Anything. What were you thinking of?'

'I just felt sorry for her. She was wandering the streets. Her fur was all hanging off . . .'

'Her fur was hanging off? Oh, this gets better and better.' Two of the Captain's phones were ringing, but she didn't answer them.

'And she had this limp, and she'd walk a few steps, then let out this scream, then walk a few more steps and scream again.'

'Well, now *I'm* screaming, Lister. I want that cat, and I want it now! D'you think we have quarantine regulations just for the hell of it? Just to make life a bit more unbearable? Well, we don't. We have them to safeguard the crew. A spaceship is a closed system. A contagious disease has nowhere else to go. Everybody gets it.'

'She's better now. Fur's grown back, I've fixed her leg. She's fine.'

'It's impossible to tell. You got the cat from a space colony. There are diseases out there, new diseases. The locals develop an immunity. Now, get that cat down to the lab. Double-time.'

'Sir . . .'

'You're still here, Lister.'

'What are you going to do with the cat?'

'I'm going to have it cut up, and run tests on it.'

'Are you going to put it back together when you've finished?'

The Captain closed her eyes.

'You're not, are you?' persisted Lister. 'You're going to kill it.'

'Yes, Lister, that's exactly what I'm going to do. I'm going to kill it.'

'Well, with respect, sir,' said Lister, taking a cigarette from his hat band, 'what's in it for the cat?'

Lister smiled. The Captain didn't.

'Lister, give me the cat.'

Lister shook his head.

'We'll find it, anyway.'

'No, you won't.'

'Let me put it like this' – the Captain reclined back in her chair – 'give me the frigging cat.'

'Look, she's fine, there's nothing wrong with her.'

'Give me the cat.'

'Apart from anything else, she's pregnant.'

'She's *what*? I want that cat.'

Lister shook his head again.

'Do you want to go into stasis for the rest of the jag and lose three years' wages?'

'No.'

'Do you want to hand over the cat?'

'No.'

'Choose.'

SEVENTEEN

11.05.

Rimmer hurried out of the lift and down Corridor 4: delta 799 towards the exam hall.

Under his high-neck zipped flightsuit he had everything he needed to pass the exam. On his right thigh, in tiny script, were all the basic principles of quantum mechanics. Time dilation formulae covered his right calf. Heisenberg's uncertainty principle took up most of his left leg, while porous circuit theory and continuum hypotheses filled his forearms.

Rimmer had never done anything illegal before. He hadn't so much as got a parking ticket on his home moon, Io. He'd never even fiddled his expenses, which, quite frankly, even the Captain did.

He'd never cheated; never. Not because he was of high moral character, but simply because he was scared. He was terrified of being caught.

He walked into the clinically white exam room. The adjudicating officer glanced at his watch and nodded towards the one empty desk, where an exam paper lay face-down, and returned to reading his novel.

He knows, thought Rimmer, his face glowing like Jupiter's Red Spot. *He knows from the way I walked into the room. He knows.*

Rimmer ducked his body low into his chair, so just his head remained above the table top, and peered past the backs of the examinees in front of him, waiting for the adjudicator to make his move. Waiting for him to leap forward and rip off his flimsy flightsuit. exposing his shame: his illustrated body, Rimmer's cheating frame.

For a full ten minutes Rimmer watched the officer quietly reading his novel. *All right*, thought Rimmer, *play it like that. The old cat and mouse game.*

Another ten minutes went by. Still the officer taunted him by doing nothing. Nothing.

At 11.45 Rimmer decided the adjudicator *didn't* know, and it was safe to begin. Safe to . . . cheat!

He turned over the exam paper and started to read the questions. Something appeared to be sucking oxygen out of the room, and he seemed to have to take two breaths to his usual one, just to keep conscious.

Buh–BUB.

Buh–BUB.

Buh–BUB!

His heartbeat was deafening; when someone turned round, he was convinced they were going to say: 'Can you keep your heartbeat down a bit? I'm trying to concentrate.'

'ASTRONAVIGATION EXAMINATION – PART ONE,' he read. Then underneath: ' ANSWER FIVE QUESTIONS ONLY.'

Just five, thought Rimmer. *I'm not going to make that mistake again.*

'QUESTION ONE.'

As he looked at the question, the letters seemed to come off the page and sway, out of focus, like distant figures disappearing in a heat haze on a desert road. He blinked. Two tears of sweat ran past his eyes and tumbled onto the page. He ran his hands through his hair and wiped the perspiration off his face with his palms, then blinked twice more, and brought the question into focus.

'$\Omega f\copyright \dagger \Delta \leqslant \diamondsuit^{\lceil}\int\int \dagger \not\equiv \nleqslant' \# \S f \copyright \Omega \Omega^{\cdot\cdot} \pi \mu^{\sim} \int\int \sqrt{} \, /_{\varsigma} \sqrt{} \, \dagger \not\equiv \nleqslant \, ^{\cdot\cdot} \S \P \P \cdot \Omega \Sigma \circledR \S \infty \, ^{\cdot\cdot} \Delta \mathring{a}$'

Oh God, thought Rimmer, *I've forgotten how to read.*
He blinked several more times.

'DESCRIBE, USING FORMULAE WHERE APPROPRIATE, THE APPLICATION OF DE BURGH'S THEORY OF THERMAL INDUCTION IN POROUS CIRCUITRY.'

That was his left forearm! The answer was there! The formulae were there! All he had to do was slide back his sleeve, copy it all down and he was one-fifth of his way into that officers' club.

He looked at the other questions. There were three others he could do. And he could do them perfectly. Eighty per cent. He only needed forty! There was a whole hour to go.

HE WAS AN *OFFICER*!!

Arnold J. Rimmer, Astronavigation Officer, Fourth Class. Already, in his mind's eye, ticker-tape was cascading from rooftops as he sat in the open-top limousine waving to the adoring Ionian crowds.

He snapped out of it. No time for complacency. Fifteen minutes per question. It was enough.

Let's go-o-o-o-o! he screamed, silently. He glanced nonchalantly around. No one was watching.

Casually he rested his hand on his wrist, and slowly slid back the sleeve. The adjudicating officer turned a page in his novel.

Rimmer looked down at his arm.

An inky black blob stared up at him.

His body had betrayed him. It had conspired to drench him in sweat; it had dissolved his best chance ever of getting that glimmering gold bar.

He looked at his right hand. The answer to the question 'Describe, Using Formulae Where Appropriate, the Application of De Burgh's Theory of Thermal Induction in Porous Circuitry' was there, somewhere, hiding in the black blobby mess.

Rimmer decided to take a chance in a million. It was the longest of long shots.

With careful precision he placed his inky hand on the answer sheet and pressed as hard as he could. Maybe, just maybe, when he removed his hand, his tiny copperplate writing would reassemble itself legibly on the page.

He removed his hand.

There in the middle of the page was a perfect palm print, with a single middle finger raised in mocking salute.

An idiotic grin spread across Rimmer's face as he picked up his pen and signed the bottom of the page.

Slowly he clambered to his feet, saluted the adjudicating officer, and woke up on a stretcher on his way to the medical bay.

EIGHTEEN

Petrovitch led the way and Lister followed, flanked by two unnecessary security guards. They stopped at the door to the stasis booth.

'Last chance, Lister. Where's the cat?'

Lister just shook his head.

'Three years in stasis for some stupid flea-bitten moggy? Are you crazy?'

Lister wasn't crazy. Far from it.

He'd first heard about the stasis punishment from Petersen. Now that the booths were no longer used for interstellar travel, their only official function was penal. Lister had spent six long, boring evenings, shortly after Kochanski had finished with him, poring over the three-thousand-page ship regulation tome, and had finally tracked down the obscure clause.

The least serious crime for which stasis was a statutory punishment was breaking quarantine regulations. When *Red Dwarf* had stopped for supplies at Miranda, he'd spent the last afternoon of his three-day ship leave and all his wages buying the smallest, healthiest animal with the best pedigree he could find. For three thousand dollarpounds he'd purchased a black longhaired cat with the show name 'Frankenstein'. He'd had her inoculated for every known disease, to ensure that she didn't actually endanger the crew, and smuggled her aboard under his hat.

A week later he started to panic. The ship's security system still hadn't detected Frankenstein's presence.

It was tricky.

On the one hand he wanted to get caught with the cat, but he didn't want the cat to get caught and dissected. Eventually he hit on the idea of having his photograph taken with the cat, and sending off the film to be developed in the ship's lab.

Finally, and much to his relief, they'd caught him. Three years in stasis was everything he'd hoped for. OK, his wages would be suspended, but it was a small price to pay for walking into a stasis booth, and walking out a subjective instant later in orbit around the Earth.

He'd hidden Frankenstein in the ventilation system. The system was so vast she would be impossible to catch, and also provided her with access for foraging raids to the ship's food stores.

So, all in all, as Lister stepped into the stasis booth, he was feeling pretty pleased with himself, or, at least, as pleased as anyone could expect to feel who was actually as miserable as hell.

Petrovitch gave him one last, last chance to surrender the cat, which Lister naturally refused.

As the cold metal door slammed behind him, he sat on the cold smoothness of the booth's bench and exhaled. Suddenly a warm, green light flooded the chamber, and Lister became a non-event mass with a quantum probability of zero.

He ceased, temporarily, to exist.

NINETEEN

20.17.

A red warning light failed to go on in the Drive Room, beginning a chain of events which would lead, in a further twenty-three minutes, to the total annihilation of the entire crew of *Red Dwarf*.

20.18.

Rimmer was released from the medical bay, and told to take twenty-four hours' sick leave. He was halfway along Corridor 5: delta 333, on his way back to his sleeping quarters, when he changed his mind and decided to spend the evening in a stasis booth.

The medical orderly had informed him of the Lister situation, and that just about capped a perfect day in the life of Arnold J. Rimmer. On top of everything, Lister was about to gain three years on him. By the time they got back to Earth, Lister would be exactly the same age, while he would be three years older. Even with his illicit stasis-boothing, Rimmer could only hope to snatch three months; four at best. So Lister would gain two-and-three-quarter whole years, and he was already younger than Rimmer to start with. It seemed totally unfair.

To cheer himself up, he decided to spend the evening in a state of non-being, and vowed to begin work in the morning on an appeal against Lister's sentence, so he could get him out of the stasis booth and make him start ageing again.

20.23.

Navigation officer Henri DuBois knocked his black cona coffee with four sugars over his computer console keyboard. As he mopped up the coffee, he noticed three red warning blips on his monitor screen, which he wrongly assumed were the result of his spillage.

20.24.

Rimmer got out of the lift on the main stasis floor and made a decision which, in retrospect, he would regret forever.

He decided to comb his hair.

20.31.

The cadmium II coolant system, located deep in the bowels of the engine corridors, stopped funtioning.

20.36.

Rimmer stood in the main wash-room on the stasis deck and combed his hair. He combed his hair in the usual way, then decided to see what it would look like if he parted it on the opposite side. It didn't look very good, so he combed it back again. He washed his hands and dried them on a paper towel. If he had left at this point and gone directly to a stasis booth, he wouldn't have died. But, instead, he was seized by one of his frequent superstition attacks.

He rolled the paper towel into a ball and decided if he could throw it directly into the disposal unit, he would eventually become an officer. He took careful aim, decided on an overarm shot, and tossed his paper ball.

It missed by eight feet.

He retrieved the paper and decided if he got it in the disposal unit three times on the run, it would make up for the miss. The miss would then be struck from the superstition record, and not only would he become an officer, but within three weeks he would get to have sex with a beautiful woman.

Standing directly above the disposal unit, he dropped and retrieved the paper ball three times. Combing his hair one last time, he left the wash-room, idly wondering just who the beautiful girl might be, and headed for a stasis booth.

20.40.

The cadmium II core reached critical mass and unleashed the deadly power of a neutron bomb. The ship remained structurally undamaged, but in 0.08 seconds everyone on the Engineering Level was dead.

20.40 and 2.7 seconds.

Rimmer placed his hand on the wheel lock of stasis booth 1344. He heard what sounded like a nuclear wind roaring down the corridor towards him. It was, in fact, a nuclear wind roaring down the corridor towards him.

What now? he thought, rather irritably, and was suddenly hit full in the face by a nuclear explosion.

0.57 seconds before he expired, Rimmer realized he was going to die. His life didn't flash before him. He didn't think of his parents, or his brothers or his home. He didn't think of the failed exams or the wasted time in the stasis booths. He didn't even think about his one, brief love affair with Yvonne McGruder, the ship's female boxing champion.

What he did, in fact, think of was a bowl of soup. A bowl of gazpacho soup.

Then he died.

Then everyone died.

TWENTY

Deep in the belly of *Red Dwarf*, safely sealed in the cargo hold, Frankenstein nibbled happily from a box of fish paste, while four tiny sightless kittens suckled noisily beneath her.

Part Two

Alone in a Godless
universe, and out
of Shake'n'Vac

ONE

The hatch to the stasis booth zuzz-zungged open, and a green 'Exit now' sign flashed on and off above Lister's head.

Holly's digitalized faced appeared on the eight-foot-square wall monitor.

'It is now safe for you to emerge from stasis.'

'I only just got in.'

'Please proceed to the Drive Room for debriefing.' Holly's face melted into the smooth greyness of the blank screen.

'But I only just got in,' insisted Lister.

He walked down the empty corridor towards the Xpress lift. What was that smell? A musty smell. Like an old attic. He knew that smell. It was just like the smell of his grandmother's cellar. He'd never noticed it before.

And what was that noise? A kind of hissing buzz. The air-conditioning? Why could he hear the air-conditioning? He'd never heard it before. He suddenly realized it wasn't what he was hearing that was odd, it was what he *wasn't* hearing. Apart from the white noise of the air-conditioning, there was no other sound. Just the lonely squeals of his rubber soles on the corridor floor. And there was dust everywhere. Curious mounds of white dust lying in random patterns.

'Where is everybody?'

Holly projected his face onto the floor in front of Lister.

'They're dead, Dave,' he said, solemnly.

'Who is?' asked Lister, absently.

Softly: 'Everybody, Dave.'

'What?' Lister smiled.

'Everybody's dead, Dave.'

'What? Everybody?'

'Yes. Everybody's dead, Dave.

'What? Petersen?'

'Yes. They're *all* dead. *Everybody* is dead, Dave.'

'Burroughs?'

Holly sighed. 'Everybody is dead, Dave.'

'Selby?'

'Yes.'

'Not Chen?'

'Gordon Bennet!' Holly snapped. 'Yes, Chen! Everybody. Everybody's dead, Dave.'

'Even the Captain?'

'YES! EVERYBODY.'

Lister squeaked along the corridor. A tic in his left cheek pulled his face into staccato smiles. He wanted to laugh. Everybody was dead. Why did he want to laugh? No, they couldn't all be dead. Not everybody. Not *literally* everybody.

'What about Rimmer?'

'HE'S DEAD, DAVE. EVERYBODY IS DEAD. EVERYBODY IS DEAD, DAVE. DAVE, EVERYBODY IS DEAD.' Holly tried all four words in every possible permutation, with every possible inflection, finishing with: 'DEAD, DAVE, EVERYBODY *IS*, EVERYBODY IS, *DAVE*, DEAD.'

Lister looked blankly in no particular direction, while his face struggled to find an appropriate expression.

'Wait,' he said, after a while. 'Are you telling me *everybody's* dead?'

Holly rolled his eyes, and nodded.

The enormous Drive Room echoed with silence. The banks of computers on autopilot whirred about their business.

'Holly,' Lister's small voice resonated in the giant chamber, 'what are these piles of dust?'

The dust lay on the floors, on chairs, everywhere, all arranged in small, neat dunes. Lister dipped his finger in one and tasted it.

'That,' said Holly from his huge screen, 'is Console Executive Imran Sanchez.'

Lister's tongue hung guiltily from his mouth, and he wiped the white particles which had once formed part of Console Executive Imran Sanchez onto his jacket cuff.

'So, what happened?'

Holly told him about the cadmium II radiation leak; how the crew had been wiped out within seconds; how he'd headed the ship pell-mell out of the solar system, to avoid spreading nuclear contamination; and how he'd had to keep Lister in stasis until the radiation had reached a safe background level.

'So . . . How long did you keep me in stasis?'

'Three million years,' said Holly, as casually as he could.

Lister acted as if he hadn't heard. Three million years? It had no meaning. If it had been *thirty* years, he would have thought 'What a long time.' But three *million* years. Three million years was just . . . stupid.

He wandered over to the chair opposite the console he'd seen Kochanski operate.

'So, Krissie's dead,' he said, staring at the hummock of dust. 'I always . . .' His voice tailed away.

He tried to remember her face. He tried to remember the pinball smile.

'Well, if it's any consolation,' said Holly, 'if she had survived, the age difference would be insurmountable. I mean, you're twenty-four, she's three million: it takes a lot for a relationship with that kind of age gap to work.'

Lister wasn't listening. 'I always thought we'd get back together. I, ah, had this sort of plan that one day I'd have enough money to buy a farm on Fiji. It's cheap land there, and . . . in a half-assed kind of way, I always pictured she'd be there with me.'

This was getting morbid. Holly tried to lighten the atmosphere.

'Well,' he said, 'she wouldn't be much use to you on Fiji now.'

'No,' said Lister.

'Not unless it snowed,' said Holly, 'and you needed something to grit the path with.'

Lister screwed up his face in distaste. 'Holly!'

'Sorry. I've been on my own for three million years. I'm just used to saying what I think.'

For some time now, well, the last two hundred thousand years to be exact, Holly had grown increasingly concerned about himself. For a computer with an IQ of six thousand, it seems to him he was behaving in a more and more erratic way.

In fact, he'd long suspected he'd gone a bit peculiar. Just as a bachelor who spends too much time on his own gradually develops quirks and eccentricities, so a computer who spends three million years alone in Deep Space can get, well, set in his ways. Become quirky. Go a little bit . . . odd.

Holly decided not to burden Lister with this anxiety, and hoped his oddness would eventually sort itself out now he had a bit of company.

Another slight concern which he tried to put to the back of his RAM was that, for a computer with an IQ of six thousand, there was a rather alarming amount of knowledge he seemed to have forgotten. It wasn't, on the whole, important things, but was nonetheless fairly disturbing.

He knew, for instance, that Isaac Newton was a famous physicist, but he couldn't remember why.

He couldn't remember the capital of Luxembourg.

He *could* recall pi to thirty thousand digits, but he couldn't say for absolute certain whether port was on the left side, and starboard on the right, or whether it was the other way round.

Who knocked Swansea City out of the FA Cup in 1967? He *used* to know. It was a mystery now.

Obviously none of this missing information was absolutely vital for the smooth running of a mining ship three million years out into Deep Space. But technically he was supposed to know more-or-less everything and, frankly, there were some worrying gaps. He could remember, for instance, that in the second impression, 1959 publication of *Lolita* by Vladimir Nabakov, printed in Great Britain by the Shenval Press (London, Hertford and Harrow), page 60 was far and away the dirtiest page. But was Nabakov German or Russian? It totally eluded him.

Maybe it wasn't important. Of course it wasn't important.

Still, it was for Holly a source of perturbation.

It's a source of perturbation, he thought. Then he wondered whether there was such a word as 'perturbation', or whether he'd just made it up. He didn't know that either. Oh, it was hopeless.

Lister sat in the empty Copacabana Hawaiian Cocktail Bar and poured a triple whisky into his double whisky, then topped it up with a whisky. Absently, he lit the filter end of a cigarette and tried to assimilate all the information Holly had thrown at him.

Everybody was dead.

Everybody.

He'd been in stasis three million years.

Three million years.

Since one drunken night outside the 'Marie Lloyd' off Regent Street, London, every step he'd taken had led him further and further from home. First it was Mimas, then Miranda, and now he was three million *years* away. Three million years out into Deep Space. Further than any human being had ever been before.

And he was totally alone.

The enormity of all this was slowly beginning to sink in when Holly dropped his final bombshell. The one about the human race being extinct.

'What d'you mean, "extinct"?'

'Well, three million years is a very good age for a species. I mean, your average genus only survives a couple of hundred thousand years, max. And that's with a clean-living species, like dinosaurs. Dinosaurs didn't totally screw up the environment. They just went around quietly eating things. And even then, they didn't get to clock up the big one mill. So the chances of the human race making it to the big three-oh-oh-oh-oh-oh-oh are practically non-existent. So I'm afraid you just have to face up to the very real possibility that your species is dead.'

Much to his surprise, Lister had let out a sob.

'Were you very close?' Holly tilted his head sympathetically. 'Well, yeah, I suppose you must have been, really.' That was a bit of an odd thing to say, he thought.

Lister took out his shirt-tail and blew his nose. 'So, I'm the last human being alive?'

'Yeah. You never think it's going to happen to your species, do you? It's always something that happens to somebody else's.'

Lister spent the next few days going to pieces.

There seemed little point in getting dressed, and so he wandered around naked, swigging from a bottle of whisky.

He didn't know what to do.

He didn't know if there was anything *to* do.

And worst of all, he didn't much care.

He slept wherever he fell, a painful, dreamless sleep. He hardly ate, and drank a small loch-worth of whisky. He didn't even *like* whisky, but beer was too cumbersome to carry around in sufficient quantities to achieve oblivion.

He lost a stone in weight, and started shouting at people who weren't there.

Every evening, at around 5 p.m. he'd stagger, stark naked, into the Drive Room and, waving his whisky bottle dangerously in the air, he'd belch incoherent obscentities at Holly's huge visage on the gigantic monitor screen.

Sometimes Lister imagined he'd heard the phone ring, and he'd rush to pick it up.

On the evening of the fifth day as he staggered through the *Red Dwarf* shopping mall, toasting invisible crowds, he keeled over and blacked out.

When he woke up in the medical unit, a man with an 'H' on his forehead was looking down at him with undisguised contempt.

TWO

'You're a hologram,' said Lister.

'So I am,' said Rimmer.

'You died in the accident,' said Lister.

'So I did,' said Rimmer.

'What's it like?'

'Death?' Rimmer mused. 'It's like going on holiday with a group of Germans.' He cradled his head in his hands. 'I'm so depressed I want to weep. To be cut down in my prime – a boy of thirty-one, with the body of a thirty-year-old. It's unbearable. All my plans; my career, my future; everything hinged on my being alive. It was *mandatory*.'

'What happened to me? Did I black out?'

'Excuse me, I'm talking about my being dead.'

'Sorry. I thought you'd finished.'

'I'm so depressed,' repeated Rimmer, '*so* depressed.'

Over the next couple of days, Lister slowly recovered in the medical bay. One morning, while Rimmer was off reading the *How to Cope With Your Own Death* booklet for the fifteenth time, Lister took the opportunity to ask Holly why he'd brought Rimmer back.

'You'd gone to pieces. You couldn't cope. You needed a companion.'

'But *Rimmer*??'

'I did a probability study,' lied Holly, 'and it turns out Rimmer is absolutely the best person to keep you sane.'

'Rimmer?'

Holly's disembodied head tilted forward in a nod.

'Why not Petersen?'

'A man who buys a methane-filled twenty-four bed-roomed bijou residence on an oxygenless moon whose only distinction is that it rotates in the opposite direction from its mother planet – you seriously expect me to bring him back to keep you sane? Gordon Bennett – he couldn't even keep himself sane, let alone anyone else.'

'Yeah, but at least we had things in common.'

'The only thing you had in common was your mutual interest in consuming ridiculous amounts of alcohol.'

'Selby? Chen?'

'Ditto.'

'What about Krissie?'

'Dave, she finished with you.'

'But *Rimmer*?? Anyone would have been better than Rimmer. Anyone. Hermann *Goering* would have been better than Rimmer. All right, he was a drug-crazed Nazi trans-vestite, but at least we could have gone dancing.'

'It was Jean-Paul Sartre,' said Holly, thinking it may very well actually have been Albert Camus, or Flaubert, or perhaps it was even Sacha Distel, 'who said hell was being trapped for eternity in a room with your friends.'

'Sure,' said Lister, 'but all Sartre's mates were French.'

'I think I'm thinking, therefore I might possibly be,' Rimmer said aloud as he padded silently around the sleeping quarters in his hologramatic slippers. Try as he might, he couldn't even begin to grapple with the metaphysics of it all.

'I think I might be thinking, therefore I may possibly be being.' It was mumbo-jumbo to Rimmer. It was worse than Emerson, Lake and Palmer lyrics.

'I'm *so* depressed.'

He hated being dead.

When he was a boy on Io, he remembered witnessing an

'Equal rights for the Dead' march, where holograms from all the moons of Jupiter had rallied for better conditions.

The Dead were generally given short shrift throughout the solar system. They were banned from most hotels and restaurants. They found it almost impossible to hold down a decent job. And, even on television, although holograms featured occasionally, they were generally only included as token deads. Not a single golf club throughout known space had a dead member.

The living had a very uncomfortable relationship with holograms in general, reminding them as they did of their own mortality. Also there was a natural resentment towards 'Deadies' – to become a hologram, outside of the Space Corps, you had to be one of the mega-rich. The horribly expensive computer run-time, and the massive power supply that was needed, kept hologramatic afterlife very exclusive indeed.

Sitting on the shoulders of his brother, Frank, the six-year-old Rimmer had booed and jeered with the rest of the crowd. Encouraged by Frank, he'd actually personally thrown a stone, which had passed silently through the back of a hologram woman marching in line.

'Deadies! Dirty Deadies!'

And now he was one of them.

A dirty Deady.

Well, he wasn't going to let it get him down any more. He wasn't going to let it stand in his way. He was dead, there was no use bleating about it. Was that a reason to quit? Did Napoleon quit when he was dead? Did Julius Caesar quit when he was dead?

Well . . . yes.

But that was before the hologram was invented. And that was the advantage he had over two of the greatest men in history. He may not have been the most successful person who ever lived when he was alive but, by God, he'd make up for that in his death.

There was still that ziggurat to climb. There was still that gold bar to achieve.

Nelson had one eye and one arm. Caesar was an epileptic. Napoleon, the man himself, suffered so badly from gonorrhoea and syphilis, he could barely pee. It seemed a veritable boon to Rimmer that the only disability he appeared to have was being dead!

First thing tomorrow, he thought, *I'm going to get the skutters to paint a sign to hang over my bunk.* And he pictured it in his mind's eye, on polished oak:

'TOMORROW IS THE FIRST DAY OF THE REST OF YOUR DEATH.'

THREE

HNNNnnnnNNNNNKRHHhhhhhhhHHHHHH
HNNNnnnnNNNNNKRHHhhhhhhhHHHHHH

A sound like a buzz-saw played through an open-air rock festival's PA system awoke Rimmer from a dream about his mother chasing him through a car-park with a sub-machine-gun.

He swung his legs over the bunk, and tried to locate the sound of the buzz-saw played through an open-air rock festival's PA system. It was Lister, snoring.

HNNNnnnnNNNNNKRHHhhhhhhhHHHHHH
HNNNnnnnNNNNNKRHHhhhhhhhHHHHHH

The snore drilled into Rimmer's skull – perfectly even, up and down, followed by a catarrhy trill, and then the worst part of all: the silence. The silence that always made him think Lister had stopped snoring. One second. Two seconds. Three seconds. He has, he has stopped snoring! Four seconds. Fi . . . then, the snort, then the revolting semi-choking sound as the mucus shifted around his cavernous nasal system, and back onto the perfectly even snore.

HNNNnnnnNNNNNKRHHhhhhhhhHHHHHH
HNNNnnnnNNNNNKRHHhhhhhhhHHHHHH

Rimmer stood up and leaned over Lister's sleeping form. There was a half-empty metal curry tray lying on his chest, which rose and fell in rhythm with his grinding snore.

Rimmer's first impulse was to reach over and pinch his nose, but, of course, he couldn't. He couldn't shake him either, or turn him on his side. He couldn't even take a thin piece of piano wire and slowly garrotte him. If he hadn't been a hologram, this would definitely have been his favourite option.

He arched over, until his mouth was in whispering distance of Lister's ear. Then he screamed: 'STOP SNORING, YOU FILTHY SON OF A BASTARD'S BASTARD'S BASTARD!!!'

Lister jerked awake. 'What?'

'You were snoring.'

'Eh?'

'You were snoring.'

'Oh,' said Lister, lying back down. 'Sorry.'

Within three seconds Lister was back asleep. And within ten, he was snoring again.

HNNNnnnn NNNNNKR HHhhhhhhh HHHHHH
HNNNnnnn NNNNNKR HHhhhhhhh HHHHHH

The man was impossible to live with! He was an animal! He was an orang-utan! He was a hippo! He was like one of those little grey monkeys you see at the zoo who openly masturbate whenever you go round with your great-aunt Florrie! He was quite the most revoltingly heinous creature it had ever been Rimmer's misfortune to encounter. What further proof did you need that God did not exist? As if He'd allow this . . . this onion! to become the last surviving member of the human race. He symbolized everything that was cheap and low and nasty and tacky about Mankind. Why *him*? A man whose idea of a change of clothing was to turn his T-shirt inside out, so that the stench was on the outside! Who used orange peel and curry cartons as makeshift ashtrays. Who would frequently tug out a huge great lump of rotting, fetid meat from one of the cavities in his teeth and announce proudly that it could feed a family of four! Who bit his nails – his toenails! He would actually sit there, with his foot in his mouth, and trim his nails by biting them. And then – the most hideous thing of all – he would eat the cuttings! Eating your toenails, for God's sake! This was the Last Man. The Last Human Being. A person who could belch *La Bamba* after eleven pints of lager. A man who ate so many curries he sweated Madras sauce. Revolting! His bed sheets looked like someone had just given birth to a baby on them. And he destroyed things! Not on purpose: he was just such a clumsy, slobby, ham-fisted son-of-a-prostidroid somehow he always destroyed things. Rimmer remembered once showing him a photograph of his mother and, five seconds later, turned round to see him absently using it as a toothpick! He once lent him his favourite album, and when it came back there was a footprint over James Last's face! And raspberry jam seeds buried in the groove. How is that possible? To get jam on a record? Who listens to James Last and eats raspberry jam? And the inner sleeve was missing! And there was a telephone number and a doodle on the lyric sheet! Destroyed!

HNNNnnnn NNNNNKR HHhhhhhhh HHHHHH
HNNNnnnn NNNNNKR HHhhhhhhh HHHHHH

How could anyone possibly live with this man??

HNNNnnnn NNNNNKR HHhhhhhhh HHHHHH
HNNNnnnn NNNNNKR HHhhhhhhh HHHHHH

How could it be that here, snoring like an asthmatic warthog, was the last representative of the human race? How was it possible that this man was alive, while *he* was dead?

How???

HOW???

HOW????

FOUR

Only two days earlier Lister had finally got round to collecting all his personal belongings from Vacuum Storage, and now here he was, sitting on his bunk, packing them all up again to take them back to Vacuum Storage.

He'd asked Holly to turn the ship around and head back to Earth. Maybe the human race *was* extinct, maybe it wasn't. Maybe they'd evolved into a race of super-beings. Maybe they'd wiped one another out in some stupid war and the ants had taken over. But where else was there to go?

Earth was home. He had to find out if it still existed, even if it did take another three million years to get back. So he'd decided to go back into stasis. What else was there to do? He certainly had no intention of hanging around with only a highly neurotic dead man for company.

He looked down at his vacuum storage trunk. He really did have a pretty feeble collection of belongings: four cigarette lighters, all out of gas; a copy of the *Pop-up Karma Sutra* — *Zero gravity version*; a hard ball of well-chewed gum, which he'd bought at a bar in Mimas from a guy who guaranteed it had once been chewed by Chelsea Brown, the famous actress; a pair of his adoptive grandmother's false teeth, which he'd kept for two reasons: (a) sentimental, and (b) they were just the thing for opening bottles of beer; his bass guitar with two strings (both G); three hundred and fifty Zero-Gee football magazines; and his entire collection of Rasta-Billy-Skank DAT tapes.

And, of course, there were his goldfish.

He wandered over to the three-foot-long oblong tank and peered into the murky green water. At first, he couldn't see a thing through the slimy silt. He flicked on the underwater illumination switch and pressed his face to the side of the tank. Gradually, through the gloom, he made out a moving silhouette. As his eyes adjusted, he saw it was Lennon, swimming happily in and out of the fake plastic Vatican. But he couldn't see McCartney.

He rolled up his sleeve and swirled his arm around in the stagnant filth, releasing a pungent, evil smell. Finally he located the missing fish, lodged in the papal balcony above St Peter's Square. It was dead.

He shook his head, and smacked the fish violently against the corner of Rimmer's slanting architect's desk, then held the fish to his ear and listened. Nothing.

Picking up Rimmer's Space Scout knife, he flicked out a blade and opened up the fish like a watch.

There was the problem! A loose battery. He prodded it back into place and snapped the fish closed. McCartney blinked back into life. He dropped the piscine droid into the water and watched as it happily swam off through the arch of the plastic Sistine Chapel, backwards.

'Ye-es,' said Lister. 'Brutal.'

Rimmer walked in through the hatchway and spotted Lister's vacuum trunk. 'What are you doing?'

Rimmer listened in mounting disbelief as Lister outlined his plan. 'What about me? What am I supposed to do on my own for three million years?'

'Well, I dunno. I haven't really thought about it.'

'No. Exactly.'

'Come on – you can't expect me to hang around here. Why don't you get Holly to turn you off till we get home?'

'Because, dingleberry brain,' Rimmer rose to his feet, 'if by some gigantic fluke the Earth still exists, and if, by an even greater stretching of the laws of probability, the human race is still alive, and if during the six million years we've been away they haven't evolved into some kind of super race, and we can still understand them; if all that comes to pass – when I get back to Earth, the reasons for me being brought back as a hologram will no longer apply, and my personality disc will be neatly packed away in some dusty vault that nobody ever goes in. And that will be the end of Rimmer, Arnold J.'

'You never know. When we get back, it might turn out that they've found a cure for Death.'

Rimmer sucked in his cheeks and rolled his eyes around in their sockets.

'Well, you never know,' said Lister, feebly.

'Oh yes. I expect doctors' waiting rooms are absolutely heaving with cadavers. "Ah, Mrs Harrington. Dropped dead again, eh? Never mind."' Rimmer mimed scribbling a prescription. '"Take two of these, three times a day, and try not to get run over by another bus."'

'I'm going into stasis,' said Lister, picking up his vacuum trunk, 'and that's that. You don't seriously expect me to spend the rest of my life alone here with you.'

'Why not?'

'Fifty-odd years? Alone with you?'

'What's wrong with that?'

Lister stopped and put down his trunk. 'I think we should get something straight. I think there's something you don't understand.'

'What?' said Rimmer.

'The thing is,' said Lister as kindly as he could: 'I don't actually like you.'

Rimmer stared, unblinking. This really was news to him. He didn't like Lister, but he always thought Lister liked him. Why on Io shouldn't he like him? What was there not to like?

'Since when?' he said, with a slight crack in his voice.

'Since the second we first met. Since a certain taxi ride on Mimas.'

'That wasn't me! That guy in the false moustache who went to an android brothel? That wasn't me!'

Rimmer was outraged at Lister's accusation. Even though it was true, he felt it was so out of kilter with his own image of himself, he was able to summon up genuine indignation. As if he, Arnold J. Rimmer, would pay money to a lump of metal and plastic to have sexual intercourse with him! It just wasn't like him.

True, he did it, but it wasn't like him!

'I've never been to an android brothel in my life. And if you so much as mention it again, I'll . . .' Rimmer faltered. He suddenly realized there wasn't very much he *could* do to Lister.

'I don't get it. What point are you trying to make?'

'The point I'm trying to make, you dirty son of a fetid whoremonger's bitch, is that we're friends!' Rimmer smiled as warmly as he could to help disguise the massive incongruity he'd walked straight into.

'Sniff your coffee and wake up, Rimmer; we are not friends.'

'I know what you're referring to,' Rimmer nodded his head vigorously. 'It's because I gave you a hard time since you came aboard, isn't it? But don't you see? I had to do that, to build up your character. To change the boy into a man.'

'Oh, do smeg off.'

'I always thought you saw me as a sort of big brother character. Heck — we don't always get on. But then, what brothers do? Cain didn't always get on with Abel . . .'

'He killed him.'

'Absolutely. But underneath all that they were still brothers, with brotherly affection. Heaven knows, I didn't always get on with my brothers — in fact once, when I was fourteen, I needed mouth-to-mouth resuscitation after all three of them held my head down a toilet for rather too long – but we laughed about it afterwards, when I'd started breathing again.'

'You're not going to persuade me not to go into stasis. I am not spending the rest of my life with a man who keeps his underpants on coat hangers.'

Rimmer held up his outspread palms in a gesture of innocence. 'I'm not trying to persuade you.'

'Then what's all this about?'

'I don't know. I'm not sure what anything's about any more.'

Here comes the emotional blackmail, thought Lister.

'It's not easy, you know, being . . . dead.'

'Uhn,' Lister grunted.

'It's so hard to come to terms with. I mean . . . death. Your own death. I mean, you have plans . . . so many things you wanted to do, and now . . .'

'Look – I'm sorry you're dead, O K? It was cruddy luck. But you've got to put it behind you. You're completely obsessed by it.'

'Obsessed??'

'It's all you ever talk about.'

'Well, pardon me for dying.'

'Frankly, Rimmer, it's very boring. You're like one of those people who are always talking about their illnesses.'

'Well!' said Rimmer, his eyes wide in astonishment.

'It's just boring. Change the disc. Flip the channel. Death isn't the handicap it once was. For smeg's sake, cheer up.'

'Well!' said Rimmer. And he couldn't think of anything else to say. So he said 'Well!' again.

'And quite honestly, the prospect of hanging around and having to listen to you whining and moaning, and bleating and whingeing for the next three quarters of a century, because you happen to have snuffed it, does not exactly knock me out.'

'Well!' said Rimmer.

'Fifty years alone with you? I'd rather drink a pint of my own diarrhoea.'

'Well!'

'Or a pint of somebody else's, come to that. Every hour, on the hour, for the next seventy years.'

'I can't believe' – Rimmer was shaking – 'you've just said that.'

Holly faded into focus on the sleeping quarters' vid-screen.

'Oi,' he said, rather un-computerlike, 'I've just opened the radiation seals to the cargo decks. And there's something down there.'

'What do you mean?'

'Some kind of life-form.'

'What is it?'

'I can only see it on the heat scanner. I don't know what it is – I only know what it isn't.'

'What isn't it, then?'

'It isn't human.'

FIVE

Lister clutched the bazookoid – the heavy portable rock-blasting mining laser – to his chest, and checked again that the pack on his back was registering 'Full Charge'.

Light flitted through the wire mesh of the rickety lift as it clumsily juddered its way down into the bowels of the ship.

Three miles of lift shaft. Over five hundred floors, most of them stretching the six-mile length of the ship.

These were the cargo decks, where all the supplies were stored.

The tiny, exposed cage shuddered and rocked slowly past floor after floor.

Down.

Perhaps twenty floors of food, vacuum-sealed, tin mountains, stretching out beyond vision.

Down.

Four floors of wood – a million chopped trees stacked in silent pyramids.

Down.

Floors of mining equipment.

Down.

Floors of raw silicates, mined from Ganymede.

Down.

Floors of water, stored and still in enormous glass tanks.

And down.

And the only sound was the metallic squealing of the lift cable as it plunged them deeper and deeper into the gloomy abyss.

'I don't know why *I'm* scared. I'm a hologram. Whatever it is, it can't do anything to me.'

'Thanks. That makes me feel really secure.'

The gloom enveloped them. The light on Lister's mining helmet cut only twenty feet into the darkness. Lister flipped down the helmet's night-visor and switched the beam to infra red.

Down.

Then, something strange. These floors were empty. Hundreds of cubic miles of supplies were missing! Food, metal, wood, water – missing.

'It's gone!'

'What has?' Rimmer squinted blindly into the darkness.

'Everything.'

'What d'you mean, everything?'

'All the supplies. The last ten floors – they were all empty.'

'I'm *so* glad I'm already dead. I'm so, so glad.'

'You want to shut the smeg up?'

Down.

D

o

w

n

In the bottom right hand corner of Lister's visor a small green cross began to flicker.

'Oh, smeg. There *is* something here.'

'Where?'

The cross crept up the visor. Lister wanted to say: 'The next floor,' but he couldn't. He couldn't speak.

The lift coughed to a stop. The whine of the motor faded to nothing.

There it was.

Stretching before them, six miles in length, half-lit and desolate.

A huge, impossible city.

A *city*!

The lift doors folded open – *cher-chunk*! – and they stepped out onto the rough cobbled street.

Crudely fashioned igloo-shaped dwellings lined the roadway; hummocks of carved wood, without doorways. Each had only a slit, perhaps a yard wide and less than a foot high, cut six feet from the ground.

Lister checked the charge on the bazookoid back pack, and they both started cautiously down the street. Before them was a crossroads. The igloo hummocks stretched out in every direction. The flashing cross in Lister's visor throbbed more insistently, and indicated they should turn right.

'What *is* this place?'

Lister slung the bazookoid over his shoulder and scrambled up one of the hummocks. He poked his head through a slit and peered into the dim interior.

'Some kind of house. But it's tiny. Just enough room for two people to crouch in and peer out of the gash at the top. Whatever lived here really liked confined spaces.' Built into a tiny recess in the wall was a small bookcase containing six books. Lister reached in and managed to grab three of them. He dropped down from the hummock.

Rimmer peered over his shoulder as he opened each book in turn. Every single page in every book was blank. Lister slipped the books into his haversack, grabbed the bazookoid, re-checked the charge, and they moved off again.

After five minutes or so, they reached a square. Rows of benches faced a television screen attached to a video recorder. Lister ejected the disc. It bore the ship's regulation supply logo.

'What is it?' asked Rimmer.

'"The Flintstones".'

They turned left. More hummocks. Another square, but this time set out like a street café: tables with parasols; wooden chairs. And in the centre: a table, fully laid, with two gold candelabra, both lit. A meal, half-eaten, sat steaming on a plate.

The blip on Lister's visor was pulsing faster than ever.

'It's here!' Lister's finger tightened on the beam button of the bazookoid. 'Whatever it is, it's right here!'

A flash.

A pink blur flashed from the top of a hummock, pinning Lister to the floor, and sending the weapon skittering across the cobbles.

Rimmer watched, half-paralysed, as the pink neon-suited man with immaculate coiffeur sniffed Lister, looked up with a puzzled expression, sniffed him more deeply, then finally got to his feet, took out a clothes brush and smoothed out his suit.

'Sorry, Man,' he said, 'I thought you were food.'

SIX

From the moment he discovered that the cadmium II had achieved critical mass, Holly had less than fifteen nanoseconds to act. He sealed off as much of the ship as possible — the whole cargo area, and the ship's supply bay. Simultaneously, he set the drive computer to accelerate far beyond the dull green-blue disc of Neptune in the distance, and out into the abyss of unknown space. Then he read the Bible, the Koran, and other major religious works: he covered Islam, Zoroastrianism, Mazdaism, Zarathustrianism, Dharma, Brahmanism, Hinduism, Vedanta, Jainism, Buddhism, Hinayana, Mahayana, Sikhism, Shintoism, Taoism and Confucianism. Then he read all of Marx, Engels, Freud, Jung and Einstein. And, to kill the remaining few nanoseconds, he skipped briefly through Kevin Keegan's Football — It's a Funny Old Game.

At the end of this, Holly came to two conclusions. First, given the whole sphere of human knowledge, it was still impossible to determine the existence or not of God. And second, Kevin Keegan should have stuck to having his hair permed.

In the hold, Frankenstein's four offspring began to breed. Each litter produced an average of four kittens, three times a year. At the end of the first year, the second generation of kittens started to breed too. They also produced three annual litters of three to four kittens.

When Frankenstein died, at the great old age of fourteen, she left behind one hundred and ninety-eight thousand, seven hundred and thirty-two cats.

198,732 cats, who continued to breed.

*

Still Red Dwarf *accelerated.*

Holly witnessed at first hand phenomena which had never been witnessed before. He saw phenomena which had only been guessed at by theoretical physicists.

He saw a star form.

He saw another star die.

He saw a black hole.

He saw pulsars and quasars.

He saw twin and triplet sun systems.

He saw sights Copernicus would have torn out his eyes for, but all the while he couldn't stop thinking how bad that book was by Kevin Keegan.

The cats continued to breed.

Red Dwarf *continued to accelerate.*

The forty-square mile cargo hold was seething with cats.

A sea of cats.

A sea of cats, sealed from the radiation-poisoned decks above, with nowhere to go.

Only the smartest, the biggest and the strongest survived.

The mutants.

The mutants, who had rudimentary fingers instead of claws, who stood on their hind legs, and clubbed rivals to death with crudely-made clubs. Who found the best breeding mates.

And bred.

Felis erectus was born.

Red Dwarf, *still accelerating, passed five stars in concentric orbits, performing a breathtaking, mind-boggling stellar ballet.*

Not that Holly noticed.

He'd been on his own now for two million years and was no longer interested in mind-boggling stellar ballets. What he was really into was Netta Muskett novels. The young doctor had just told Jemma she had only three years to live, as he held her in his powerful masculine grip, his dark brooding eyes piercing her very soul. Outside, the suns danced into a perfect pentagon and span, end over end, like a gigantic Catherine wheel.

But Holly didn't see it. He was too busy reading Doctor, Darling.

Then there was a plague.

And the plague was hunger.

Less than thirty Cat tribes now survived, roaming the cargo decks on their hind legs in a desperate search for food.

But the food had gone.

The supplies were finished.

Weak and ailing, they prayed at the supply hold's silver mountains: huge towering acres of metal rocks which, in their pagan way, the mutant Cats believed watched over them.

Amid the wailing and the screeching one Cat stood up and held aloft the sacred icon. The icon which had been passed down as holy, and one day would make its use known.

It was a piece of V-shaped metal with a revolving handle on its head.

He took down a silver rock from the silver mountain, while the other Cats cowered and screamed at the blasphemy.

He placed the icon on the rim of the rock, and turned the handle.

And the handle turned.

And the rock opened.

And inside the rock was Alphabetti spaghetti in tomato sauce.

And in the other rocks were even more delights. Sugar-free baked beans. Chicken and mushroom Toastie Toppers. Faggots in rich meaty gravy. All sealed in perfect vacuums, preserved from the ravages of Time.

God had spoken.

And Felis sapiens was born.

Holly was gurning. He was pulling his pixelized face into the most *bizarre and ludicrous expressions he could muster. He'd been gurning now for nearly two thousand years. It wasn't much of a hobby, but it helped pass the time.*

He was beginning to worry that he was going computer-senile. Driven crazy by loneliness. What he needed, he decided, was a companion.

He would build a woman.

A perfectly functioning human woman, capable of independent thought and decision-making. Identical to a real woman in the minutest detail.

The problem was he didn't know how.

He didn't even know what to make the nose out of.

So he gave the whole scheme up as a bad idea, and started gurning again.

And there was a war between the Cats.

A bloody war that laid waste many of their number.

But the reason was good.

The cause was sensible.

The principle was worth fighting over.

It was a holy war.

Some of the Cats believed the one true father of Catkind was a man called Cloister, who saved Frankenstein, the Holy Mother, and was frozen in time by the evil men who sought to kill her. One day Cloister would return to lead them to Bearth, the planet where they could make their home.

The other Cats believed exactly the same thing, except they maintained the name of the true Father of Catkind was a man called Clister.

They spent the best part of two thousand years fighting over this huge, insuperable theological chasm.

Millions died.

Finally, a truce was called.

Commandeering the fleet of shuttles from the docking bay, half the Cats flew off in one direction, in search of Cloister and the

Promised Planet, and the other half flew off in the opposite direction, in search of Clister and the Promised Planet.

Behind them they left the ones who were too weak to travel: the old, the lame, the sick and the dying.

And one by one, they died.

Soon only two remained: one a cripple, one an idiot.

They snuggled together for warmth and companionship.

And one day, to the cripple and the idiot, a son was born.

SEVEN

So the last human being alive, a man who had died, and a creature who'd evolved from cats, stood around the metal table that was bolted to the floor of the sleeping quarters and listened to a computer with an IQ of six thousand, who couldn't remember who'd knocked Swansea City out of the 1967 FA cup, explain what the hell was happening.

'So he's a Cat,' said Lister for the fourteenth time.

The Cat took a small portable steam iron out of his pocket and started pressing the sleeve of his jacket.

Outwardly, at least, he was human in appearance – there was a slight flattening of his face: his ears were a little higher on his head; and two of his gleaming upper teeth hung down longer and sharper than the others, so they peeked, whitely, over his lips whenever he grinned. Which he did a lot.

He didn't seem to have a trace of super-ego. He was all ego and id – monumentally self-centred and, if he'd been human, you would have described him as vain. But you couldn't apply human values to Cats – there seemed to be very little connection between the two cultures. The invention which proved the turning point in Cat history wasn't Fire or the Wheel: it was the Steam-operated Trouser Press.

Getting information out of the Cat wasn't easy: if you asked him too many questions, he just got bored, and went off to take one of the five or six showers he appeared to need daily.

He didn't have a name. He found it difficult to understand the idea. He was of the unshakeable conviction that he was the absolute centre of the entire universe, the reason for its being; and the notion that someone might now know who he was was beyond his comprehension.

'What about in relationships?' Lister had persisted.

'Re-la-tion-ships?' The Cat rolled the word around on his tongue. The Cats had learned English from the vast number of video discs and training films that were stored in the cargo decks, waiting for delivery to Triton. But most human concepts eluded them.

'Yeah, you know, between a man cat and a woman cat. What do you call each other?'

'Hey, you.'

'What? In the entire relationship, you never refer to each other by name?'

'You know how long a Cat relationship lasts? Three minutes. First minute's fine; second minute, you feel trapped! Third minute, you've got to leave.'

The very thought of a relationship which lasted longer than three minutes brought the Cat out in a cold sweat, and he had to go and take another hot shower.

And so the evening progressed.

When the Cat wasn't showering or snoozing, he was preening. He appeared to have secreted about his immaculate person an arsenal of combs and brushes, none of which seemed to spoil the line of his immaculate pink suit.

For the most part, detail's of the Cat's background remained obscure. He found the concept of 'parents' bewildering. He couldn't believe there was ever a time he wasn't born. When he put his mind to it, he did recall two other Cats who used to be around, but most of the time they'd avoided each other. One of them, he reckoned, had probably been his mother — because she wouldn't sleep with him. In fact, she'd got quite angry at his approaches and hit him on the head with a large frying pan.

The other must have been his father; a deeply religious Cat who was constantly reciting the Seven Cat Commandments: 'Thou shalt not be cool; Thou shalt not be in vain; Thou shalt not have more than ten suits; Thou shalt not partake of carnal knowledge with more than four members of the opposite sex at any one session; Thou shalt not slink; Thou shalt not hog the bathroom; and Thou shalt not steal another's hair-gel.'

In the Dark Ages of religious intolerance, these laws were laid down by Cat priests to keep their race in check. It was only through denying certain lusts, certain natural urges to be cool and stylish, they said, that a Cat could find redemption. Strict punishments were meted to transgressors: Cats caught slinking in public would have their shower units removed; Cats condemned as vain would have their hair-driers confiscated, and be forced to wear fashions some two or three seasons old.

'Paisley? With thin lapels and turn-ups?? But that was last spring! Please, no! Have mercy!'

The Cat finally tired of the relentless questioning and announced it was time for its main mid-evening snooze. He casually leapt up on top of Rimmer's locker, curled up in the impossibly small space and fell immediately into a deep and satisfying sleep.

'What are we going to do with him?' Rimmer asked. Lister sat at the table, playing with his locks. He was thinking. Watching Lister thinking always reminded Rimmer of a huge, old, rusty tractor trying to plough furrows in a concrete field.

Finally, he looked up. 'He's coming with us. Back to Earth.

Disappointment filtered through Rimmer's brittle smile.

'You're still going into stasis then? You're taking him with you?'

'Why not?'

No reason, he thought. *No reason at all. So long as you don't give two short smegs about Arnold J. Rimmer.*

EIGHT

'Jump here, jump back . . . Waaaah.'

The Cat slinked down the corridor, pulling a clothes rack on wheels which was packed with suits. Blue suits, green suits, red suits. Polka dots, stripes, checks. Silk suits, fur suits, plain suits. Each one he'd made himself during the years he'd been trapped down in the cargo hold.

'Jump up, jump down . . .' The cat spun round and did a little dance, without breaking stride.

He reached the Vacuum Storage floor, where Lister was waiting impatiently.

'What are you doing?'

'I'm doing what you said do.'

'I said "Bring a few basic essentials you can't leave behind."'

'Right,' agreed the Cat, 'and this is all I'm taking. Just this and the other ten racks. Travel light, move fast. Waaaaah.' He spun on the spot.

'You can't pack all this in Vacuum Storage – it'll take ages.'

The Cat's face drooped. He'd spent the last two hours trying to whittle his enormous collection down to his favourite hundred suits. He'd been *cruel* with himself. The yellow DJ with green piping had *gone*. The imitation walrus hide with the fake zebra collar was *history*! And his red PVC morning suit with matching top hat and cane – down the *tube*!

'You can take two suits,' Lister said firmly, 'and that's it.'

'Two suits?' the Cat laughed mockingly. 'Two? Then I'm staying, buddy.'

'You can't stay. When I come out, you'll be dead.'

'Two suits *is* dead.'

'Pick.'

The Cat walked up and down the racks, then he walked up and down the racks again. Then he went behind the racks and walked up and down them on the other side. 'How many did you say it was? Ten?'

'Two.'

'Oh, man.' The Cat walked up and down the racks again.

Lister walked up to the rack, grabbed two suits, and thrust them roughly into the vacuum trunk. 'OK, those are the two you're taking.'

The Cat picked up the arm of the first suit on the rack and shook it by the sleeve. 'Bye, man.' He tapped it on its padded shoulder and went to the next one.

Lister sighed. 'I'd better say so-long to Rimmer.'

'Bye, baby,' said the Cat to his next suit; 'gonna miss you.'

Lister walked off down the corridor. 'We're going into stasis in ten minutes. I'll meet you in the sleeping quarters.'

'Hey,' the Cat called, 'if I cut off my leg and leave it behind, can I take three?'

It didn't make sense.

As Holly flicked through the four zillion megabytes of navicomp data, and simultaneously cross-checked the information against all the sensor status databanks, he found it impossible to avoid the conclusion that *Red Dwarf* was 0.002 seconds away from doing something completely impossible.

It was about to break the light barrier.

True, the average cruising speed for a vessel the size of *Red Dwarf* was 200,000 miles an hour.

True, they had been accelerating constantly for the last three million years.

True, the ship was now clocking up 669,555,000 miles an hour, which was just 45,000 miles an hour below the speed of light.

And true, in 0.0019 seconds they would break the light barrier.

The thing was: it wasn't possible.

Light is the speed limit for the universe.

Nothing travels faster than light.

All of which was good. What wasn't so good was that *Red Dwarf* was about to do exactly that.

In 0.0017 seconds.

It didn't make sense.

Holly reprogrammed the Drive computer to slow down. Which the Drive computer did. But because they were accelerating so fast, slowing down merely meant they were accelerating slightly less quickly than they were before. However, they were still accelerating. So they were slowing down, but still going faster.

That didn't make much sense to Holly either.

The only thing that was clear was that by the time they'd slowed down enough to be actually slowing down, in the sense of going slower – rather than the kind of slowing down that meant they were actually getting faster, albeit faster more slowly – they would already have broken the light barrier.

Which was impossible.

And they were due to do this in 0.0013 seconds.

Holly hummed softly.

Holly had only uncovered all this when he'd tried to chart the ship's return course to Earth.

At first he'd assumed it was possible to do a three-point turn or loop the loop, but according to his calculations it would take the best part of three hundred and fifty thousand years just to do a fairly sharpish U-turn.

Then Holly got his plan. If he could manoeuvre *Red Dwarf* into orbit around a planet, they could use the gravitational pull to slingshot out 180° later on a heading back to Earth.

Brilliant!

Who said he was getting computer-senile?

Of course, this Fancy Dan astrobatics talk was all a tiny bit irrelevant, because they were about to break the light barrier, and Holly was fairly convinced that in so doing they would all be instantly reduced to their component atoms.

And as far as he could tell this was going to happen in 0.000 seconds.

Oh dear.

That was now.

NINE

At the same instant, Lister was everything and he was nothing. His mass was infinite and his mass was non-existent.

As he watched, his legs stretched out beneath him, as if he were teetering on the top of the World Trade Centre, staring down at his tiny feet miles below.

His face buckled and rippled. His eyelashes hung down over his cheeks like huge palm trees.

He was all colours and he was no colours. Instinctively, he reached out an arm to steady himself, and it telescoped away across the now-infinite space of the sleeping quarters as if it were elastic.

He turned to get his bearings, and found himself looking at the back of his own head.

And then he was falling, falling into himself, and when he opened his eyes he discovered his head was in his stomach; then just as quickly he mushroomed back out, and his head was the shape and size of an Egyptian pyramid.

He tried to walk. A mistake. His legs became hopelessly tangled. He forgot how many he had, and where they should go. Each step was like trying to construct a wayward deck-chair. And then he fell over. But he didn't go down, he went up.

He folded round on himself, to form a perfect cylinder, and everywhere he looked there was him.

Him him him him him him him him him him him him him him him him . . .

And all the hims started screaming as they spun, cutting orbits around themselves, like electrons.

And then it stopped.

And he was just standing in front of the washbasin, his razor in his hand, looking at his soaped-up face in the mirror.

Holly appeared on the sleeping quarters' monitor.

'Whoops!' he said: 'My fault,' and grinned contritely.

'What happened?'

'We've broken the light barrier.'

'I thought that was impossible.'

'Nah,' said Holly.

'So are we travelling at light speed, now?'

'Faster.'

'Is everyone O K?'

'Rimmer's a bit shaken up. He's still running around in circles in the technical library.'

'What about the ship?'

'Well, now it's got back to its original mass, it's feeling much perkier,' said Holly, and left to devote all his available run-time to navigating a ship that was now travelling beyond measurable speed.

Lister stepped into the northern hatchway of the recreation room, on his way to the technical libary to find Rimmer. Down the centre of the recreation room were dozens of baize-covered tables in various shapes and sizes: pool, snooker, cuarango and flip. The walls were lined with 3-D video booths – *Italian Driver* was Lister's favourite: one of the most thrilling and dangerous games around, the object of which was to park a car in Rome. Rimmer stepped in through the southern hatchway.

'Rimmer, we've broken the light barrier . . .'

'What?' said Rimmer.

'We're going faster than the speed of light!'

'How did I do what?'

'What d'you mean: "How did I do what?"'

'Lister, don't be a gimboid.'

'I'm not being a gimboid.'

'How could I? I've just been in the library, thinking. Anyway, I've decided . . .' Rimmer paused for no discernible reason, then yelled, equally inexplicably: 'Shut up!', wheeled round 180°, and appeared to be addressing a dartboard. 'As I was saying, before I was so rudely interrupted: I've decided when you go into stasis I want to be left on. I want to stay behind.'

'Are you all right, Rimmer?'

'What things?' said Rimmer with a puzzled expression. 'Eh?'

'I said *what*?' Rimmer turned his head slowly, following some unseen object with his eyes.

'What's going on?' Lister passed his hand in front of Rimmer's eyes. Rimmer stared blankly ahead.

'You're space crazy,' Rimmer said.

'*I'm* space crazy? You're the one who's space crazy.'

'Well, it probably *is* déjà vu,' said Rimmer. 'Sounds like it.' He scratched the hologramatic 'H' on his forehead with his long, thin finger, shook his head, then walked across to the northern hatchway and stepped out.

Simultaneously, another Rimmer stepped in through the southern hatchway.

Lister whipped round just in time to see the first Rimmer's back disappearing round the corner.

'Rimmer!' he said to the Rimmer who'd just come in, 'You just this second walked out of that door.'

'What?' said this other Rimmer.

'How did you do that?' Lister's head was flicking from exit to exit.

'How did I do what?'

'Rimmer, you just went out of that door,' Lister pointed at the north exit, 'and you've just come in through this one.'

'Lister, don't be a gimboid.'

'Look, I swear on my grandmother's life, as you walked out *there* you came in *here*.'

'How could I? I've just been in the library, thinking. Anyway, I've decided . . .'

'Rimmer! I'm telling you . . .' Lister walked to the centre of the room and stood with his back to the dartboard.

'Shut up!' Rimmer yelled, wheeling around to face him. 'As I was saying before I was so rudely interrupted: I've decided when you go into stasis I want to be left on. I want to stay behind.'

'Rimmer — you've just been in and said exactly these things.'

'What things?'

'You said that. You said "What things?"'

'I said *what*?'

'And that. You said that too.'

'You're space crazy,' said Rimmer.

'Yes!' said Lister, nodding, 'And then you said it was probably déjà vu.'

'Well, it probably *is* déjà vu,' said Rimmer. 'Sounds like it.'

'Well go on then. Scratch your "H", shake your head and walk out.'

Rimmer scratched the hologramatic 'H' on his forehead with his long, thin finger, shook his head, then walked across to the northern hatchway and stepped out.

He'd caught the lift and was heading back towards the sleeping quarters before Lister caught up with him.

'Rimmer! Wait! Listen to me . . .'

Suddenly, the Cat raced out from the sleeping quarters, and ran past them, clutching a bloodied handkerchief to his mouth.

'My tooth! My tooth! I think I lost my tooth!'

Lister stopped. 'Cat — what happened?'

The Cat raced by, ignoring him.

Rimmer stood in the entrance to the sleeping quarters.

'Look,' he said quietly.

The Cat was standing motionless by the bunks, his lips slightly parted in a half-smile of disbelief.

'Correct me if I'm wrong,' said Rimmer, 'but the Cat just rushed past us, and now he's standing here.'

'Did you get him?' said the Cat to Lister.

Lister turned to Rimmer. 'You see? Something weird is happening.'

'I was just sitting here,' said the Cat, 'just waiting, like you said to wait. Then this appallingly handsome guy who was an exact replica of me appeared, and started singing about fish.'

'It's something to do with light speed,' said Lister.

Rimmer called for Holly.

Holly was busy. He was busy worrying.

He'd given up trying to navigate the ship at super-light speed. He was fairly certain they'd already passed directly through the middle of seven planets, and at least one sun. It was completely impossible to avoid them, because they only appeared on his navicomp after the event.

Still, for some reason the ship seemed to have survived intact, so he decided not to worry about it.

Another slight concern was that *Red Dwarf* seemed to be following another *Red Dwarf*. And they, in turn, seemed to be being followed by yet another. In fact, when Holly examined it closely, they seemed to be flying in a convoy of at least twenty-six *Red Dwarf*s. Holly reasoned he couldn't do much about it, so he decided not to worry about this either.

In fact, there was nothing he could do about anything. At least, not until they dropped below light speed, which, according to his calculations, was seventy-eight hours away. But Holly had a very low opinion of his own calculations, so he wasn't going to put too much faith in that.

'What? What? What? What is it? I'm busy. I'm trying to navigate.' Holly's digitalized face appeared blurry and ill-defined.

'What's the problem? You've got an IQ of six thousand, haven't you?'

'Look, I've got to steer a ship the size of a small South American republic at speeds hitherto unencountered in the realm of human experience. We're travelling faster than the speed of light – we pass through things before I've even *seen* them. Even with an IQ of six thousand, it's still brown trousers time.'

'Just tell us what's happening.'

'You're seeing future echoes. Because we're travelling faster than light, we're overtaking ourselves in time. You're catching up with things you're about to do, before you've actually done them. Future echoes,' he repeated. 'OK?'

'So,' said Lister, 'the Cat is going to break his tooth some time in the future?'

'What tooth? Nobody's going to break *my* tooth.'

'How long is this going to last?'

'Until the reverse thrust takes effect and we drop below light speed.' Holly's image closed one eye and did some mental arithmetic which was probably wrong. 'Seventy-three hours and fourteen minutes,' he said as confidently as he could.

'*Nobody* is going to break my tooth.'

'Look! Look!' Rimmer spluttered. 'There's another one!'

A photograph was slowly materializing on Lister's bunk-side table.

It was a photograph of Lister. A photograph of Lister wearing a white surgical gown, standing outside the ship's medical unit. His eyes were dark and weary, but he was grinning. In his arms, wrapped in silver blankets, were two new-born babies.

'Two babies?' Lister looked up at the Cat who was craning over his shoulder.

He reached out to pick up the photograph, but his hand passed through it, and the picture slowly evaporated.

'Where do we get two babies from, without a woman on board?'

TEN

Lister was having an argument with the dispensing machine when he heard the explosion.

It was a simple dispute, and the dispensing machine was completely in the wrong. Lister had ordered his customary breakfast of prawn bangalore phall, half-rice, half-chips, seven spicy poppadoms, a lager-flavoured milkshake and two Rennies. The machine had delivered a raspberry pavlova in onion gravy.

'There's something wrong with your voice recognition unit.'

'Coming right up,' said the dispensing machine, and served up two lightly grilled kippers.

'No, you don't understand. There's a malfunction somewhere.'

'No problem at all,' said the machine. 'Rare, medium, or well done?' then dispensed forty-three pounds of raw calf's liver.

'Forget it. Forget the food. Can you just give me a coffee?'

'No sooner said than done,' said the machine pleasantly, and a Christmas pudding, flambéd in brandy, rolled out of the dispensing hatch, onto the floor, and set fire to Lister's trouser bottoms.

Lister was still stamping out the Christmas pudding when the explosion rocked the ship.

When he arrived breathless in the Navicomp Chamber, Rimmer was staring, still in shock, at the Drive panel.

'What was *that*?' shouted Lister.

Slowly Rimmer turned his head and looked up.

'Brace yourself for a bit of a shock: I just saw you die.'

'You saw what??'

'Well, I did warn you to brace yourself.'

'What? When? You didn't give me much of a chance.'

'I gave you ample bracing time.'

'No you didn't. You didn't even pause.'

'Well, I'm sorry. I've just had a rather disturbing experience. I've just seen someone I know die in the most hideous, hideous way.'

'Yeah! Me!'

'It was horrible.' Rimmer screwed up his face and shuddered in distaste. 'You were standing by the navicomp . . .'

'I don't want to know!'

'You don't want to know how you die?'

'No. 'Course I smegging don't.'

Suddenly the room seemed very dark and cold to Lister. 'Was it quick?' he asked quietly.

'We-ell. I wouldn't say it was *super* fast. Not if you count the thrashing about and the agonized squealing.' He shuddered again.

'You're enjoying this, aren't you?'

'What a horrible thing to say.'

'It was definitely me?'

'Yup!' Rimmer grinned.

'I don't want to know about this.' He sucked absently at one of his locks. 'How old did I look?'

'How old are you now?'

'Twenty-five. How old did I look?'

'I'd say . . .' Rimmer clicked his tongue '. . .mid-twenties.'

'Smeg!' Lister got up and kicked the navicomp. 'I'm not ready.' He kicked it again. 'I'm not smegging ready!'

'Yes, you did seem surprised. Especially when the arm came off.'

'So you saw my face? You got a good look at my face? It was actually me? It was *my* face?'

'Yes, you were wearing your stupid leather deerstalker with the furry earmuffs.'

Lister snatched off his leather deerstalker with the furry earmuffs. 'OK. I'll never wear a hat. I'll never wear it again. Then it can't happen.' He flung the cap across the navicomp, and it scudded along the floor.

Rimmer smiled. 'But it *has* happened. You can't change it, any more than you can change what you had for breakfast this morning.'

'But it *hasn't* happened, has it? It has will be have going to have happened, but it hasn't actually *happen* happened.'

'The point of it is, it *has* happened. It's just it hasn't taken place yet.'

Lister stared blankly into space, playing with his hair, while Rimmer tried to wrestle back the smirk that was making a break for his face.

'All right. OK. OK. The Cat, right?' Lister got to his feet. 'The Cat broke his tooth in a future echo, right?'

'I'm listening.'

'If I can stop him breaking it . . .'

'Can't be done.'

'. . . then I can stop me from dying!'

'Can't be done. Unfortunately.'

'So . . . how would the Cat break his tooth?'

Lister sat quietly, tugging at a loose piece of rubber on the toecap of his boot.

Rimmer watched him, whistling a Dixieland jazz version of *Death March in Saul*.

'Eating something . . .'

'Can't be done, me old buckeroo. Your number is up'.

'Eating something hard . . .'

'Can't be done-a-roonied. Sadly.'

Lister stood up, his eyes alive, and pelted out of the navi-comp chamber.

'Where are you going?' Rimmer got to his feet.

'My goldfish!' Lister's voice echoed from the corridor. 'Trying to eat my robot goldfish!'

Plop.

Plop, kerplop, plop . . .

The Cat lay listlessly on Rimmer's bunk. Several of his shirts were slung on a line across the sleeping quarters, dripping noisily into receptacles.

Plop.

Plop, kerplop, plop . . .

He hated laundry day. It always made him tired. Wearily he picked up another dirty shirt, unfurled his tongue and started cleaning it with long, methodical, rough, wet licks, stopping occasionally to top up his tongue with washing-up powder.

When it was finished, he hung the shirt on the line with the others.

Plop, kerplop, plop . . .

He really didn't feel like attacking his sock pile right now, so he got up and started mooching around the quarters, looking for something else to do.

He picked a book from Rimmer's shelf and ran his nose across one or two pages, but he couldn't make any sense of it. It appeared to be covered in funny little blobs, which didn't smell of anything.

Cats didn't communicate by writing. They communicated by smell. To 'read' a piece of Cat literature, you ran your nose along a line, which released various impregnated scents from the page.

There were two hundred and forty-six smell-symbols in the Cat lexicon. Each could be qualified by smaller, subtler smells which altered the meaning. Symbols could also mean completely different things in different contexts. For instance, the smell for 'fear' in a different setting could also mean 'very bad', 'noxious', 'toilet' or sometimes even 'estate agent'.

The Cat decided to amuse himself by trying to read the contents of Lister's dirty laundry basket. Much to his surprise, some of it translated quite well into Cat prose. In fact one T-shirt contained a sentence about a fearful, very bad estate agent going to a noxious toilet.

Then he noticed the goldfish.

He watched them for a while. One of them was swimming backwards. He'd never actually seen a live fish, but he was aware of some primal instinct they stirred deep within his stomach.

Even though he'd eaten less than an hour ago, he found a little hunger pain squeaking *'Let's eat the fish'*. He had a small, half-hearted dialogue with the hunger pain, but it was fairly insistent.

'*Come on, let's eat the fish!*'

'I'm not hungry.'

'*Eat it, eat it, come o-o-o-on.*'

The Cat put his hand into his jacket pocket and pulled out an already buttered roll. He usually kept one handy.

He began his food ritual by singing mockingly at the snack.

> '*I'm gonna eat you little fishie . . .*
> *I'm gonna eat you little fishie . . .*
> *I'm gonna eat you little fishie . . .*
> *'Cause I like eating fish.*'

To give the fish a fighting chance, he stood with his back to them. Then in a single movement he swivelled round, flicked one of the fish out of the tank with the back of his hand, and caught it in the bread roll.

'Too *slow*, little fishie,' he chided his goldfish sandwich. 'Too slow for *this* Cat.'

He raised the squirming roll to his mouth and started to bite down through the bread.

'Noooooooo!' screamed Lister.

The Cat half turned and saw Lister flying towards him like a berserk caber, his face contorted, his mouth forming a distorted, elliptical 'O'.

'Nooooooooooooooooooooooooooooooooooooooooooooooooooooo!'

The Cat was still smiling, in anticipation of his fishie nibble, when Lister crashed into him. They smacked into the table and tumbled onto the hard, grey deck.

The fish roll skidded across the floor. Lister sprang off the softly-moaning Cat, grabbed the roll, and looked inside.

McCartney was still wriggling away.

Intact.

Unbitten.

'I did it,' Lister said quietly. 'I DID IT!!' he screamed, not so quietly. 'I did it. I got the fish. I'm not going to die!' He did a victory dance, like a Zero-Gee ceiling receiver who'd just scored the winning touch-up.

Rimmer stood in the doorway.

The Cat clambered to his feet. 'My tooth!' He put a handkerchief to his mouth; it came away bloody. 'You're crazy!'

Lister came towards him. 'Let me see . . .'

The Cat raced out of the sleeping quarters. 'My tooth! My tooth!' he was yelling. 'I think I lost my tooth!'

Lister stared at the floor, at the small piece of white enamel that was lying under the chair taunting him. A one-toothed grin.

'Well,' Rimmer's smirk was as big as Yankee Stadium, 'allow me to be the very first to offer my deepest commiserations.'

ELEVEN

Lister spun the cap off the bottle of Glen Fujiyama, Japan's finest malt whisky, and poured a generous measure into a pint mug. Rimmer lay on his bunk, whistling pleasantly, his hologramatic eyes a-twinkle. Every opportunity he got, he tried to catch Lister's eye and wink at him cheerily.

Lister took a gulp of whisky. 'You're loving this, aren't you?'

'Oh, you're not still going on about your impending death, are you? For heaven's sake,' fake Scouse accent: 'change der record. Flip der channel. Death isn't der handicap it once was. For smeg's sake, cheeer up.'

'You are, aren't you? You're loving it.'

'Holly – I'd like to send an internal memo. Black border. Begins: "To Dave Lister. Condolences on your imminent death."' Rimmer half closed his eyes. 'What's that poem? Ah, yes . . .

> Now, weary traveller,
> Rest your head,
> For, just like me,
> You'll soon be dead.'

'You're really sick, you know that?'

'Come o-o-o-on, –' Rimmer made the 'on' last three full seconds – 'it's all you ever talk about. Frankly, Lister, it's very boooooring.'

'You are, you're loving it.'

'You're obsessed.'

'You realize when I die, you're going to be on your own.'

'Can't wait.'

'I thought you didn't want that. I thought that's what you were bleating on about before.'

'No, what got me down before wasn't being on my own. It was the idea that you were doing so much better than me. Staying young, and being alive; it was all too much to take. Now, me old buckeroo, the calliper's on the other foot.'

Lister gave up trying to argue. It was just adding to Rimmer's pleasure.

'I remember my grandmother used to say: "There's always some good in every situation."'

'Absolutely, absolutely,' agreed Rimmer; 'and looking on the bright side in this particular situation, you *are* about to do the largest splits you've ever done in your life.'

'So, I get blown up, right?'

'Bits of you do. What's that thing – I think it's part of your digestive system – the long purply thing with knobbly bits? You only ever see them hanging in Turkish butcher shops. Well, whatever it is, that fair flies across the Navicomp Chamber. It was like a sort of wobbly boomerang.'

'Smeg off!'

'Temper.'

'I don't want to die.'

'Neither did I.'

'But it's not fair. There's so much I haven't done.'

Lister started to think about all the things he hadn't done. For some reason one of the first things that came to his mind was the fact that he'd never had a king prawn biriani. Whenever he'd seen it on the menu, he'd always played safe and ordered chicken or lamb. Now he never would have a king prawn biriani.

And books. There were so many he'd meant to read, but hadn't found the time.

'I've never read . . . I've never read . . .' Actually, when he thought about it, he realized he'd never read *any* book. It wasn't that he didn't *like* literature, it was just that generally he waited for the film to come out.

And a family. He'd always assumed one day he'd have a family. A *real* family, not an adopted one. A *real* one. And he'd always wanted to spend a lot of time doing the thing you had to do if you wanted to get a family. He hadn't done nearly enough of that. Not nearly enough. A lot, but not nearly enough.

He was dimly aware that Rimmer was speaking, and Lister grunted occasionally to give the impression he was listening. But he wasn't. He was remembering his old job, back on Earth. His old job parking shopping trolleys at Sainsbury's megamarket, built on the site of the old Anglican cathedral.

One time the manager had caught him asleep in the warehouse. He'd constructed a little bed out of bags of salt, hidden from view behind a wall of canned pilchards. The manager had two GCSEs, a company car and a trainee moustache. He'd lectured Lister for an hour about how, if he applied himself, within five years he could be a manager himself, with a company car – and, presumably, a trainee moustache. On the other hand, the trainee moustache warned him, if he didn't apply himself he'd be parking shopping trolleys for the rest of his natural.

Lister, who knew he was no genius, also knew for absolute certain he was one hundred and forty-seven times smarter than the manager. Nonetheless, he'd found this pep-talk extraordinarily disturbing. He knew he didn't want to spend all his life parking shopping trolleys, and equally he couldn't get excited about becoming stock control manager at Sainsbury's Megastore, Hope Street, Liverpool.

The manager took him by the lapels and shook him. He told Lister he had to make the grade and become an SCM, or his life would 'never amount to *shit*.'

And now, as he sat there knowing he'd probably only got a few hours to live, it occurred to him for the first time ever that the pompous goit with the trainee moustache would probably turn out to be right. And that hurt. That really hurt.

And that was how he spent most of the evening. Tugging at the whisky bottle, reviewing his crummy life. And it wasn't the mistakes he made that haunted him, it was the mistakes he hadn't got *round* to making. He flicked through the catalogue of missed opportunities and unfulfilled promises. He thought about the magnificently unlikely string of coincidences which had brought him into being. The Big Bang; the universe; life on Earth; mankind; the zillions-to-one chance of the particular egg and sperm combination which created him; it had all happened. And what had he done with this incredible good fortune? He'd treated Time like it was urine, and pissed it all away into a big empty pot.

But no, it wasn't true: he'd had triumphs, a little voice from the whisky bottle was telling him. He'd been at the Superdome that night in London when the Jets played the Berlin Bandits in the European divisional play-offs, when Jim Bexley Speed, the greatest player ever to wear the Roof Attack jersey, had the greatest game of his great career. He'd seen that famous second score when Speed had gone round nine men, leaving the commentators totally speechless, for the first time in history for fully nine seconds. That was a triumph. Just being there. He was alive and *there* that night. How many men could say that?

Then there was that time at the Indiana Takeaway in St John's Precinct when he'd tasted his first shami kebab, and become hopelessly and irrevocably hooked on this Indian hors d'oeuvre. True, he'd dedicated a good deal of the rest of his life searching for another truly perfect shami kebab. And, true, he'd never found one. But at least he'd tasted *one*. One food-of-the-gods, perfect shami kebab. How many men could say that?

And then there was K.K. True, they'd only dated for five weeks. And the last week had been a bit sour. But four weeks of Kristine Kochanski being madly in love with him. Kristine Kochanski, who was so beautiful she could probably have got a job on the perfume counter at *Lewis's*! And she'd fallen in love with *him*! For four weeks! Four whole weeks. How many men could say that? Not that many, probably.

And that night in the Aigburth Arms when he played pool. That night when, for some unknown reason, everything he tried came off. The Goddess of Bar Room Pool looked down from the heavens and blessed his cue. Every shot *tnuk*! Straight in the back of the pocket. They couldn't get him off the table. He was unbeatable. Three and a half hours. Seventeen consecutive wins. He became a legend. He never played pool again, because he knew he wasn't that good. But that night in the Aigburth Arms he became a *legend*. A legend at the Aigburth Arms. How many men could say that?

The whisky bottle clanked emptily against the rim of his glass. He'd drunk half a bottle of whisky in two hours. How many men could say that?

He was drunk. How many men could say that?

He fell asleep in the chair. How many men could say that?

At three in the morning he was woken up by Holly.

'Emergency. There's an emergency going on. It's still going on, and it's an emergency.'

Rimmer sat up in bed, his hologramatic hair pointing stupidly in every compass direction. 'What is it?'

'The navicomp's crashed. It can't cope with the influx of data at light speed. We've got to hook it up to the Drive computer and make a bypass.'

Lister slung his legs over the bunk. 'The navicomp? The navicomp in the Navicomp Chamber?'

'If we don't fix it, the ship will blow up in about fifteen minutes and twenty-three seconds.'

Lister jumped down to the floor. 'This is it, then.'

Rimmer looked at him. 'Don't go.'

'What d'you mean "Don't go"? You said yourself I can't avoid it. Let's get it over with. What was I wearing?'

'Your leather deerstalker, and that grey T-shirt.'

Lister pulled on his deerstalker with deliberate precision. Then he walked across to the washbasin and lifted the metal towel rail off its support. 'Let's go.'

'What's that for?'

Lister patted the towel rail against his left palm. 'I'm going out like I came in – screaming and kicking.'

'You can't whack Death on the head.'

'If he comes near me, I'll rip his tits off.'

Then he was gone.

TWELVE

The Navicomp Chamber was fogged with acrid smoke from the melted insulating wires, and a thick cable swung from the ceiling, jumping and sparking like a dying electric python. A manic high-pitched screeching from the wounded navigation computer rose and fell as around the perimeter of the chamber monitor screens popped and shattered one by one.

Lister, his eyes streaming, fumbled for the bypass unit strapped to the wall and, following Holly's shouted instructions, dragged it across the broken glass and hooked it up to the main terminal.

He opened the bypass casing. Inside were twelve switches.

'Start at the one numbered twelve,' Holly was yelling, 'and leave a one second gap between each switch.'

He closed his eyes and rested his finger on the twelfth switch.

He flicked it down.

The pitch of the wailing navicomp increased by an octave. A green light flickered on beside the number twelve.

He moved his finger across to the eleventh switch.

Click.

Eeeeeeeeee. Another octave higher.

A green light.

The tenth switch.

Click.

The console monitor above Lister's head exploded, and vomited shards of glass into the smoke.

Another green light.

The switch numbered nine.

Another green light.

Eight.

Then seven.

And that was half way.

Number six.

Click.

A red light.

'Turn it off,' Holly said. 'Turn it off before . . .'

Lister flicked it off, waited, and flicked it back on.

Eeeeeeeeeeeeeee.

Green.

Five to go.

A maximum of five seconds before his purple knobbly thing was destined to fly across the room.

Click.

Click.

Click.

Just two left. Two little switches.

Lister wanted it to happen now. The penultimate switch. He didn't want to have to flick on the last one *knowing*. Knowing it would be the one to kill him. He wanted to have that slight element of surprise. But he was disappointed.

Click.

Green light.

EEEEEEEEEEEEEEEE.

The pitch of the screeching navicomp was now so high it was almost beyond his hearing threshold. Hardly a noise — more a feeling. A pointed squeal, a maniac sawing away at the top of his skull. Black smoke thrust its arm down his throat and started to yank out his lungs.

Lister stared at the last switch.

He rested his finger on it and felt its smoothness.

Then he screamed.

He screamed and pressed it.

And nothing.

Just silence.

Then a red light, that flickered to green, then back to red.

And then steady, steady green.

GREEN.

There was a huge BOOM!

Followed by a second huge BOOM!

And a third.

And Lister realized it was his heartbeat.

He sucked deeply at the foul, smoke-laden air. It tasted good.

And for the second time in twenty-four hours he did the touch-up shuffle. His feet rooted to the spot, he swayed from his waist and moved his arms in counter-motion.

He was alive.

THIRTEEN

The *Red Dwarf* Central Line tube hissed to a halt, and Lister danced out onto the platform. He had a sudden urge for chocolate – white milk chocolate, which he hadn't had since he was a kid – so he slipped a fifty pennycent bit into the machine and tugged on the drawer, but the drawer was stuck. For some reason this filled him with delight. The drawers were always stuck on station platform chocolate machines. Some things don't change. He laughed too much, then jumped on the escalator and leapt three steps at a time to catch up with Rimmer.

They stood on the escalator. Every advert they passed, Lister sang the advertising jingle.

'I don't know why you're so chirpy.'

'I'm alive!'

'But it's going to happen: I saw it happen. It just hasn't happened when we thought it would happen.'

'Who cares? The point is: it hasn't happened.'

'Correction: it has happened. It just hasn't happened yet.'

'Don't let's get into that again.'

'Lister – I saw it. I saw you die. It was you. I'm sure it was you.'

'What about the photograph? The two babies? That hasn't happened yet. Maybe none of it's going to happen.'

'It's going to happen.'

'It's really browning you off, isn't it, that I haven't died yet?'

The escalator pushed them off at the top. Lister leapt over the turnstile barrier, and Rimmer walked through it.

'No, it's not that. It's just your dunderheaded refusal to accept the pointless cruelty of existence. That's what gets my goat.'

Lister shook his head sadly.

When they walked into the sleeping quarters an old man was lying on Lister's bunk.

When he smiled his age lines crinkled like wrapping paper. He raised his robotic left arm. The hand was a metallic prosthesis, but the little finger had been customized so its top joint was a bottle opener. He used it to flick open a bottle of self-heating saké, and took a healthy swig. His white hair was plaited into three-foot long locks, and his right eye was missing. In its place was a telephoto lens, which zoomed and clicked, and focused in unison with his good eye.

And it was quite clear the old man was Lister.

He looked towards the door, but didn't appear to see them.

The watch on the future echo's good right arm emitted a series of squeaks. He turned it off and smiled. Lister made out a curious tattoo on his future self's forearm. It appeared to be burned into the flesh; some kind of formula. It was fading, but it looked like 'U = BIL'. Lister was craning closer to read it when the old man spoke.

'So, you're here,' he said. Lister's voice, but with a slight quaver. 'I can't see you, and I can't hear you, but I know you're here. Rimmer, you're going to say it's impossible.'

'It is impossible,' said Rimmer, 'I saw you die.'

The old man looked, more or less, in Lister's direction. 'Hello, Dave. This is me, I mean, you. I mean, I am you. I mean, I am you as an old man. I know you're here, because when I was your age I saw me at my age telling you at your age what I'm about to tell you. And you've got to tell you, too, when you get to be me.'

'Well,' said Rimmer, 'thank heavens you've still got all your marbles.'

'The person you saw die, Rimmer, was Bexley's son.'

Rimmer frowned. 'Who's Bexley?'

'I was always going to call my second son Bexley,' said Lister, 'after Jim Bexley Speed.'

'Dave – it wasn't you that Rimmer saw in the Navicomp Chamber, it was Bexley's boy. It was your grandson.'

Lister sat heavily into a chair. It was too much to take in. He wasn't going to die in the navicomp accident. He was going to have a son, who was also going to have a son. And so his son's son would die.

'You have two sons,' the old Lister was saying, 'and six grandchildren.'

'But one of them dies.'

'Everyone dies,' said the old Lister. 'You're born, you die. The bit in between is called "Life". And you have all those times together still to come. Enjoy.' He smiled.

The old man's watch went off again. 'I haven't got much time. Get your camera and go to the medical unit.'

'What's at the medical unit?' Lister fumbled in his locker for his camera.

Lister's older self began to grow translucent.

'What about me?' Rimmer walked up to the bunk. 'What happens to me?'

'He can't hear us, Rimmer – he's from the future.'

'Ah, but if I ask you what happens to me now you'll remember it, and when you get to be *him* you'll be able to tell me.'

'Brutal.' Lister grabbed the camera from his vacuum storage trunk and raced out.

'Don't waste time. Run,' the old Lister called after him.

'What happens to me, Old Man? Do I become an officer? Do I ever get a body again? Do we get back to Earth?'

The old man took another swig of saké and stared,

unseeing, through Rimmer's imploring face.

'Oh, Rimmer,' he said suddenly, 'you wanted to know what happened to you.'

'Yes! What happened to me?'

'Come close,' the old Lister beckoned; 'Come close. Closer.'

Rimmer inclined his ear to the old man's mouth.

'You wanted to know your future?'

'Yes please,' Rimmer whispered reverently, and stood on tip-toe so his ear hovered barely millimetres from the future echo's mouth.

The old Lister breathed in deeply, then belched loudly into Rimmer's ear.

He was still laughing when he vanished.

Rimmer caught up with Lister just outside the medical unit. Lister was hastily fitting an instafilm into the camera.

A jolt rocked the ship, and Lister went crashing against a wall, dropping the film. 'Smegging hell.' He picked it up and fumbled it into the camera. 'Smeg!' It was upside down.

Holly flicked up on the wall monitor.

'Deceleration achieved! We're slowing down, dudes. We'll be below light speed in thirty-five seconds precisely.'

'What's going to happen now? Are we going to see my funeral or something?'

'No – we're *de*celerating now,' said Holly. 'The faster we were going, the more into the future the future echoes were. But since we've just started slowing down, the future echoes should get nearer to the present.'

A baby started crying.

Then another baby started crying.

Standing in the doorway of the medical unit was another Lister – more or less the same age Lister was now. He was wearing a white surgical gown. And in his arms were two babies wrapped in silver thermal blankets.

'I can't see you, and all that guff,' Lister's future echo said, 'but I'd like you to meet your twin sons. This is Jim, and this is Bexley.'

Lister brought them into focus in the viewfinder, and rested his finger on the camera trigger.

'Say "cheese", boys.' The future echo struck a pose and grinned.

The two babies wailed louder than ever.

Click.

The future echoes faded away.

The camera ejected the qik-pik, and an image of Lister holding two babies in silver blankets slowly coloured into focus.

Lister turned, and started to walk back to the sleeping quarters. Rimmer followed him. 'How are you supposed to get two babies when we don't have a woman on board?'

'I dunno,' Lister grinned, 'but it's going to be a lot of fun finding out.'

FOURTEEN

Captain Yvette Richards ran her fingers through the bristles of her crew cut, and craned forward to look at the spectrascope of the sun they were approaching. It was perfect. She let out a Texan yelp.

'We *got* it!'

Flight Co-ordinator Elaine Schuman leaned over her shoulder and peered at the console. 'It's a supergiant?'

'You betcha!' said Richards, and yelped again.

'Time to celebrate,' said Schuman.

Kryten, the service mechanoid, handed round styrofoam cups of dehydrated champagne, and topped them up with water.

The eight-woman, two-man crew yelped and cheered and partied, while Kryten handed round more champagne and irradiated caviare niblets, which he'd been saving specially.

It had taken the crew of *Nova 5* six months to find a blue supergiant — a star teetering on the edge of its final phase in the right quadrant of the right galaxy. Another month, and they would have ruined the whole campaign. They certainly felt they had good reason to celebrate.

Sipping her champagne Kirsty Fantozi, the star demolition engineer, started programming the nebulon missile. It had to explode at just the right moment to trigger off the reaction in the star's core which would push it into supernova stage. A star in supernova would light up the entire galaxy for over a month, giving off more energy than the Earth's sun could in ten billion years. It would be a hell of a bang.

One undetected bug in Fantozi's programming could ruin everything. Not only did she have to push the star into supernova, she had to time it so the light from the explosion would reach Earth at exactly the right moment. The right moment was the same moment as the light from the other one hundred and twenty-seven supergiants, which were also being induced into supernovae, reached Earth.

For anyone living on Earth the result would be mind-fizzlingly spectacular. One hundred and twenty-eight stars would appear to go supernova simultaneously, burning with such ferocity they would be visible even in daylight.

And the hundred and twenty-eight supernovae would spell out a message.

And this would be the message:

'COKE ADDS LIFE!'

For five whole weeks, wherever you were on Earth, the huge tattoo would be branded across the day and night skies.

Honeymooners in Hawaii would stand on the peak of Mauna Kea, gazing at sunsets stamped with the slogan. Commuters in London, stuck in traffic jams, would peer through the grey drizzle and gape at the Cola constellation. The few primitive tribes still untouched by civilization in the jungles of South America would look up at the heavens, and certainly not think about drinking Pepsi.

The cost of this single, three-word ad in star writing across the universe would amount to the entire military budget of the USA for the whole of history.

So, ridiculous though it was, it was still a marginally more sensible way of blowing trillions of dollarpounds.

And, the Coke executives were assured by the advertising

executives at Saachi, Saachi, Saachi, Saachi, Saachi and Saachi, it would put an end to the Cola war forever. Guaranteed. Pepsi would be *buried*.

OK, it wasn't wonderful, ecologically speaking. OK, it involved the destruction of a hundred and twenty-eight stars, which otherwise would have lasted another twenty-five million years or so. OK, when the stars exploded they would gobble up three or four planets in each of their solar systems. And, OK, the resulting radiation would last long past the lifetime of our own planet.

But it sure as hell would sell a lot of cans of a certain fizzy drink.

Fantozi finished the program and fired the nebulon missile off into the heart of the star. She finished her styrofoam cup of champagne and flicked on her intercom.

'Let's turn this son-of-a-goit around and go home.'

The nose cone of *Nova 5* slowly swung around to begin the jag back to Earth.

The seven crew members who were in stasis didn't survive the crash.

As the ship bellied onto the cratered surface of the ice-clad moon, it caught the edge of a jagged precipice which ripped open the port side like a key on a sardine can, and the stasisees spewed out into the deadly methane atmosphere.

Captain Richards, who'd taken the first three-month watch along with Schuman and Fantozi, had been playing solo squash when Kryten had dropped in to the leisure suite to inform her politely that the ship's steering system had gone all cockamamie, and the computer had gone doo-lally.

She'd raced up to the Drive Room to find chaos. The computer was reciting fifteenth-century French poetry, and the steering system was on fire.

'What in hell is happening?'

'*Étoilette, je te vois . . .*' the computer said soothingly.

Kryten sprayed the steering system with a portable extinguisher. 'I don't understand what's going on, Miss Yvette.'

'Schuman! Fantozi!' Richards barked into the intercom. 'Get in here – we're in *deep* smeg!'

'It's a complete mystery,' said Kryten.

'*Que la lune trait à soi . . .*'

'One minute he was fine,' Kryten shook his head, 'the next he was acting like this.'

Richards tore at the panel housing to engage the back-up computer.

'*Nicolette est avec toi . . .*'

'I mean, if I'd known he was going to go mad on us, I wouldn't have bothered cleaning him.'

'Say *what*, Kryten?'

'I mean, what is the point of treating him to a complete spring-clean, polishing all his bits and bobs with beeswax, and scrubbing his terminals with soapy water, if he's going to go all peculiar?'

'You *cleaned* the computer?'

'What? Can't you tell? He's absolutely sparkling. Just look inside.'

Richards peered into the computer's circuit board casing. Foaming, soapy water bubbled and smoked beneath the gleaming, newly-polished innards.

'*M'amiette a le blond poil,*' the computer gurgled, and blew soap bubbles out of its voice simulation unit.

'Kryten – did you clean the back-up computer too?'

Kryten look away modestly.

'Did you, Kryten?'

'Please, Miss Yvette – I don't want thanks.'

'Did you?' She grabbed him roughly by his shoulders.

'The only thanks I need is knowing that you appreciate a job well done.' His lipless mouth twisted into a plastic grin.

Schuman burst into the Drive Room, wearing a towel, rat-tails of wet hair bouncing behind her.

'What's happening?'

Fantozi raced past her and up to the fizzling flight console. Her eyes darted over the digital read-outs. She typed quickly on the old-fashioned five-button keyboard.

'There's no way in!' She tried again. 'We can't get manual – the flight console won't let us in!'

'Well, it should be working one hundred and ten per cent,' Kryten said; 'it's even cleaner than the computers.'

Nova 5 dug a three and a half mile smoking furrow like a giant, twisted grin in the icy surface of the moon, and finally came to rest in two separate pieces at the bottom of a mountain range. The red-hot metal of the hull screamed and hissed, warped and twisted in the cruel suddenness of its icy bath. Gradually it stopped protesting, and with a sigh surrendered to its final resting place.

Silence.

Kryten looked down at his legs. They were thirty feet away, at the other end of the Drive Room. *Nova 5* tilted like a dry-ski slope. He dragged his torso down the incline, over to the body of Yvette Richards. Blood pumped from a gash in her thigh, and her leg was twitching involuntarily. She was breathing.

Just.

Kryten looked down at the mess of wires that were hanging out of the end of his torso, located one he didn't need very much, yanked it out, and tied it in a tourniquet round the top of her thigh.

Richards' eyes blinked open. 'Is everyone O K?'

Fantozi was groaning under a pile of debris. Kryten hauled his half-body to the mound of twisted metal, and started pulling her out. Both her legs were broken. Kryten made rudimentary splints out of his hip rods, and bound them with wires torn from his midriff.

'Thanks, Kryten.' Her mouth split into a dry smile, then she passed out.

Schuman crawled in from the corridor, her ankle twisted

almost backwards, with cuts on her face and hands. 'Hey, Richards,' she grinned, 'nice landing. Remind me never to lend you my car.'

Kryten lugged what was left of himself over to Schuman and, without warning, snapped her twisted ankle back into place. She screamed and punched him in the head.

'We've lost the others' – Richards was looking at the security cameras – 'and half the ship. We've still got the stores and the medical unit. And, since we're all still breathing, we can assume the atmosphere generator is still operational and the crash seal held. I guess Kryten hadn't gotten round to cleaning it yet.'

'We'd better get you all down to the medical unit,' said Kryten. 'Excuse me, Miss Elaine: would you be so kind as to pass me my legs?'

FIFTEEN

Holly was lost.

When he'd finally managed to wrestle *Red Dwarf* down to below light speed, he'd found a small electric-blue moon with a suitable gravity, plunged into its orbit and performed the 180° slingshot manoeuvre needed to turn the ship around.

But now he was lost.

The thing about being in Deep Space is the universe looks exactly the same from wherever you are. It's a sort of gigantic version of the Barbican Centre. And although they were now *supposed* to be on a course heading back for Earth, Holly wasn't totally one hundred per cent convinced his calculations were absolutely, right-on-the-button correct.

There are two ways to cope when you're lost: the first way you get out a map, discover where you are, work out where you want to go, and plot out a route accordingly. The second method was the method Holly was using. Basically, you keep on going, hoping that sooner or later you'll come across a familiar landmark, and muddle through from there.

So far nothing had looked very familiar. Occasionally he spotted a constellation he thought they may have passed before, but he couldn't swear to it; and every so often they passed the odd multi-ringed gas giant with a red spot at the pole, but, frankly, multi-ringed gas giants with red spots at their poles were ten a penny.

On his way out of the solar system, all those years ago, he'd started to compile what he hoped would be the definitive

A to Z of the universe, with galaxies, planets, star systems, street names and everything. But he'd fallen behind in the last couple of millennia, and had lost heart in the whole project.

It was the same with his diary. Each year he began to log the events of the voyage in eloquent detail. But every year, by January the thirteenth, he'd generally forgotten to keep it up, and the rest of the diary just comprised a few important birthdays: his creator's, his own, Netta Muskett's and Kevin Keegan's. And the only reason he included Kevin Keegan's was to remind himself not to send him a card, because he'd written *Football – It's A Funny Old Game*.

So, until he spotted a star or a planet he recognized, Holly amused himself by devising a system totally to revolutionize music.

He decided to decimalize it.

Instead of the octave, it became the decative. He invented two new notes: 'H' and 'J'.

Holly practised his new scale: 'Doh, ray, me, fah, soh, lah, woh, boh, ti, doh.' It sounded good. He tried it in reverse.

'Doh, ti, boh, woh, lah, soh, fah, me, ray, doh.'

It would be a whole new sound: Hol Rock.

All the instruments would have to be extra large to incorporate the two new notes. Triangles, with four sides. Piano keyboards the length of zebra crossings. The only drawback, as far as Holly could see, was that women would have to be banned from playing the cello unless they had birthing stirrups, or elected to play it side-saddle.

This exercise in restructuring the eight-note musical scale helped keep his mind off a number of major perturbations. One of these was that they were running worryingly low of a number of major supplies which had been consumed by Catkind during Lister's stay in stasis.

Checking the supply list was a bit like opening a bank statement. Sometimes, when you're feeling good and things are going well, you can *take* the news, even though you know it's going to be hideous. Other times, most of the time, that bank statement can stay unopened for *weeks*. The ranks of figures lurk inside the missive like warped hobgoblins; evil, deranged, waiting to leap out and suck out your life force. Pandora's box in an envelope.

That's pretty much how Holly felt about the ship's inventory. The last time he'd mustered enough courage to take a peek, he'd discovered some goose-pimpling shortages. Although they had enough food to last fifty thousand years, they'd completely run out of Shake'n'Vac. They had little fruit, few green vegetables, very little yeast, and only one After Eight mint, which he was sure no one would eat because they'd all be too polite to take it.

So, to take his mind off the problem, Holly began singing his first decative composition, *Quartet for nine players in H sharp minor*. He'd just reached the solo for trombone player with three lungs when the incoming message reached the ship's scanning system.

Since Lister realized he couldn't possibly go into stasis, on the grounds that the future echoes of himself had told him that he didn't, he decided he wouldn't, and instead he'd tried to make the best of a difficult situation. While he waited for the babies to show up, whenever and however that was, he elected to have some fun.

He'd found a jet-powered space bike in the docking bay, and was overhauling it with a view to going on a joy ride through an asteroid belt.

With a rag soaked in white spirit, he sat on his bunk methodically cleaning the greasy machine parts which were scattered all over his duvet, while Rimmer paced up and down the metal-grilled floor of the sleeping quarters.

'*Mi esporas ke kiam vi venos la vetero estos milda,*' said the language instructor on the vid-screen, and left a pause for the translation.

Rimmer paced.

'Errm ... uhhhh ... uhmmmm ... Wait a minute ... I know this ... Ooooh ... hang on ... don't tell me ... Urrrh ...'

Without looking up from the jet manifold he was fervently greasing, Lister chimed: 'I hope when you come the weather will be clement.'

'I hope when you come the weather will be clement,' the woman on the vid-disc concurred.

'Don't tell me. I would have got that.'

'*Bonvolu direkti min al kvinsela hotelo?*' the recorded instructor prompted.

'Ahhh, yes ... this is one from last time ... I remember this ... Ooooh ...'

Lister took the screwdriver out of his mouth. 'Please could you direct me to a five-star hotel?'

'Wrong, actually. Totally, completely and utterly, totally wrong.'

'Please could you direct me,' the instructor said, 'to a five-star hotel?'

'Lister – would you please shut up?'

'I'm just helping you.'

'I don't need any help.'

Rimmer had decided to put his demise behind him, and vowed to make his death as rich and fulfilling as was humanly possible. And so, he had taken up again his Esperanto language studies.

Although technically Esperanto wasn't an official requirement for promotion, officers were generally expected to be reasonably fluent in the international language.

'*La mango estis bonega! Dlej korajn gratulonjn´ al la kuiristo.*'

Rimmer snapped his fingers. 'I would like to purchase the orange inflatable beach ball, and that small bucket and spade.'

'The meal was splendid!' the woman translated. 'My heartiest congratulations to the chef.'

Rimmer squeaked. 'Is it??' He asked the vid to pause.

'You've been studying Esperanto for eight years, Rimmer. How come you're so hopeless?'

'Oh, really? And how many books have you read in your entire life? The same number as Champion, The Wonder Horse. Zero.'

'I've read books,' lied Lister.

'We're not talking about books where the main character is a dog called "Ben". Not books with five cardboard pages, three words a page, and a guarantee on the back which says: 'This book is waterproof and chewable.'

Lister sprayed some W D40 onto a spark plug. 'I went to art college.'

'You?'

'Yeah.'

'How did *you* get into art college?'

'Usual way. The usual, normal, usual way you get into art college. Failed all my exams and applied. They snapped me up.'

'Did you get a degree?' Rimmer's pulse quickened: Please *God*, don't let him have a degree!

'Nah. Dropped out. Wasn't there long.'

'How long?'

Lister looked up and tried to work it out. 'Ninety-seven minutes. I thought it'd be a good skive, but I took one look at the timetable and checked *out*. It was ridiculous. I had lectures first thing in the middle of the afternoon. Half past two every day. Who's together by then? You can still taste the toothpaste.'

He shuddered at the memory and went back to cleaning his bike parts.

Rimmer shook his head and re-started the language tape.

'*La menuo aspektas bowege – mi provos la kokidajon.*'

'Ah, now this one I *do* know . . .'

Holly's image replaced the woman's on the monitor, and smoothly delivered the correct reply.

'The menu looks excellent; I'll try the chicken.'

'Holly, as the Esperantinos would say,' Rimmer made the Ionian sign for 'Smeg off' with his two thumbs: '*"Bonvolu alsendi la pordiston — lausajne estas rano en mia bideo"*, and I think we all know what that means.'

'Yes,' said Holly, 'it means: "Could you send up the Hall Porter — there appears to be a frog in my bidet?"'

'Does it?' Rimmer was genuinely surprised. 'Well, what's that one: "Your father was a baboon's rump, and your mother spent most of her life with her pants round her ankles, up against walls with astros"?'

'Look,' said Holly, suddenly remembering why he was there, 'you'd better come down to the Communications suite. We're getting an S O S call.'

SIXTEEN

Lister grabbed a cup of tea from the dispensing machine, they collected the Cat and caught the Xpress lift down to Comm: level 3.

'Aliens,' said Rimmer, his eyes gleaming with the possibilities; 'it's aliens.'

Rimmer believed passionately in the existence of aliens. He was convinced that, one day, *Red Dwarf* would encounter an alien culture with a technology so far in advance of mankind's they would be able to provide him with a new body. A new start.

'It's aliens,' he repeated; 'I know it.'

'Your explanation for anything slightly odd is aliens,' said Lister. 'You lose your keys, it's aliens. A picture falls off the wall, it's aliens. That time we used up a whole bog roll in a day, you thought *that* was aliens.'

'Well, we didn't use it all.' Rimmer shot him his best Rod Sterling *Twilight Zone* look. 'Who did?'

'*Aliens* used up our bog roll?'

'Just because they're aliens, it doesn't mean they don't have to visit the smallest room. Only, they probably do something weird and alienesque; like it comes out of the top of their heads, or something.'

Lister sipped his tea and mulled the concept over. 'Well,' he concluded, 'I wouldn't like to get stuck behind one in a cinema.'

*

A huge screen a hundred metres square hung down over the communication consoles, and four speakers, each the size of a fairly roomy Kensington bedsit, throbbed gently as Holly tried to establish contact by repeating a series of standard international distress responses over and over again in a variety of different languages.

'It's from an American ship, private charter, called *Nova 5*,' said Holly tonelessly. 'They've crash-landed. I'm trying to get them on optical.'

'Oh.' Rimmer sighed with disappointment. 'So it's not aliens.'

'No. They're from Earth. I hope they've got a few spare odds and sods on board. We're a bit short on a few supplies.'

Lister sipped his tea. 'Like what?'

'Cow's milk,' said Holly. 'We ran out of that yonks ago. Fresh *and* dehydrated.'

'What kind of milk are we using now, then?'

'Emergency back-up supply. We're on the dog's milk.'

Lister froze, the styrofoam cup resting on his lips, the tea half-way down his throat. He swallowed. 'Dog's milk?'

'Nothing wrong with dog's milk. Full of goodness, full of vitamins, full of marrowbone jelly. Lasts longer than any other kind of milk, dog's milk.'

'Why?'

'No bugger'll drink it. Plus, of course, the advantage of dog's milk is: when it's gone off, it tastes exactly the same as when it's fresh.'

Lister dropped his cup into a waste chute. 'Why didn't you tell me, man?'

'What? And put you off your tea?'

'Something's happening!' Rimmer pointed at the Comm screen, which fizzled and buzzed with static.

Slowly an image formed: the flat angular features of a mechanoid face, the head without curves, the mouth without lips.

'Thank goodness, thank goodness. Bless you!' Kryten clapped his hands together. 'We were beginning to despair . . .'

'We?' said the Cat, arching his brow.

'I am the service mechanoid aboard *Nova 5*. We've had a terrible accident. Seven of the crew died on impact; the only survivors are three female officers, who are injured but stable.'

'Female?' The Cat looked at Lister. 'Is that "female" as in "soft and squidgy"?'

'I am transmitting medical details.'

Digitalized pictures of Richards, Schuman and Fantozi flashed up on the screen, followed by reams of medical data.

RICHARDS, Yvette. Age 33. Rank: Captain. Compound fracture, left fibula. Blood type O . . .

FANTOZI, Kirsty. Age 25. Rank: Star Demolition Engineer. Multiple fractures, both legs. Blood type A . . .

SCHUMAN, Elaine. Age 23. Rank: Flight Co-ordinator. Severe fractures, right ankle. Blood type O . . .

The Cat's eyes darted across the significant details. 'Three. All injured and helpless. This is tremendous!'

Rimmer turned from the screen and smoothed down his hair. 'Tell them,' he said, a new tone of authority in his voice, 'Tell them the boys from the *Dwarf* are on their way! Or my name's not Captain A. J. Rimmer, Space Adventurer!'

'Oh, thank you, Captain. Bless you. I'll tell them.'

Kryten shut down transmission.

'Captain?' Lister inclined his head forward and looked up at Rimmer through his eyebrows, as if peering over a pair of imaginary spectacles. 'Space Adventurer?'

'It's good psychology. What am I supposed to say? "Fear not, we're the blokes who used to clean the gunk out of the chicken soup machine? Actually we know smeg-all about space travel, but if you've got a blocked nozzle we're your lads"? That's going to have them oozing with confidence, isn't it?'

'Hey, Head,' the Cat said to Holly, 'how far are we away?'

'Not far. Twenty-eight hours?' he guessed.

'Only twenty-eight hours!' The Cat leapt to his feet. 'I'd better start getting ready! I'm first in the shower room. Waaaaah!' he screamed with delight. 'I'm so excited, all six of my nipples are tingling!'

'Look,' said Lister, 'this is a mission of mercy. We're taking an injured crew urgently needed medical supplies. We're not going down the disco on the pull.'

'Dum dum *dum* dum dum *dum* dum dum . . .'

Disco music thundered out of Lister's eight-speakered portable wax-blaster, which vibrated and slid across the metal surface of the sleeping quarters' table.

'Dum dum *dum* dum dum *dum* dum dum . . .' Lister mimicked the synth-tymp as he glided rhymically over to his metal locker and pulled out his underwear drawer. One sock remained. He tutted, and grooved across to his dirty laundry basket.

'Dum dum *dum* dum . . .'

He pulled out two very hard, very stiff, rather dangerous-looking yellow socks. Holding them at arm's length, he sprayed them liberally with Tiger deodorant, then put them on the table and hit them several times with a small toffee hammer.

'Dum dum *dum* dum dum *dum* . . .'

He moon-walked back to the locker, reverently took out an old brown paper bag, and fished out his lucky-scoring underpants.

They had at one time been blue. Now they were a yellowy-grey with holes in the cheeks, and the elastic hung out of the waist band. He held them in his arms like he was holding the Turin Shroud. These were the underpants he'd happened to be wearing the night he met Susan Warrington. Susan had got him drunk, and taken advantage of his tender years on the ninth hole — par four, dogleg — of Bootle Municipal Golf Course.

He'd worn them again the night Alison Bredbury's dad had to be rushed off to hospital with a heart attack, leaving him alone with Alison, the key to the drinks cabinet and her parents' double bed.

From then they'd achieved in his mind a mystic quality. He'd worn them sparingly, not wanting to use up their magic powers.

Obviously they'd not always been successful. In fact, a lot of the time they hadn't been successful. And slowly the dreadful thought began to occur to him that they might be just a rather ordinary pair of dog-eared Y-fronts, and not some talismanic, spell-kissed, warlock-woven, sorcery-spun article of enchantment. They were just a pair of knickers.

But then . . .

Then he discovered if he wore them backwards . . . all their magical properties returned!

Kristine Kochanski.

For four whole weeks she was madly in love with him. For four whole weeks he'd worn his backward boxers. Not daring to risk an ordinary pair, he'd washed them each night and worn them backwards throughout their relationship.

Naturally she'd asked him why. He told her he had twenty-one pairs of identical briefs, and he always dressed in a hurry. She bought him new pairs, and forced him to wear them. Like a fool, he did. And soon after their relationship had ended.

'Dum dum *dum* dum . . .' He slipped on the sacred shorts, backwards *and* inside-out.

'No prisoners,' he said aloud, and glided over to the ironing board.

He lifted the iron off his best green camouflage pants and

pulled them on. He felt air on his buttock, and when he checked in the mirror he found an iron-shaped hole clean through the right cheek.

'Dum dum *dum* dum dum *dum* . . .'

He rifled through his locker, found the colour he was looking for, and sprayed the exposed buttock with green car touch-up paint.

He looked in the mirror again. From a distance you honestly couldn't tell. True, he smelled like a newly-painted Cortina, but that would fade in time. He slipped on his favourite London Jets T-shirt and stood back to take in the whole picture: the freshly hammered socks, the cleverly inverted underpants, and the neatly sprayed trousers. Hey, he knew it wasn't perfection, but *God*, it was close.

'Oh, you're not on the pull, eh?' Rimmer stood in the doorway wearing a dashing white officer's uniform, complete with banks of gleaming medals, and gold hoops of rank which ran the length of his left arm, which Holly had grudgingly simulated for him.

Look at him! Rimmer thought. *He's really trying. He's wearing all his least smeggy things. That T-shirt with only two curry stains on it — he only wears that on special occasions. Those camouflage pants with the fly buttons missing.*

'You're toffed up to the nines!' he said out loud.

'That's rich, coming from someone who looks like Clive of India.'

'Oh, it's started.' Rimmer dusted some imaginary dust off his gold epaulette. 'I knew it would.'

'What has?'

'The put-downs. It's always the same every time we meet women. Put me down, to make yourself look good.'

'Like when?'

'Remember those two little brunettes from Supplies? And I said I'd once worked in the stores, and they were very interested, and asked me exactly what I used to do there?'

'And I said you were a shelf.'

'Right. Exactly.'

'So? They laughed.'

'Yes! At me. At my expense. Just don't do it, OK? Don't put me down when we meet them.'

'How d'you want me to act then? How d'you want me to behave?'

'Just show a little respect. For a start, don't call me Rimmer.'

'Why not?'

'Because you always hit the RIMM at the beginning. *RIMM*-er. You make it sound like a lavatory disinfectant.'

'Well, what should I call you?'

'I don't know. Something a bit more pally. Arnie? Arn, maybe? Something a bit more . . . I don't know. How about: "Big Man"?'

'Big Man?'

'How about "Chief", then? "The Duke"? "Cap", even. What about "Old Iron Balls"?'

Rimmer could see he wasn't really getting anywhere. 'OK, then,' he tried, 'how about the nickname I had at school?'

'What? Bonehead?'

Impossible! Lister couldn't *possibly* have known his nickname at school was 'Bonehead'. No one knew this. Not even his parents. 'What on Io makes you think my nickname at school was Bonehead?'

'Well, it had to be, didn't it?'

'What?'

'It was a guess.'

'Well, it was a guess, as it turns out, that was completely way off the fairway and into the long grass. The nickname to which I was referring was "Ace".'

'You're nickname was never "Ace". Maybe "Ace-hole".'

'There you go again! Knock, knock, knock. Why can't you build me up instead of always putting me down?'

'For instance?'

'Well, I don't know. Perhaps if the chance occurs, and it comes up naturally in the course of the conversation, you could possibly drop in a mention of the fact that I'm, well . . . very brave.'

'Do what?'

'Don't go crackers. Just, perhaps, when my back's turned, you might steer the dialogue round to the fact that I . . . died, and, well, I was pretty gosh-darn brave about it.'

'You're pretty gosh-darn out of your smegging tree, Rimmer.'

'Or you could bolster up my sexual past. Why don't you just casually hint that I've had tons of women? Would that break your heart, would it? Would that give you lung cancer, to say that?'

Rimmer arched threateningly close to Lister's face, his eyes bulging: 'Just *don't* put me down, OK?'

SEVENTEEN

'Come on, everyone – they're here! They're in orbit! Heavens! There's so much to do.' Kryten rushed down the sloping corridor, pausing only to water a lusciously green plastic pot plant.

Things were going very well. Very well indeed. The girls had been quiet and really most forlorn of late. Being marooned light years from home with scant hope of rescue had been very trying, to say the least. He'd done his best to keep them entertained, to keep their spirits high, but over the last few weeks, he'd felt intuitively that they were losing hope.

Even his Friday night concert parties, usually the highlight of the week, had begun to be greeted with growing apathy. Miss Yvette was especially guilty of this. She hadn't particularly enjoyed them from the beginning, and had told him so.

The concert parties always began in the same way. After baths and supper Kryten would clear the decks while the girls played cards, or read. At nine sharp the lights would be dimmed, and Kryten would tap-dance onto a makeshift stage in the engine-room, singing *I'm a Yankee Doodle Dandy*, juggling two cans of beeswax. And then he'd go into his impressions. His best one was of Parkur, the mechanoid aboard the *Neutron Star*, but none of the girls knew him, so it never went down that well. Then there were the magic tricks. Or, to put it more accurately, the magic *trick*. He would lie in a box and saw himself in half. It wasn't much of a trick because he actually did saw himself in half. And then the evening suffered a slight hiatus while they waited the forty minutes it took for Kryten to reconnect his circuitry.

Then he'd round off the evening with a selection of hits from *The Student Prince*. And then they'd play prize bingo. The prize in the prize bingo was always a can of Jiffy Windo-Kleen. Nobody ever wanted a can of Jiffy Windo-Kleen, so Kryten always got it back and was able to use it as the next week's prize.

In an odd kind of way Kryten was grateful for the accident. His life had taken on a new vitality. He was *needed*. The girls depended on him. His days were full. There was the cooking, the changing of the bandages, the physiotherapy, the concert parties. And, of course, there was the cleaning.

Kryten took almost orgasmic delight in housework. Piles of dirty dishes thrilled him. Mounds of unwashed laundry filled him with rapture. An unmopped floor left him dry-mouthed with lust. He loved cleaning things even more than he loved things being clean. And things being clean sent him into a frenzy of ecstasy.

And at night, when everyone was safely tucked in bed and all the chores were done and there was absolutely nothing left to clean, then, and only then, he'd sink into his favourite chair, cushions aplump, and watch *Androids*.

Androids was a soap opera, aimed at the large mechanoid audience who had huge buying power when it came to household goods. Kryten had all one thousand, nine hundred and seventy-four episodes on disc. He'd seen them all many times, but he still winced when Karstares was killed in the plane crash. He still wept when Roze left Benzen. He still laughed and slapped his metal knee when Hudzen won the mechanoid lottery and hired his human master as a servant. And he always cheered when Mollee took on the android brothels, put the pimps into prison and set the prostidroids free.

Androids, he told himself, was his one vice. That, and the single chocolate he allowed himself each viewing, to conserve supplies. When he watched *Androids* he wasn't just a mechanoid, marooned light years from nowhere, with three demanding dependants and a never-ending schedule of work.

He was somewhere different. Somewhere glamorous. Somewhere else.

He was Hudzen, winning the lottery and hiring a human to serve him. He was Jaysee, swinging the mega-quidbuck deals, dining in the best restaurants, living in his vast penthouse atop the Juno Hilton.

He was someone else.

Kryten rushed down the slope and onto the main service deck, where the girls were breakfasting.

'Come on! They're here!' He clapped his hands.

Richards, Schuman and Fantozi didn't move. They hadn't moved, in fact, for almost three million years.

The three skeletons sat round the table, in freshly-laundered uniforms, and grinned.

'I don't know what's so funny,' said Kryten. 'They'll be here any moment, and there's so much to *do*!' He clucked and shook his head. 'Miss Elaine, honestly: you haven't even made an effort. *Look* at your hair.'

He fussed over to the table, and took out a hairbrush.

'What a mess you look.' He hummed *Stay Young And Beautiful*, and combed her long blonde wig with smooth, gentle strokes. When her hair was just so, he stood back and eyed her critically. He wasn't *quite* satisfied. He took out a lipstick that matched her uniform and touched up her makeup.

'Dazzling. You could go straight on the cover of *Vogue*.'

He shuffled down the table.

'Miss Yvette! You haven't *touched* your soup. It's no wonder you're looking so pasty.' He patted her gingerly on the shoulder. There was a long, slow creaking noise, and the skeleton slumped face down into the bowl of tomato soup. Kryten threw up his hands in horror. 'Eat nicely, Miss Yvette! What *will* that nice Captain Rimmer think if he sees you eating like that?' He hoisted the skeleton back onto the chair, sprayed her with a squirt of Windo-Kleen, and gave her head a quick polish.

'Now then, Miss Kirsty.' He waddled over to the remaining skeleton and looked her up and down: the trendy knee-length boots, the chic, deep red mini-skirt and the peaked velvet cap cocked at a racy angle.

'No,' he beamed, putting the hairbrush away. 'You look absolutely *perfect!*'

EIGHTEEN

The Cat slinked down the docking bay gantry in his gold, hand-stitched flightsuit, carrying a two-feet-high, cone-shaped matching space helmet under his arm.

He climbed up the boarding steps into Blue Midget, where Lister and Rimmer were sitting in the drive seats waiting for him. He jumped into the cramped cabin, struck a pose like King of the Rocket Men, legs splayed, chest puffed out, hand on one hip, and said: 'Put your shades on, guys. You're looking at a nuclear explosion in lurex.' He gleamed a smile at them and fluttered his eyes.

'You're looking good,' said Lister, craning round.

'Looking *good*?? Did I hear the man say, "Looking only *good*??" Buddy, I am a plastic surgeon's *night*mare. Throw away the scalpel; improvements are impossible.'

'A spacesuit,' said Rimmer, 'with cufflinks?'

'Listen,' said the Cat, dusting the console seat before arranging himself on it, 'you've got to guarantee me we don't pass any mirrors. If we do, I'm there for the *day*.'

Lister flicked on the remote link with Holly.

Holly appeared on the screen looking somehow different. Lister scrutinized the image. He couldn't quite work out what it was.

'All right, then, dudes? Everybody set?'

Lister twigged. 'Holly, why are you wearing a toupé?'

Holly was upset. He spent some considerable time corrupting his digital image to give himself a fuller head of hair. 'So it's not undetectable, then? It doesn't blend in naturally and seemlessly with my own natural hair?'

'It looks,' said Lister, 'like you've got a small, furry animal nesting on top of your head.'

'What is wrong with everybody?' Rimmer straightened his cap. 'Three million years without a woman, and you all go crazy.'

He's right, thought Holly, *who am I trying to impress? I'm a computer! How humiliating to have that pointed out by a hologram!* Out of spite he instantly simulated a large and painful boil on the back of Rimmer's neck, and made it start to throb.

Blue Midget, the powerful haulage transporter originally designed to carry ore and silicates to and from the ship, looked strangely graceful as it flickered between the red and blue lights of the twin sun system above the howling icy green wasteland of the moon that had become *Nova 5*'s graveyard.

Lister peered through the furry dice dangling from the windscreen. 'Nice place for a skiing holiday.'

Rimmer stared unblinkingly at the tracking monitor. 'Nothing yet,' he said helpfully. He slipped his finger down the collar of his shirt where a large boil was really beginning to hurt.

Lister struggled hopelessly with the twelve gear levers. Each provided five gears, making it sixty gears in all, and Lister hadn't yet been in the right one throughout the twenty-minute jag.

The tracking monitor started delivering a series of rapid bleeps.

'We've got it!' Rimmer cried. 'Lat. twenty-seven, four, Long. seventeen, seven.'

Lister looked at him like he was speaking Portuguese.

'Left a bit, and round that glacier.'

'Oh, right.'

*

Lister landed appallingly in forty-seventh gear. Blue Midget stalled, bounced and rocked, before settling to rest with an exhausted sigh. Lister pushed in the buttom marked 'C'. The caterpillar tracks, telescoped out of their housing, rotated down to the icy emerald surface and hoisted the transporter ten feet above the ground.

'Hey,' said the Cat, impressed, 'You really can drive this thing.'

'Actually,' said Lister, 'I thought that was the cigarette lighter.'

The red-hot wiper blades melted green slush from the windscreen as Blue Midget rose and fell over a series of icy dunes. As they reached the peak of the next range, they saw, in the hollow below the broken wreck, jutting out of the landscape like a child's discarded toy.

The gearbox groaned and rattled as they made their slippery descent down into the crater.

'Yoo-hoo!' the Cat squealed in falsetto, and waved madly out of the port side window.

'Ah, come in, come in.' Kryten ushered them in from the airlock. 'How lovely to meet you,' he said, and bowed deeply.

'Cârmita,' said Rimmer, speaking too loudly. 'What a delightful craft – reminds me of my first command.' He turned and hissed to Lister: 'Call me *Ace*.'

Lister pretended not to understand and walked off down the spotless, newly painted white corridor after Kryten, who was chattering banalities about the weather.

'Green slush again. Tut, tut, tut.'

The Cat flossed his teeth one last time, and followed them.

Kryten, used to the strange tilt, walked speedily down the thin corridor, listing at an odd angle.

He went through a large, pear-shaped hatchway, and they followed him across what must have been the ship's Engine-

Room. Even Lister, who knew next to nothing about these things, could tell *Nova 5*'s technology was far in advance of *Red Dwarf*'s. Taking up three-quarters of the room was the strangest piece of machinery Lister had ever seen: it was like a huge series of merry-go-rounds stacked one on top of the other and turned on their sides. Each of these was filled with silver discs joined by thick gold rods, and at the end was what looked like an enormous cannon.

'What's that?' asked Lister.

'It's the ship's Drive,' Kryten replied. 'It's the Duality Jump.'

'What's a Duality Jump?'

'Don't be thick, Lister. Everybody knows what a Duality Jump is,' said Rimmer, lying.

Kryten scurried through the pear-shaped exit, and Lister practically had to sprint out of the engine-room to catch up with them two corridors later.

Suddenly, the Cat swivelled, as they passed a full-length mirror recessed in the wall. His heart pounded, his pulse quickened. He felt silly and giddy. He was in love.

'You're a work of Art, baby,' he crooned softly at his reflection.

Lister turned and shouted: 'Come on!'

'I can't. You're going to have to help me.'

Lister picked up his golden-booted foot and started to yank him down the corridor. Unable to help himself, the Cat hung on to the mirror. His gloved fingers squeaked across the glass surface as Lister pulled him free.

'Thanks, Man,' the Cat said gratefully. 'That was a bad one.'

'I'm so excited,' said Kryten, shuffling along and absently dusting a completely clean fire-extinguisher. 'We all are. The girls can hardly stop themselves from jumping up and down.'

'Ha ha haaa,' brayed Rimmer, falsely. 'Cârmita, Cârmita.'

'Ah!' said Kryten, '*Vi parolas Espekanton, Kapitano Rimmer?*'

'I'm sorry?'

'*Vi parolas Espekanton, Kapitano Rimmer?*'

'Come again?'

'You speak Esperanto, Captain Rimmer?'

'Ah, *oui, oui, oui. Jawol. Si, si.*' Rimmer searched desperately through his memory for the appropriate phrase. Mercifully it came to him. '*Bonvolu alsendi la pordiston lausajne estas rano en mia bideo.*'

'A frog?' said Kryten. 'In which bidet?'

'Ha ha haaaaa,' brayed Rimmer, even less convincingly. 'It doesn't matter. I'll deal with it myself.'

Kryten walked round the corner and down the ramp on to the service deck.

'Well, here they are,' he said.

Without looking where Kryten was beckoning, Rimmer bent down on one knee and swept his cap in a smooth arc. 'Cârmita!' he purred.

Lister and the Cat tumbled in behind him.

Their eyes met the hollow sockets of the three grinning skeletons sitting around the table.

There was a very, very long silence.

It was followed by another very, very long silence.

'Well,' said Kryten, a little upset, 'isn't anybody going to say "Hello"?'

'Hi,' said Lister, weakly. 'I'm Dave. This is the Cat. And this here is Ace.'

Rimmer still hadn't closed his mouth from forming the final vowel of Cârmita. Lister leaned over and whispered to him conspiratorially: 'I think that little blonde one's giving you the eye, Cap.'

'Now,' Kryten clapped his hands, 'you all get to know one another, and I'll run off and fetch some tea.' He staggered off up the slope.

'I don't believe this,' said Rimmer, massaging the 'H' on his forehead.

Lister looked at him. 'Be strong, Big Man.'

'Our one contact with intelligent life in over three million years, and he turns out to be an android version of Norman Bates.'

'So, they're a little on the skinny side,' said the Cat, ever hopeful. 'A few hot dinners, and who knows?'

Lister walked up to the table and put his arms around two of the skeletons' shoulders.

'I know this may not be the time or the place to say this, girls, but my mate, Ace here, is incredibly, incredibly brave . . .'

'Smeg off, dogfood face!'

'And he's got tons and tons of girlfriends.'

'I'm warning you, Lister.'

Kryten raced back down the slope, carrying a tray which held several plates of triangular-shaped sandwiches, a pot of steaming tea, and a plate with seven of his precious chocolates on it. As he laid out the cups on the table, he looked up, suddenly aware of the lack of conversation.

'Is there something wrong?' he asked.

'Something wrong??' said Rimmer, aghast. 'They're dead.'

'Who's dead?' asked Kryten, pouring some milk into the cups.

'They're dead,' Rimmer waved at the three skeletons. 'They're all dead.'

'My God!' Kryten stepped back in horror. 'I was only away two minutes!'

'They've been dead for centuries.'

'No!'

'Yes!'

'Are you a doctor?'

'You only have to look at them,' Rimmer whined. 'They've got less meat on them than a chicken nugget!'

'Whuh . . . whuh . . . well, what am I going to do?' Kryten stammered. 'I'm programmed to serve them.'

'Well, the first thing we should do is, you know . . . bury them,' said Lister quietly.

'You're *that* sure they're dead?'

'Yes!' Rimmer shouted.

Kryten waddled over to Richards's leering skeleton. 'What about this one?'

Rimmer sighed. 'Look. There's a very simple test.' He walked up to the head of the table. 'All right,' he said, 'hands up any of you who are alive.'

Kryten looked on anxiously. To his dismay, there was no response. He made frantic signals, coaxing the girls to raise their hands.

'OK?' said Rimmer finally.

Kryten's shoulders buckled, and he dropped limply into a chair, totally defeated.

'I thought they might be . . . but I wouldn't allow myself . . . I didn't want to admit . . . I . . . I'm programmed to serve them . . . It's all I can do . . . I let them down so badly . . . I . . .'

Lister shuffled uncomfortably.

'What am I to do?' Kryten said plaintively. A buzzer went off in Kryten's head. It was his internal alarm clock telling him it was time for Miss Yvette's bath. Automatically he raised himself, and then, remembering, sank back down again. He took a sonic screwdriver from his top pocket, flipped a series of release catches on his neck, removed his head and plonked it down unceremoniously on to the table.

'What are you doing?' said the Cat.

'I'm programmed to serve,' said Kryten's head. 'They're dead. The programme is finished. I'm activating my shut-down disc.'

'Woah!' said Lister. 'Slow down.'

Kryten's hands twisted the right ear off his disembodied head and pressed a latch which flipped open his skull.

'Kryten – listen to me . . .'

Kryten started removing the minute circuit boards from inside his brain, and stacking them neatly on the table.

'Kryten . . .'

He tugged out several batches of interface leads, neatly wrapped them up and placed them tidily beside the rest of his mind.

Finally he located his shut-down programme. 'Sorry about the mess,' he said, and switched himself off.

His eyes rotated back into the plastic of his skull; his body slumped forward in his seat and crashed onto the floor.

NINETEEN

'It's driving me batty. Must you do it here?' Rimmer surveyed the array of android organs spread higgledy-piggledy all over the sleeping quarters. 'What's this on my pillow? It's his eyes!'

'I'm trying to fix him,' said Lister, holding Kryten's nose in one hand and poking a pipe cleaner soaked in white spirit up his nostril with the other.

It had taken them a week to transport the two broken halves of the *Nova 5* back to *Red Dwarf*. They had needed all six of the remaining transporter craft, operating on auto pilot, to wrench the ship free of the centuries-old methane ice, but after five days of maximum thrust the small transporters had finally yanked the wreck clear, and hauled it slowly and precariously up to the orbiting *Red Dwarf*.

The Drive section of *Nova 5* held few surprises – Kryten had meticulously updated the inventory every Tuesday evening for two million years. Most of the food was still vacuum-stored. Lister had been delighted to discover they had twenty-five thousand spicy poppadoms and a hundred and thirty tons of mango chutney; enough, he pointed out at the time, to keep him happy for the best part of a month.

There was, thankfully, nearly two thousand gallons of irradiated cow's milk, and Lister had insisted the dog's milk be flushed out into the vacuum of space, where it had instantly frozen, leaving a huge dog-milk asteroid for some future species to ponder over.

'Why d'you have to keep his bits all over my bunk?'

'So I know where they are.'

'Yes, well, I'm sorry, but I refuse to have somebody else's eyes on my pillow.'

'Look – I'll have him finished by this afternoon.'

'You've been saying that for two months. What's this in my coffee mug? It's a big toe.'

'Rimmer, will you just smeg off and leave me to it?'

'What the smeg do you want to repair him for anyway? He's just a mechanoid. A mechanoid that's gone completely barking mad.'

'I want to find out about that duality drive – I want to know if we can fix it. And . . . I dunno . . . I feel sorry for him.'

'Sorry for him? He's a machine. It's like feeling sorry for a tractor.'

'It's not. He's got a personality.'

'Yes, a personality that should be severely sedated, bound in a metal straightjacket and locked in a rubber room with a stick between his teeth.'

'I think I can fix that.'

'You think it's just like repairing your bike, don't you? Spot of grease, clean all his bits, re-bore his carburettor, and bang! he's as good as new.'

'Same principle.'

'He's got a defect in his artificial intelligence. You'd need a degree in Advanced Mental Engineering from Caltech to set him to rights.'

Lister prodded one of Kryten's circuit boards with a soldering iron. The noseless head fizzed momentarily into life.

'Ah-ha,' it said, in rapid falsetto, 'elephant rain dingblat VietNam.' The eyes on Rimmer's pillow rotated and blinked. 'Telephone sandwich kerplunk armadillo Rumplestiltskin purple.'

'Well,' said Rimmer. 'Once again you've proved me wrong.'

*

HNNNnnnnNNNNNKRHHhhhhhhHHHHHHH
HNNNnnnnNNNNNKRHHhhhhhhHHHHHH

Rimmer looked at his bunkside clock. 2.34 a.m.

HNNNnnnnNNNNNKRHHhhhhhhHHHHHH
HNNNnnnnNNNNNKRHHhhhhhhHHHHHH.

Rimmer clambered down from his bunk and looked over at Lister's sleeping body. He was still holding one of Kryten's circuit boards in one hand, and a sonic screwdriver in the other.

And I'm supposed to keep you sane? he thought. *Who the smeg is supposed to keep ME sane?*

Rimmer closed his eyes and tried to sleep.

HNNNnnnnNNNNNKRHHhhhhhhHHHHHH
HNNNnnnnNNNNNKRHHhhhhhhHHHHHH

It was useless. He got Holly to simulate his red, black, white, blue, yellow and orange striped skiing anorak, and decided to check out the salvage operation in the shuttle bay.

Rimmer voice-activated the huge corrugated lead doors of bay 17, which yawned open to reveal the two halves of the wreck of *Nova 5*.

Even though it was the early hours of the morning, the massive salvage operation was in full flow. Rimmer looked down from the gantry at the battalions of skutters who were still unloading supplies from the mainly undamaged front section. Another group of skutters wielding laser torches were still trying to cut their way through the hull of the rear section. Even with the most powerful bazookoid lasers, their progress had been slow — barely two centimetres a day through the metre-thick strontium/agol alloy.

But what really interested Rimmer was the second half of

Nova 5. He'd gone through some of the ship's computer files, and had every good reason to suspect that the 'dead' segment contained something that might very well change his life.

He stood on the gantry, hands in his ski anorak pockets, watching the skutters lasering their way through the hull.

'How long before we're in?' he asked Holly.

'Two, maybe three days.'

There was a noise: the sound of creaking metal buckling and ripping as the huge, arch-shaped door, which the laser torches were cutting into the craft's hide, slowly teetered forward and fell like a medieval drawbridge, crushing all eight skutters.

'Maybe even sooner,' added Holly unconvincingly.

Rimmer raced down the gantry steps and across the steel floor of the hangar, to the newly burned entrance in the stern section of the hulk of *Nova 5*.

He peered into the dusty gloom. Floor lights glowed dimly down the length of the corridor. He summoned two skutters away from their unloading duties and, sending them ahead, stepped inside. The corridor was still warm from the laser torches. Electric cables and dismembered circuitry hung down from the ceiling like dead tubers in a petrified forest.

Rimmer inched his way along the corridor as the skutters' headlights cut swathes through the murky gloom. Most of the doors were open, or hanging off their hinges. There was a sensation, a feeling he couldn't explain, that the ship wasn't dead – that there was something there. Something alive.

Slowly he worked his way around the tortured topography of the first deck, then clambered down the broken spiral staircase, and found himself on the stasis corridor.

Most of the booths had been scooped clean by the scalpel-sharp corner of the glacier in the crash. Three remained. Two of them were punctured and, inside, the once-human occupants had been fossilized into the walls by centuries upon centuries of patient ice.

The third was occupied.

Skeletal legs jutted through a gash in the stasis booth door. The impact of the crash had driven the incumbent's limbs through the reinforced glass.

Rimmer peered in through what remained of the observation window. Somehow the rest of the body had been preserved, wedged half in and half out of the stasis booth. The legs had withered with age, while the upper body remained in suspended animation.

Timeless.

Unaging.

Unharmed.

Rimmer's voice activated the door. Surely he couldn't be . . . alive. The door lock twirled and the door arced open.

The man opened his eyes and looked down at his legs. His scream cut through Rimmer like a shard of jagged glass. Then he stopped screaming and died of shock.

Rimmer's heart went on a cross-country run around his body. It bounced off his stomach, caromed into his ribcage, and tried to make a forced exit through his windpipe. It was still hammering around his chest cavity like a deranged pinball when he finally stopped running four decks up.

He fell into a twilit recreation room and was on his haunches, still trying to suck air into his reluctant lungs, when he turned and saw the figure standing by the fruit machine.

His brain uttered a silent expletive, and his heart put on its spiked shoes and went for another lap.

TWENTY

The figure turned to face him. The hologramatic 'H' on her forehead glinted fluorescently in the blue light of the Games Room.

'Ah, there you are,' she smiled. 'Where's Yvette? I've been waiting for ages.'

'Yvette who?'

'I needed those course calculations.' She walked six paces towards him and held out her hand.

'Thank you,' she said, and disappeared.

Suddenly she reappeared at the fruit machine with her back to him.

'Are you OK?' said Rimmer, getting to his feet.

She turned.

'Ah, there you are,' she smiled; 'Where's Yvette? I've been waiting for ages. I need those course calculations.'

Yet again she stepped towards him, held out her hand – and vanished reappearing once more at the other side of the room.

'Ah, there you are,' she smiled again, and Rimmer left.

'Quark dingbat fizzigog Netherlands,' said Kryten's disembodied head. 'Smirk Windo-Kleen double-helix badger.' Then there was the *fzzzt* of a circuit shorting, and his eyes blinked closed. A thin whisp of smoke curled up from his open skull.

Lister cursed. He peeked into Kryten's mechanoid brain,

tutted, and fished out a half-eaten three-day-old cheese sandwich with chilli dressing. He prodded around with his soldering iron, absently biting into the sandwich.

The Cat walked in with his lunch on a tray, and sat down at the table.

'If you try and take this food, you're in serious personal danger.'

'I'm not going to try and take it.'

'Just don't even think about it.' The Cat pulled an embroidered lace lobster bib out of his top pocket and tied it around his neck. From his inside pocket he produced a solid silver case, lined with velvet and containing an exquisite set of gold cutlery with hand-carved mother of pearl handles, which he placed either side of his plate. He rubbed his hands together and went into his food-taunting eating ritual.

'I'm gonna eat you, little chickie,' he chanted at the chicken marengo; 'I'm going to eat you, little chickie. I'm gonna eat you, little chickie. 'Cause I like eating chicks.'

The song finished, he looked away from the food like a baseball pitcher checking the bases, then suddenly flicked the chicken off the plate and, in the same, smooth movement, caught it in mid-air with the same hand, and put it back on the plate.

'Too slow, chicken marengo,' he chided. 'Too slow for this Cat.'

'Why don't you just *eat* it?'

'It's no fun if you don't give it a chance.'

'But it's dead. It's *cooked*.'

'Woah!' The Cat slapped his hand down on the plate, sending the chicken spinning into the air and over his shoulder. He kicked away from the chair, somersaulted backwards, and caught it in his mouth before it hit the ground.

'Hey – this chicken is faster than I thought!' He put the chicken back on the plate, and had just started to juggle the potatoes when Rimmer walked in.

'Gentlemen,' he beamed broadly, 'there's someone I'd like you to meet. Someone who's a deep personal friend of mine. Someone who, I'm sure, will enrich all our lives. Someone, I've decided, who will be a more interesting and stimulating bunk-mate for myself, which is why I intend to move in with this someone to the spare sleeping quarters next door. Gentlemen . . .'

Rimmer gestured like a medieval courtesan, and into the open doorframe stepped someone Lister and the Cat recognized instantly.

There in the hatchway, standing beside Arnold J. Rimmer, was another, completely identical Arnold J. Rimmer.

TWENTY-ONE

After Rimmer left the woman by the fruit machine, he rounded up the skutters, and they made their way down the broken stairwell to *Nova 5*'s hologram simulation suite.

Her personality disc, scarred and warped, spun round and round in the drive, aimlessly projecting her through the same piece of dialogue for the zillionth time, in pointless perpetual motion.

The woman's name had been Nancy O'Keefe. A Flight Engineer, Second Class, she'd been the highest ranking casualty in the ship's rear section. What remained of the computer's intelligence had automatically recreated her, even though her database was corrupted beyond repair in the accident.

Rimmer told the skutter to eject the disc, and started searching through the rest of *Nova 5*'s personality library.

One by one he went through the eight-woman, two-man crew. One by one the skutters' clumsy claws placed each of the discs in the drive, and booted them up. And one by one all ten members of *Nova 5* were resurrected before him. Each in some way was corrupted.

All ten discs were unplayable.

The frustration of it!

For two cruel hours, while he went through each of the discs, he'd been able to entertain the prospect that at last he could acquire a companion. A hologramatic companion, who could understand how it felt to be dead. How it felt to be a hologram. How it felt. Someone who could *touch* him. Yes — holograms could touch. Someone *he* could touch. To *touch* again! To *be* touched!

But, no.

Denied. All ten discs warped, scratched, ruined. All ten discs destroyed in the crash.

Rimmer sat down and tried to think. What if . . . what if he could copy his own disc from the *Red Dwarf* hologram library, and then use *Nova 5*'s disc drive to simulate a duplicate him?

Two Arnold Rimmers.

Two hims.

Who better as a companion than his own self!

Arnold J. Rimmer 1 and Arnold J. Rimmer 2.

Brill-smegging-illiant.

TWENTY-TWO

'*How To Be a Winner – an Introduction to Poweramics.*'

'Ours,' said the two Rimmers simultaneously.

Lister tossed the book onto the computer trolley, with the rest of the Rimmers' belongings, and picked another off the shelf.

'*Cooking With Chillies,*' he read.

'Yours,' the Rimmers chanted in unison.

Lister tossed it back on the shelf, then turned and opened the locker marked 'Rimmer, A. J. B Sc, S Sc', which long ago Lister had learned stood for 'Bronze Swimming Certificate' and 'Silver Swimming Certificate', and started to heap all the contents onto the trolley. Twenty pairs of identical military blue underpants, all on coat hangers in protective cellophane wrapping, the pyjamas with the dry-cleaning tags pinned to the collars, the piles of *Survivalist* weaponry magazines, and his one CD – *Billy Benton and his choir sing the Rock'n'roll greats.*

'What about these posters?' asked the duplicate Rimmer.

'They're mine,' said Lister.

'I know they're yours, but the Blu-Tack isn't.'

'You want to take the Blu-Tack?'

'Well, it is *mine,*' pointed out the original; 'I did pay for it, with *my* money.'

'I think there's one of your old finger-nail clippings under the bunk. I'll put that in too, shall I?'

Rimmer Mark 2 eyed him narrowly. 'Don't try and be amusing, Lister; it doesn't suit you.'

For no reason that Lister could see, both Rimmers *howled* with laughter at this last remark, bending at the waist and thumping their knees.

'Great put-down, Arnie,' said the original Rimmer through a mask of tears.

Lister looked on, bemused.

The duplicate stood up, still giggling. 'I'll go and check how the skutters are coping with the redecoration plans.'

'See you, Big Man,' said the copy, stepping out of the hatchway.

'Catch you later, Ace,' said Rimmer, with a look of total infatuation.

'You're a very, very weird person,' said Lister, dropping a wedge of neatly ironed black socks onto the trolley. 'In fact, both of you are.'

Rimmer was oblivious to criticism. 'What an idea. What a genius idea. Using *Nova 5*'s hologram unit to generate a duplicate me. That's the best smegging day's work I ever did.'

'Of all the people you could have brought back – anyone in the *Red Dwarf* crew – you decide to copy your own disc, and bring back another you? That's turning narcissism into a science!'

'I wanted a companion. Who more interesting and stimulating than myself?'

'Why didn't you bring back one of the girls?'

'Because all the girls thought I was a prat.'

'Well, one of the guys, then?'

'They all thought I was a prat, too. Everybody thought I was a prat except for me. Which is why I brought back the Duke. Old Iron Balls himself.'

'Bonehead 2 – how could there be only one?'

'I don't have to take this any more,' Rimmer sighed happily; 'I don't have to take the put-downs, the smart-alec quips, the oh-so-clever snide asides. It's the dawn of a new era for me, Listy. No more you, with your stupid, annoying habits. No more you, holding me back, dragging me down.'

'Me? How did I drag you down?'

'Oh, let me count the ways.'

'What ways?'

'Humming.'

'Humming?'

'You hummed persistently and maliciously for eight months, every time I sat down to do some revision.'

'So, you're saying you never became an officer because you shared your quarters with someone who hummed occasionally?'

'Not occasionally. *Constantly*.'

'You failed your Astronavigation exam eight times before we even met.'

'There you go again – always ready with the smart-alec quip.'

'That's not a quip, it's a fact.'

'There you go again, putting me down.'

'So, what else did I do, besides hum?'

'Everything. Everything you ever did was calculated to hold me back, put me down and annoy me.'

'Like what?'

'Exchanging all the symbols on my revision timetable, so that instead of taking my Engineering finals I went swimming.'

'They fell off. I thought I'd put them all back in the right place.'

'Swapping my toothpaste for a tube of contraceptive jelly.'

'That was a joke!'

'Yes. The same kind of joke as putting my name on the waiting list for experimental pile surgery. The point is: you have always stopped me from being successful – that is a scientific fact.'

'Rimmer, you can't blame me for your lousy life.'

'Not just you. It's been all my bunk-mates. Pemberton, Ledbetter, Daley . . . all of you.'

'It's always the same. It's never *you*, is it? It's always

someone or something else. You never had the right set of pens for G & E Drawing . . . your dividers don't stretch far enough . . .'

'Well, they don't!' protested Rimmer.

'In the end, you can't turn round and say: "Sorry I buggered up my life – it was Lister's fault".'

'It's too late, my life's already been buggered up. It's my death that concerns me now, and I have no intention of buggering that up' – Rimmer turned on his heels – 'because I'm getting out of here and moving in with myself.'

TWENTY-THREE

Blackness.

Nothingness.

Then a sound.

'Jjjjjdt!'

Then the sound again:

'Jjjjjdt!'

What did that sound mean?

The sound again, but this time it was different. He recognized the sound. He remembered hearing it before. It was language. But he'd forgotten what it meant.

'Kryjjjjjdt.'

A name. A name he should have known.

'Kryjjjdtn.'

His name!

'Kryten? Kryten?'

A flash of green light. Then black lines drew themselves across his field of vision. Then the lines melted away, and he was looking at a message:

'Mechanoid Visual System, Version IX.05. © Infomax Data Corporation 2296.'

And then sight.

Floods of brilliant colours: blues, reds, yellows dancing nonsensically before him.

He focused. There was a man's face grinning at him.

'Ye-es!' said the face. 'Bru-taaaaal!'

'Hgvd Mumber Daffd,' said Kryten.

Lister twiddled about inside his head with a sonic screwdriver.

'Hello, Mr David,' said Kryten.

'Ye-es!' said Lister again. 'I've done it! You're back in action.' He put Kryten's skull-piece back into place, fastened the latches and replaced his ear. 'How d'you feel?'

'Everything seems to be functioning,' said Kryten flatly.

'Listen', said Lister, leaning over him, 'there's something I need to know: what's the duality jump? What is it? What does it do?'

A plastic frown rippled across Kryten's brow. 'It powers the ship. It's a quantum drive – it allows you to leap from one point in space to another. Why?'

'How does it *work*?'

'I'm just a mechanoid. I don't know these things.'

'How does it work, Kryten?' Lister insisted.

'It's something to do with Quantum Mechanics and Indeterminism''. Something about when you measure electrons, they can be in two places at the same time.'

Kryten seemed strangely reluctant to talk about it, and kept stressing it was a 'human matter' and not really the kind of thing mechanoids should concern themselves with, but, bit by bit, Lister wheedled what he could out of Kryten, and doggedly pieced together what he needed to know.

When you made a duality jump, it seemed, you temporarily coexisted at two points in the universe; you then 'chose' one of these points to 'be' in. In this way you could leapfrog across the universe, not bound by the limits of Space/Time.

'So, how long,' Lister pressed, 'would it take a duality jump to get back to Earth?'

'Oh . . . a long time.'

'How long?'

'You'd have to make about a thousand jumps.'

'How *long*?'

'Two . . .' Kryten mused '. . . perhaps even *three* months.'

'Three months!' Lister was already into the touch-up shuffle.

'But there's no fuel! It decayed centuries ago.'

'What kind of fuel does it need?'

'I don't know. I'm just a mechanoid.'

'Kryten, pleeeease.'

Kryten, shifted on the bench and twisted his fingers uncomfortably. 'I'm just a mechanoid. I just clean things.'

'But you know, don't you?'

'Only because I heard Miss Yvette talk about it once. But I'm not *supposed* to know.'

'What is it?'

'Uranium 233. Whatever that is.'

'Ye-e-e-es!' Lister thumped the table. 'Nice one, Krytie.'

'Well, if that's all, Mr David' – Kryten smiled his lipless smile – 'I'd like to be shut down again now, please.'

'What are you talking about? It took me four months to fix you.'

'But there's no point in my being on-line. I was programmed to serve the crew of *Nova 5*. They're dead now, therefore, my program is completed.'

'So? You've got to start a new program.'

Kryten tilted his head and arched a hairless eyebrow. 'To serve whom?'

'To serve no one. To serve yourself.'

'But I *have* to serve someone. I was created to serve. I serve, therefore I am.'

Lister forced back his fur-lined leather deerstalker with the heels of his palms in exasperation. 'Kryten – chill out, OK? Loosen up. Re-lax. Just hang, will you? Chill the smeg out.'

'Why?'

'Because I say so.'

Kryten's face seemed to brighten. 'Is that an order?' he said hopefully.

'Why?'

'Well, if it's an *order*, that's different.'

'It *is* an order,' Lister smiled. 'Chill out.'

Kryten was perched stiffly on a tall bar stool in the Copacabana Hawaiian Cocktail Bar, staring at the dry martini cocktail, stirred, two olives, standing before him. He didn't really like dry martinis, shaken or otherwise, but he'd ordered it because it was the drink Hudzen always had when he went to the Hi-Life Club in *Androids* and to Kryten it was the zenith of sophistication.

He knocked back the martini in a single gulp, paused a few seconds, then regurgitated it back into his glass and stirred it round for a while with his cocktail stick. He wasn't very good at enjoying himself, he decided. He'd much rather have been cleaning something. He would much rather have been re-varnishing the dance floor or shampooing all two thousand, five hundred and seventy-two crushed velvet seats.

Still, Mister David had ordered him to 'chill out', to 'hang', so 'hang' was what he must do. He sank the cocktail once more, and brought it back up again.

He flicked through his vocabulary database for a definition of 'hang (vb. slang)'. 'Reduce tension' he read once again; 'lose rigidity; cease working, worrying etc.; allow muscles to become limp; relax, enjoy oneself.' Kryten relaxed his muscles. His head lolled back, his arms hung loosely by his sides, and he fell off the bar stool onto the purple carpet.

He climbed back onto the stool, and started to worry that he hadn't ceased worrying. He looked around at the flashing disco lights on the empty dance floor. He became aware for the first time that music was pumping out of the speakers. If he was really to carry out Mister David's orders to the letter, he supposed, he was obliged to get down and dance. With a sigh of resignation he took his martini cocktail and waddled over to the dance floor. The only dance he knew was the tap dance to *Yankee Doodle Dandy*.

The music playing was Hugo Lovepole's sexy ballad *Hey Baby, Don't Be Ovulatin' Tonight*. Kryten set his drink on the floor, stamped his right foot until he got in time with the smoochy beat, and began tap-dancing furiously.

And that was how the two Rimmers found him as they strolled through the recreation decks, taking their early evening constitutional.

It had been a very pleasant stroll – quite the nicest evening Rimmer had spent for years. His duplicate was a total delight. They had each other in tucks; reminiscing, talking over old glories, old girlfriends. The simple, manly joy of chewing the fat with a like-minded, right-thinking colleague.

At last he had someone with whom he could share ideas he'd always been to embarrassed to propound before. Such as his French dictation theory of life.

Rimmer believed there were two kinds of people: the first kind were history essay people, who started life with a blank sheet, with no score, and accumulated points with every success they achieved. The other kind were the French dictation people: they started off with a hundred per cent, and every mistake they made was deducted from their original perfect score. Rimmer always felt his parents had forced him firmly into the second group. Everything he'd ever done was somehow imperfect and flawed – a disappointment. Years before, when he'd been promoted to Second Technician, he felt he hadn't *succeeded* in becoming a Second Technician, rather, he'd *failed* to become a First Technician. While he expounded the theory, his double nodded in agreement and murmured encouragements, such as 'Absolutely' and 'Very true.'

Right now, though, the conversation had shifted and Rimmer was listening with mounting glee as his double reminded him of their one-night stand with Yvonne Mc-Gruder.

'What a body! What a body!' the double was chuckling:

'And hers wasn't bad either!' Rimmer guffawed.

They paused as across the disco floor they caught sight of Kryten clickety–clacking frenetically.

'What on Io do you think you're doing?' the double said, bemused.

'I'm chilling out, sirs,' said Kryten. 'I'm hanging.' Click, click, click, tap, tippy-tap, tip.

'You're what?' said Rimmer.

'I'm getting mellow' – clicky-clack, tip, tip – 'I'm coasting. I'm chilling out.'

Kryten suddenly felt ridiculous, and stopped.

'How long have you been fixed?' Rimmer asked.

Kryten was wondering why there were two identical-looking Rimmers addressing him, but he felt that as a mech-anoid it would have been impertinent to ask. 'Since 12.15 hours, sirs.'

'It's seven-thirty in the evening. Have you been messing about all that time?' said the double.

'I was carrying out Mr David's orders, Mr Arnold, sir. He ordered me to relax.'

'Oh, and I suppose you do everything you're ordered to?'

'Yes, sir. I do, sir.'

'Really?' The two Rimmers hiked eyebrows at each other.

'Yes. I'm programmed to serve, sirs.'

The double pointed to Kryten's drink. 'Eat that cocktail glass.'

'Right away, sir,' said Kryten, and ate the glass.

'So,' Rimmer mused, 'if I said to you "spring-clean the entire sleeping quarters deck," I suppose you'd do that too, would you?'

'Of course, Mr Arnolds.'

'Splendid!' said Rimmer.

'Splendissimo!' said his digital doppleganger.

TWENTY-FOUR

The lift doors split open and disgorged a tired but happy Lister onto the habitation deck corridor. He'd spent the last two days and a night down in the technical library, then another morning liaising with Holly in the geology lab. In the last fifty-six hours he'd learned many things. He'd started off thinking that the structure and composition of planet crust and rock formations were incredibly boring. But now he was absolutely certain of it. Still, he now knew more about uranium production and mining techniques than he knew about the London Jets Megabowl-winning team of '75 – and he knew what the entire London Jets Megabowl-winning team of '75 had for breakfast on the day of the game.

This was the way it went: fissile uranium 233 could be synthesized from the non-fissile thorium isotope: thorium 232. And this was the best part: thorium 232 wasn't even rare. It was abundant in the universe. It abounded! There was lots of it! And this was confirmed when his radiometric-spectrographic survey turned up seven likely moons in this solar system alone.

Five of them would have required underground mining, so he had to rule them out. Of the remaining two, one, the more likely one, was seven months' travel away. But on the nearer moon, less than five days' journey away, there was an eighty-seven per cent probability that the ore deposits he needed were lying close to the surface. No shafts, no pit-props, no radon gas ventilation problems. Maybe he could do it. *Red Dwarf* was a mining ship – it had all the equipment: the earth-moving vehicles, the processing plants, the whole enchilada!

When he turned into his sleeping quarters, it took several moments before his tired brain registered what it was that was different.

At first he assumed he must have got out of the lift on the wrong floor, and he was now standing on the wrong deck. Then he saw his goldfish, only the water was clean, and you could see the plastic Vatican quite clearly. He looked around.

The dull grey metal walls had vanished behind a Victorian floral print in various pretty pinks. The bedspreads were in delicate cream lace, festoon blinds in a mixture of rosebud patterns hung over the viewport window. A salmon-tinted Aubusson rug swept from under the bunks to the new porcelain pedestal wash basin. The lounge area was curtained off from the bunks by red silk drapes, with gold tie-backs. The table in the middle of the room was covered in a briar rose, short-skirted circular cloth, on top of which stood rows of newly polished boots and piles of neat, crisply folded laundry.

It was appalling.

It was an atrocity against machismo.

'What the smeg is going on?'

Kryten looked up from his ironing.

'Good afternoon, Mr David, sir.'

'What have you *done*?'

'A spot of tidying.'

'What are these?' Lister snatched an unrecognizable item from the pile of laundry.

'Your boxer shorts, Mr David.'

'No way are these my boxer shorts,' said Lister. 'They bend. What have you done to this place? What is this? This bowl of scented pencil shavings?'

'Potpourri, sir.'

'Pope who? Where is everything? Where's my orange peel

with the cig dimps in it? Where's the remnants of last Wednesday's curry? I hadn't finished eating it! Where's my coffee mug with the mould in it?'

'I threw it away, sir. I threw it all away.'

'You what? I was breeding that mould. It was called "Albert". I was trying to get him two feet high.'

'Why, sir?'

'Because it drove Rimmer nuts. And driving Rimmer nuts is what keeps me going. What did you do it for?'

'The two Mr Rimmers ordered me to, sir. They even recommended the decor. They said it was very *you*.'

Lister sat down on the apple-green chintz-covered chaise longue, next to the potted plastic wisteria, and wondered where he could begin. There was something about Kryten that really disturbed him, but he wasn't quite sure what. He was a slave, and Lister hated that. For some reason, mankind seemed to be obsessed with enslaving someone: black slavery, class slavery, housewife slavery, and now mechanoid slavery. Then it hit him: it wasn't so much slavery that got to him, though get to him it did; it was the happy slave. It was the acquiescence, the assent to serve, the willingness to be a slave.

'What about you?' Lister looked up as Kryten ploughed through the ironing. 'Don't you ever want to do something just for yourself?'

'Myself?' Kryten sniggered. 'That's a bit of a barmy notion, if you don't mind my saying so, sir.'

'Isn't there anything you look forward to?'

Kryten stood, the steaming iron in his hand for a full minute, trying to think of an answer.

'*Androids*,' he said, at last. 'I look forward to *Androids*.'

'Besides *Androids*?'

Kryten had another think. 'Getting a new squidgy mop?' he ventured.

'Besides dumb soap operas and even dumber cleaning utensils?'

Kryten fell silent.

'What do you think of thorium mining?'

Kryten looked baffled.

'Follow me.'

They found the Cat on Corridor omega 577, sleeping peacefully on top of a narrow metal locker, a hairnet protecting his pompadour.

'Hey, Cat – wake up.' Lister rocked the locker.

The Cat opened one eye. 'This'd better be good. I was sleeping. And sleeping is my third favourite thing.'

'Come on. Follow me.'

A yawn split the Cat's face and made his head appear to double in size. He sprang down from the locker, arched his spine and stretched until the back of his head was touching the heels of his gold-braided sleeping slippers, and yawned again. He opened the locker door, reached inside, and draped an imitation King Penguin fur smoking jacket casually over his shoulders, before popping the top off a magnum of milk and filling a crystal goblet. He gargled petitely, urinated in the locker and followed Lister and Kryten down the corridor.

'Where are we going?'

'Mining.'

TWENTY-FIVE

The two Rimmers, dressed in identical P.E. kits jumped up in the air, flapping their arms simultaneously in time to the music and yelling encouragement at each other.

'Come on – keep it up!'

'You too!'

They landed, crouched like bullfrogs, and leapt off up into the air again.

'Jump!'

'Stretch!'

'Jump!'

'Stretch!'

'Jump!'

'Stretch!'

The Rimmers were alone aboard *Red Dwarf*.

Lister, Kryten, the Cat and twelve skutters had gone off in Blue Midget, loaded with surface mining equipment, in search of the uranium deposits on the black desert moon below. The two Rimmers were to stay behind to supervise the welding together of the two halves of *Nova 5* by the eighty-four remaining skutters. They were to oversee the restoration of the ship, to render it space-worthy again.

They were in charge!

In charge of a major operation, a gargantuan engineering challenge. And they were in charge!

Holly had estimated the operation would take two months to complete, at the very least. Well, the two Rimmers would see about that. They would do it in half that time, they decided. No, a quarter of that time. Under the excellent management of *two* Arnold Js, those skutters were going to work their little claws off! That ship would be ready in a fortnight. It would be ready, new and gleaming, by the time Lister returned with his uranium haul. Imagine his stupid little porky face, hardly able to conceal his grudging admiration. 'I've got to admit it,' he would say, 'you guys really are a great team.'

In the meantime they were getting fit, getting in shape, getting prepared for the ordeal ahead. This was day one of the new regime.

'Jump!'

'Stretch!'

'Jump!'

'Stretch!'

'And . . . rest!' The original Rimmer collapsed on the floor.

'No, keep jumping!' the double yelled, finding new strength from his other self's weakness. Red-faced, Rimmer started up again.

'You're right,' he shouted, 'keep going. Through the pain barrier.'

'Jump!'

'Stretch!'

'Jump!'

'Stretch!'

'And . . . rest!' said Rimmer again.

'What are you doing, man?' screamed his copy, still leaping.

'I'm resting. It's all going grey.'

'That's the pain barrier – beat it!'

'Absolutely!' He started jumping again. 'Up, up, up!'

'More, more, more!'

'Jump, jump, jump!'

'Stretch, stretch, stretch!'

'Rest, rest, rest?' pleaded Rimmer.

'No, no, no!' insisted the double.

They continued leaping up and down for a further minute, both too breathless to speak.

'And . . . rest!' whispered the double finally.

Rimmer landed on the floor and his legs sagged beneath him. He staggered backwards towards the bunk, and fell forward onto his knees. The glands at the back of his throat were producing saliva by the bucket-load. 'Great sesh,' he gurgled, 'that little bit extra, that's what it's all about. Driving through the pain barrier, to the brink of unconsciousness. Great sesh.'

'You . . . owe me . . . seven,' said the double on all fours, wheezing like an eighty-year-old bronchial bagpipes player.

'What?' panted Rimmer, his face quite yellow.

'I . . . did seven extra jerks . . . while you were . . . resting.'

'Come on. We're not down to counting jerks, are we? What's a couple of jerks between duplicates?'

'It's for . . . your own good. I'm . . . seven jerks fitter . . . than you. We can't . . . have that, can we?'

'I'll do them first thing in the morning, while you're asleep.'

'Now!' rasped the double.

Rimmer hauled himself onto his wobbly white legs and started to leap up in the air again. 'One . . .' he counted, 'two . . .' he counted, 'three . . .'

'That wasn't a full one. Call it a half.'

'Three and a half . . .' he counted.

'And that wasn't a full one either; call it three.'

'Four!' Rimmer leapt a full six inches off the floor.

'Three and one eighth!' the double corrected.

'Four and one eighth!'

'Three and a half,' was the verdict.

Finally, after twenty-five leaps, Rimmer's duplicate agreed he'd done seven.

'You see,' said the double, 'it's about teamwork. I drive and encourage you . . .'

'And I drive and encourage you,' gasped Rimmer. And then he was sick.

'Right' – the double rubbed his hands – 'what time shall we get up?'

'That's a good question, I.B. Early. Very early. Half past eight?'

'What, and miss half the day? How about seven?' the double ventured.

'How about six?' Rimmer topped him.

'No. Half past four!'

'Half past four? That's the middle of the night!'

'We want it to be ready in a fortnight, don't we?'

'Yes, but half past four?' Rimmer moaned. 'That's ridiculous!'

'Why's it ridiculous? You think Napoleon on the eve of the battle of Borodino said: "Wake me tomorrow at nine with two runny eggs and some toastie soldiers"?'

'You're absolutely right, Duke.'

Rimmer voice-activated the digital alarm clock and climbed thankfully onto his new bunk.

'What are you doing?' The double looked at him askance.

'I'm going to bed, Ace.'

'It's only two in the morning – we need to read up on welding techniques.'

'But we're getting up in a minute,' Rimmer said in a small, pathetic voice.

'You take metallurgy and thyratron in heat-control systems, and I'll take magnesium arc-welding, and chemical bonding techniques. Then we'll test one another, and whoever does worst has to do another hundred jumps before bunk down.'

'Once again, Arn, I hate to say it, but you're absolutely right.'

The two Rimmers finally got to bed at 3.37 a.m., and got up again fifty-three minutes later to start their morning exercises.

TWENTY-SIX

Lister crunched his way through five gear changes, and Blue Midget lurched like a drunken line-backer over the airless black desert of the unnamed moon. Helium winds whipped the sand into huge, tapering swirls that twisted across the dry, featureless landscape like a pack of children's spinning tops.

Lister landed the mining juggernaut with all the natural grace of a suicidal elephant tumbling from the Eiffel Tower.

'Nice landing, buddy,' said the Cat, digging his way out of the pile of storage lockers which had collapsed on him.

Lister threw the Cat a spacesuit. 'Put this on.'

The Cat looked at the battered old dirty silver regulation-issue spacesuit with disdain. 'Are you kidding? I wouldn't use this to buff my shoes.'

Lister clambered into his own. 'Put it on.'

'Are you seriously telling me these shoulders were *ever* in style?'

'Put it on.'

The Cat held the suit at arm's length.

'Well, maybe if I widen the lapels, put in a couple of vents, maybe some sequins down the legs . . .'

'We're going *mining*,' said Lister. 'We're not in the heats of "Come Jiving", we're going to work.'

'Hey — I do not *do* the "W" word.'

'We're all doing the "W" word,' said Lister.

Kryten stepped through the hatchway from Blue Midget's galley, carrying a tray of tea things and a plate of petits fours.

'I thought we might have some tea,' he said, setting the cups in the saucers.

'We're going smegging mining!' Lister threw his spacesuit gauntlet against the wall.

'Milk or lemon?' Kryten smiled.

'You're in charge of processing! I can't do this all on my own.'

'I'll have milk,' said the Cat.

'Is nobody listening? We're going uranium mining. It's a helium atmosphere out there. It's going to be hard, and it's going to be dangerous.'

'All the more reason,' said Kryten, 'to have a nice hot cup of tea inside you.'

Lister inflated his cheeks and expelled the air. He hunched over the orange and green flashing display of the trace computer, which beeped and blipped with annoying regularity as it processed soil samples in search of the main seam.

'Holly, have we found the main deposit yet?'

'No,' said Holly. 'I'd give it another twenty-five glimbarts.'

'What's a glimbart?'

'It's fifty nanoteks.'

'You're just making this up, aren't you?'

'No,' Holly protested feebly.

'Where is it, then?'

'I dunno,' he confessed.

'I thought you were supposed to have an IQ of six thousand.'

'Six thousand's not that much,' said Holly, aggrieved; 'it's only the same IQ as twelve thousand P.E. teachers.'

'Hey,' said the Cat, waving the cake tray, 'are there any more of these little pink ones?'

'Coming right up,' said Kryten.

Lister banged his head gently against the screen of the trace computer and wished, not for the first time, that a different sperm had fertilized his mother's egg.

TWENTY-SEVEN

It was 10.30 a.m., and Rimmer had already been up for six hours. He was standing on the deck of the cargo bay, calling out pointless orders to a group of skutters who were operating the cantilever crane, which was gently hoisting *Nova 5*'s rear section up into the air.

'Up a bit! Up! Up! More!'

The crane gingerly swung the huge tail section so it was suspended high above the ship's front half.

'Round! Round! Swing it round!' Rimmer was calling, redundantly. 'Swing it round, just like you are doing.'

This was the third day of the gruelling new regime the two Rimmers had instigated for themselves. The timetable went thus:

Rise at 4.30 a.m. Exercises till 5.00. Repair supervision, followed by lunch at 9.30. Planning meeting at 10.00. Supervision duties until supper at one o'clock in the afternoon. More supervision until second supper at 5.00 p.m. Technical reading till 6.00, then it was repair supervision all the way until supper three at 9.00. Then rest and recreation up to midnight, followed by supper four, and planning meeting until bed at 2.00 a.m.

For some reason the new regime meant having six holo-gramatic meals a day, and only two-and-a-half hours sleep.

Rimmer was near to cracking. His patience threshold was practically nonexistent, but he certainly wasn't going to be the one who said 'Let's ease off.' That would be weak and spineless – the *old* Arnold J. Rimmer, not the new, high-powered winner. Let his duplicate be the one to wimp out.

The huge chains moaned and creaked as the skutters began to lower the tail into place against the front section.

Rimmer rubbed the grey rings around his eyes, thought how tired his copy must be feeling at this moment, and suddenly got a new burst of energy.

'Down!' he shouted, unnecessarily; 'Down! Lower!'

'Big Man!' Rimmer's duplicate bounded down the gantry stairwell onto the cargo deck. Rimmer was aghast to see how fresh-faced and alert his copy appeared. Had he been cheating? Had he been secretly snoozing instead of supervising the supply inventory? It was perfectly possible. He'd been away three hours. And, quite frankly, he certainly looked a heck of a lot better than he should have done. But surely he wouldn't cheat *him*? That would be like cheating himself. That would be like cheating at patience. Wait a minute, Rimmer remembered, I *do* cheat at patience.

'Big Man,' the double repeated, 'you're doing it wrong. You should be moving the front section round to the rear section, rather than swinging the rear section round to meet the front section.'

'What the smeg difference does it make?' Rimmer snapped.

'Because if you weld them together in that position, the ship will have to take off in reverse.'

Rimmer looked round. The double was right. The ship was pointing in the wrong direction. How could he have made such a monumentally stupid error? It must be because he was tired. Then, how come his duplicate spotted it? Surely he was just as tired . . . unless . . . He had! He had been cheating!

'Stop!' the double was yelling at the two skutters operating the cantilever crane; 'Take it up again and swing it back round to where it came from.'

'Excuse me, this is my area of responsibility.'

'Swing it round! Back to where it came from. Start again!'

'Stop!' yelled Rimmer. The crane shuddered and stopped. The huge ship swung back and forth in its harness.

'No, swing it round!' the double countermanded. 'We've got to start again.'

'Stop!'

'Round!'

'What are you doing? This is *my* task! Haven't you got to rush off and have another huge great big sleep on the quiet?'

'What?' The double's face crinkled into a half-smile that announced he was lying. 'I haven't been taking secret sleeps.'

'Oh, really?' Rimmer sneered contemptuously and yelled for the skutters to stop again.

The weight of the swinging ship wrenched the back legs of the crane off the deck. The crane moaned and tilted; the ship slithered out of its harness and plummeted the four hundred yards onto the cargo deck below.

The two Rimmers watched, paralysed, as it bounced onto the steel deck before coming to rest, tail up, dinted, but structurally unharmed.

The crane eased lazily forward, then smashed down onto *Nova 5*'s rear half, slicing it neatly in two like a split banana.

TWENTY-EIGHT

Lister sat in the sealed cab of the earth remover, drumming his gauntleted fingers impatiently on the dashboard. After four days of exploratory digging they'd finally found a thorium lode, and dug a trench seventy feet deep and fifteen feet wide, which ran for a length of thirty yards. Once Lister had dug out enough three-foot slabs of raw ore to fill the eight-wheeled lunar transport vehicle (LTV), the Cat would then drive the thorium to the portalab, where Kryten would scrape away the waste soil and clay, then pack the clean ore in sealed cases aboard Blue Midget, ready to be transported back to *Red Dwarf* for refining.

At least, that was the plan.

But there were some hiccups in the procedure. And Lister was experiencing just one of those hiccups right now as he sat in the digger at the bottom of the trench with a full load, waiting for the Cat to return with the LTV. So far he'd been waiting for over an hour. He punched helplessly at the yellow furry dice dangling from the mirror, and wondered if it would have been possible to find two more incompetent and useless assistants in the entire universe to help him mine for uranium. George the Third and Brian Kidd were the only two that sprang readily to mind.

The whole of the first day had been spent teaching the Cat how to drive the LTV. Initially he had refused even to listen to Lister's instructions, until the vehicle had been customized to his liking. Now it was painted jet black, with two streaks of flame emanating from the wheel rims, twenty-four mirrors, tinted windows, and the Cat's own growling face painted on the hood. Once the vehicle was to his taste, he'd managed to pick up the basic driving skills fairly quickly, and in fact could now do wheelies and hand-brake turns even when loaded down with three tons of mineral ore.

The dashboard intercom buzzed in Lister's digger. Lister pressed the 'send' button.

'Where the smeg have you been? I've been trying to get through for an hour.'

Ffffzzzzt . . . 'Lunch,' said the Cat's voice.

'Lunch? We just had lunch two hours ago!'

Ffffzzzzt . . . 'Had it again,' said the Cat.

This was one of the major hiccups in the operation. The Cat insisted on taking regular breaks throughout the day. When he wasn't eating, he was snoozing. He took perhaps seven or eight snooze breaks every day which, he claimed, were essential: otherwise, he wouldn't have enough energy for his main evening sleep. When he wasn't eating or snoozing or sleeping, he was generally taking it easy. Lister had found him countless times aboard Blue Midget, listening to music on Lister's headphones and idly thumbing his way through a sniff book. In an average fourteen-hour working day the Cat could be relied upon to put in fifteen minutes' hard graft. So Lister found himself doing pretty much everything by himself.

Kryten was terrific. A real godsend. Provided all you needed was a plateful of triangular-shaped cucumber sandwiches with the crust removed and a pot of lemon tea. If, on the other hand, you needed someone to scrape uranium ore free of waste and pack it in sealed cases, all you got was another plateful of cucumber sandwiches and a second pot of lemon tea. Uranium recovery wasn't mechanoid work, he kept repeating. It was important and dangerous, and he couldn't accept the responsibility; and by way of a peace offering, he'd make another plate of sandwiches.

Lister finally persuaded him it was just cleaning work. Slightly bizarre cleaning work, but cleaning work nevertheless. And eventually he'd reluctantly agreed to do it. At the end of the third day, when Lister had gone across to the portalab to see how he was doing, he found the huge stack of raw ore piled up, largely untouched, in the holding tanks. Inside he found Kryten still working on his first piece of ore.

'Almost done,' said Kryten, spraying the uranium with just one more coat of beeswax, and buffing it to a gleaming finish.

Lister had banged Kryten's head with a handy piece of ore, and explained how it was important to do it a little more quickly. Since then he hadn't dared to go back and check on the mechanoid's progress.

In the meantime the Cat was back from his latest break.

Ffffzzzzt ... 'Back on the case now, buddy,' came the Cat's voice; 'Let's *work!*'

The Cat's LTV leapt off the brow of a dune, landed twenty feet beyond on its front wheels, ducking to the limit of its suspension, then reared back, its hood in the air, as the Cat wheelied up to the trench, spun on a sixpence and came to rest in a cloud of black lunar dust, in perfect parallel with Lister's digger.

Ffffzzz ... 'I'm a natural,' sighed the Cat, patting his pompadour in the rear-view mirror. 'Load me up. I have another snooze break due in one minute precisely.'

TWENTY-NINE

Rimmer sat in the hard metal chair at the hard metal table, reading the strategic account of the battle of Borodino, the critical battle in Napoleon's abortive advance on Moscow. He was taking full advantage of the fifteen minute rest and recreation period at the end of another exhausting day.

Lister's uranium party had been away now for three weeks, a full week over schedule. After the accident which smashed *Nova 5* into three pieces, the two Rimmers had gone into overdrive. Fifteen of the eighty-four skutters had exploded due to overwork. But at least *Nova 5* had been welded together so that it now lay in the original two pieces it had been before Lister left. After three weeks of back-breaking, skutter-blowing toil, they were finally back where they'd started.

Rimmer looked up at his double, who was sitting in the quarters' one easy chair, bathed in the pink glow of the student's study lamp, studying the rude paintings of Renaissance women in their book on Florentine art. When he'd drunk in enough of one painting he nodded at a skutter, who turned the page.

It was funny, the original Rimmer thought, staring at his duplicate. He'd never realized before how big his Adam's apple appeared in profile, or how small and triangular his chin was; he'd never been aware that his nostrils flared so ludicrously, or that his nose twitched like a dormouse's whenever he was concentrating. It was a stupid-looking face really.

As he watched, his double slipped a hand into his pocket, felt around and, pretending to cough, surreptitiously popped a hologramatic mint into his mouth. *Pathetic. Deeply, deeply pathetic*, thought Rimmer. *They're computer-simulated mints. There's no limit to their number. So why doesn't he offer me one?* Absently he slipped his chin below the table line and sucked a hologramatic boiled sweet from the line of three on his knee. *Because he's mean*, he thought, sucking silently; *he's pathologically mean*.

The double looked up and gave Rimmer a watery half-smile, forcing him to return to his Napoleonic diaries. The duplicate wondered idly if Rimmer knew he was beginning to lose his hair on the back of his crown, and if he knew how small and triangular his chin looked from this angle, above that megalithic Adam's apple, which bobbed up and down ludicrously, like a hamster caught in a garden hose. And why did he never offer him one of his boiled sweets? Why, instead, did he go through that absurd charade of ducking below the table and sucking them off his knee? He was mean, that was the top and bottom of it. Pathologically so.

Rimmer looked up again and noticed his double watching him. 'Good book?' he asked.

'Mmmm?' said the double, quickly swallowing his mint. 'Yes, yes. Florentine art.'

Rimmer smirked.

'What's funny?'

'Nothing,' said Rimmer, shaking his head.

'No, tell me. What is it?'

'You're looking at the rude pictures of Renaissance women. I just think it's funny.'

The double snorted through his familiar, lying half-smile. 'No, I'm not. I just happen to be intrigued by sixteenth-century art. True, there are several saucy portrayals of the Madonna sans fig leaf, as it were. But I don't particularly dwell on them.'

'Yes, you do. You're a freak for Renaissance bazongas. And the pair on page 78 in particular.'

An anger tic tugged at the double's top lip. 'Do you really think I'm the sort of pathetic, sad, weasly kind of person who could get erotically aroused by looking at paintings of matronly breasts?'

'I do it, so you must do it,' Rimmer said brightly. 'It's just, obviously, I've never seen it from the outside before. And although it is sad, pathetic and weasly, I grant you, it's also tremendously amusing. Especially the way you keep on getting the skutter to turn back to page 78 as if you've forgotten something.'

'I don't have to sit here and take this.'

'Yes. That's a good idea. Why don't you stand up and let me have a go on that chair?'

'Ohhhh —' the double smiled and nodded — 'that's what this is all about.'

'It's just it's my favourite chair,' Rimmer said petulantly, 'and you always seem to hog it.'

'It's my favourite chair too,' protested the duplicate.

'I used to be able to sit on it all the time when I was with Lister. Now I'm with you, I'm relegated to this hard metal chair, next to this hard metal table. And you get the student's pink light.'

'Well, the student's pink light just happens to be next to the comfy chair.'

'Which is why once in a while you might offer to let me sit there.'

'Well, of all the stupid things to argue about, honestly. You're tired — I think you must be working too hard.'

'I'm not working too hard,' Rimmer hissed; 'I can take it.'

'Hey — it's no disgrace to need more than two-and-a-half hours' sleep. True, a lot of the greatest people in history survived on three hours or under, but it doesn't necessarily mean you're a complete failure if you need twelve or thirteen.'

'I don't need twelve or thirteen.'

'Then why are you getting so ratty?'

'I'm not getting ratty,' Rimmer whined.

'Why do you keep putting me down, then?'

A bitter silence descended on the room. The thing that Rimmer hated more than anything was being put down. Lister did it to him, the Cat did it to him, and now he was doing it to himself. Rimmer began to regret his outburst. He didn't like to see his other self upset, and he even contemplated briefly going up to him and giving him a manly embrace. But in a moment of homosexual panic, he thought his double might get the wrong idea. Not that he would, of course, because he was him and he knew for a fact that he wasn't that way sexually tilted; so obviously his double wasn't and obviously his double would know that he wasn't either, and it was simply a manly embrace, meant in a sort of *mano a mano* kind of way . . . Perhaps he *was* tired. He certainly had good reason. He'd only had ten hours' sleep in the last twenty-one days. He was practically hallucinating with fatigue.

And whose fault was that? His double's. Rimmer didn't know how it had started, but somehow they'd got involved in a kind of 'tougher-than-you' game. Every time Rimmer suggested a schedule that was reasonably testing, his double would have to top it. And Rimmer could hardly let him get away with that, so he'd suggest something even more difficult, and then his duplicate would top that too!

Now, after twenty-one days of this, they were down to one-and-a-half hours' sleep a night. All he needed was a lie-in. Two or three days in bed and he'd be his old self again. It made sense! They'd blown up the skutters and broken the ship. If they'd spent the last three weeks in bed doing absolutely nothing at all, they'd be in exactly the same position as they were in now. He decided to suggest they take a couple of days off. Who cared if his copy saw it as a sign of weakness? He'd suggest it anyway.

'I was thinking,' he said aloud, 'about tomorrow's getting-up time.'

'So was I,' said his double. 'How about tomorrow we only have one hour fifteen minutes?'

'How about one hour?' Rimmer found himself saying automatically.

'No, better still,' said his double, 'forty-five minutes.'

Rimmer shut up, and wished he'd never spoken.

THIRTY

Blue Midget headed at breakneck speed towards the metal wall of *Red Dwarf*'s hull. Just before impact it flattened out and hugged the body of the ship, before twisting into a loop-the-loop and zipping smoothly in through the open doors of the cargo bay. It twisted side over side like a torpedo before flipping upright and coming to rest on the landing pad.

Lister eyeballed the Cat. 'That's the last time you drive,' he said.

They clambered down the boarding steps and stood on the deck of the cargo bay.

There before them *Nova 5* lay in one gleaming whole. Repaired, finished and space-worthy. Lister was stunned. True, they had been away almost three months, collecting enough thorium 232 for the jag home, but the Rimmers had done it! They'd actually done a job, and not screwed it up.

It was only at a second glance that Lister became aware of the burnt-out husks of eighty-or-so exploded skutters surrounding the ship. From *Nova 5*'s hatchway a lone skutter slowly emerged with a welding laser in its tired claw, and made its way unsteadily down the boarding ramp and onto the cargo bay floor. It glided painfully across the deck, emitting a dangerous whining sound, and arrived in front of Lister, Kryten and the Cat. It tilted its head like a quizzical dog, and exploded in an orange flare.

The three of them clumped noisily down the gantry steps on

to the habitation deck, and were half-way to the sleeping
quarters when they heard the voices.

'Shhh!' Lister held up his hand.

Faintly at first, then gradually increasing in clarity, the
sound of a heated argument filtered down the corridor.

'What did you call me?'

'I said you were a bonehead, Bonehead!'

'I'm a what?'

'It's no wonder Father despised you.'

'I was his favourite.'

'His favourite boneheady wimpy wet!'

'You filthy, smegging liar!'

'Everyone hated you. Even Mother.'

'Pardon?'

'You're a hideous emotional cripple, and you know it.'

'Shut up!'

'What other kind of man goes to android brothels, and
pays to sleep with robots?'

'THAT WASN'T MEEE!!!!'

'Of course it was you – I'm you. I know.'

'Shut UP!!'

'You've always been afraid of women, haven't you?'

'Shut UP!!!'

The argument had begun at eight o'clock, shortly after
supper. It was now five hours later, and it was showing no
signs of abating. Neither of them could remember why it had
begun or, indeed, what it was about. They just knew they
disagreed with one another. It was all-out verbal warfare.
They'd gone beyond the snide sniping stage; they'd gone past
the quasi-reasonable stage, when each pretended to put his
case coolly and logically, and would begin with phrases such
as: 'What I'm saying is . . .', 'The point I'm making is . . .',
and prevent the other from speaking with the perennial: 'If
you'd just let me finish . . .' They had made exactly the same
points in a variety of different ways for nearly two hours,

before tiredness crept in and the argument turned into a nuclear war.

Rimmer's double had launched the first nuke: the bonehead remark. Bonehead. Rimmer's nickname at school. He was really quite irrationally sensitive about it. The word yanked him back to the unhappy school-yards; reminded him of the mindless taunts of his cruel peers, of the dreadful mornings when he ached to be ill so he wouldn't have to go on the green school shuttle and have That Word daubed on his blazer in yellow chalk. He was branded. It was a brand that might fade, but would never completely disappear. He might be eighty years old, and successful as hell, but if he bumped into an old classmate he would still be Bonehead.

Before the double launched the bonehead nuke, Rimmer was unquestionably on top in the argument. The double had said something stupid, and Rimmer had been at the stage of saying: 'Give me an example of that,' knowing full well there were no examples to give. He was strutting up and down in his pyjamas, arms folded, a man in control, a man in command, when the bonehead nuke looped across without warning and blew him away.

'Pardon me, Bonehead.'

Rimmer actually physically staggered. Their arguments had never escalated this far before. They'd gone up to Def Comm Three, but never past it. Rimmer had to employ the time-honoured device of pretending not to have heard him properly, while his psyche's lone bugler sounded muster, and his tattered thoughts tried to regroup and launch an offensive.

But his double had capitalized on Rimmer's temporary silence by immediately launching three follow-up nukes in quick succession. The one about his Father hating him. KABOOM! The one about him being a hideous emotional cripple. KABOOM! And the one about him being afraid of women. KABABABOOM!

Rimmer was about to use a nuke of his own. His left leg had gone into spasm caused by rage. His eyes were wide and crazed. And he didn't care any more. He was going to use *the* nuke. The nuke to end all nukes. The total annihilation device. When his double used it instead.

'Oh, shut up,' the duplicate sneered, 'Mr Gazpacho!'

Rimmer stood, his mouth half-open, swaying dizzily. He felt as if someone had sucked out his insides with a vacuum cleaner.

'Mr What?' he half-smiled in disbelief. 'Mr What??'

'I said: "Mr Gazpacho," DEAFIE!'

'That is the most obscenely hurtful thing anyone has ever said . . .'

'I know,' the double grinned evilly.

Rimmer's hatchway slid open.

'That's the straw that broke the dromedary!' Rimmer screamed back at his double. Then he turned and padded into the corridor where Lister, Kryten and the Cat were standing.

'Ah, Lister. You're back,' he said quietly.

'Everything all right, is it?' Lister asked.

'For sure,' Rimmer smiled. 'Absolutely.'

'No problems, then?'

'Nope.'

'Everything's A-OK?'

'Yup! Things couldn't really be much hunky-dorier.'

'It's just — we heard raised voices.'

Rimmer laughed. 'That's quite an amusing thought, isn't it? Having a blazing row with yourself.'

From the sleeping quarters the double's voice screamed: 'Can you shut the smeg up, Rimmer! Some of us are trying to sleep!'

'I mean,' Rimmer continued, ignoring the outburst, 'obviously we have the odd disagreement. It's like brothers, I mean . . . a little tiff, an exchange of views, but nothing malicious. Nothing with any side to it.'

The double screeched: 'Shut up, you dead git!'

Rimmer smiled at Lister and, perfectly calm, he said: 'Excuse me – I won't be a second.'

He walked slowly down the corridor, paused outside the hatchway, and bellowed at maximum volume: 'Stop your foul whining, you filthy piece of distended rectum!'

Lister, Kryten and the Cat shuffled uncomfortably and examined the floor.

'Look, it's pointless concealing it any longer,' said Rimmer, walking back towards them. 'My duplicate and I ... we've had a bit of a major tiff. I don't know how it started but, obviously, it goes without saying: it was his fault.'

THIRTY-ONE

Lister's empty supper plate lay on the floor. Only the red, oily streaks of Bangalore Phall and half of his seventh poppadom, which he couldn't quite manage, bore evidence that he'd had a five-course Indian banquet for one.

Earth!

As he lay on his bunk, cuddling his eighth can of Leopard lager, Jimmy Stewart was asking the townfolk not to withdraw their money from the Bailey Building And Loan Company on the sleeping quarters' vid screen.

Earth!

He was watching Frank Capra's *It's a Wonderful Life*, his all-time favourite movie, but couldn't concentrate, even though it was his favourite scene. The Wall Street panic scene. The scene where Jimmy Stewart is trying to calm the hysterical mob clamouring to withdraw all their money after the Wall Street crash. But the money isn't there – the money's invested in the people's houses. Then Jimmy Stewart offers them his honeymoon money – he offers to divide out the two thousand dollars he was going to spend on his *honeymoon* – to keep them going till the bank opened again on Monday. But the fat guy in the hat steps up to the counter and still demands all his money – two hundred and forty-two dollars – and Stewart has to pay it, and he's begging people just to take what they need. And then a woman comes up to the counter and says she can manage on twenty dollars. Then up steps old Mrs Davis and asks for only seventeen dollars and fifty cents, which was the point where Lister usually started to blubber, and tears would sting his eyes, and he wouldn't dare look around the room in case anyone was watching him. But not this time.

Earth!

The movie was as great as ever, and he would never get tired of watching it, but he couldn't concentrate on anything because he knew he was finally going back home.

Earth!

He could taste it.

Nova 5 was fuelled and ready to go. The small band of skutters they'd brought back from the mining expedition were making the final checks and loading supplies. Tomorrow they were leaving. Within weeks Lister would be back on Earth!

Earth!

That septic orb. That dirty, polluted world he loved. He ached for the Brillo pad sting of a breath on a city street. The oh-so-delicious stench of the oily, turdy sea in summer. The grassy parks in spring, festooned with the thrilling vibrant colours of discarded chocolate wrappers and squidgy condoms and squashed soft drink cans. He longed to look up at a winter sky and see again the huge artificial ozone plug which sat above the Earth like an absurd toupé, constructed in his lifetime to repair the damage caused by two generations of people who wanted to flavour their sweat. Earth. It was a dump. It was a sty. But it was his home, where he belonged, and where he was finally going.

He flicked off the vid and slipped down from his bunk. It was time to tell the Rimmers. It was time to tell them that when they left tomorrow on *Nova 5*, only one of them could come.

Rimmer had been avoiding himself since the argument. He didn't know how to begin a reconciliation conversation.

Things had been said which . . . well, things had been said. Hurtful things. Bitter, unforgivable things which could never be forgotten. Equally, he couldn't just carry on as if nothing had happened. So he spent the day in the reference library, keeping out of everyone's way.

It was 4.30 p.m. when he finally swallowed the bile and slumped reluctantly into his sleeping quarters, looking curiously unkempt. His hair was uncombed and unwashed. A two-day hologramatic growth swathed his normally marble-smooth chin. His uniform was creased and ruffled. He flopped untidily into the metal armchair.

His double sat on the bunk, looking moodily out of the viewport window. As Rimmer entered he'd looked round over his shoulder, then turned back without acknowledging him.

They sat there in silence. One minute. Two minutes. Three minutes. Bitter, accusing silence. They were both masters at using silence, and right now they were using it in a bitter, accusing way. After twenty minutes of stonewalling, Rimmer could take no more.

'Look . . .' he began, 'I want to apologize for . . .' Rimmer faltered, uncertain as to precisely what he was supposed to apologize for. 'I want to apologize for everything.'

'Ohhhhh, shut up,' his double said dismissively.

Rimmer's eyes shrank, weasel-small. 'You don't like me, do you? Even though I'm you, you don't actually like me. Even though we're the same person, you actively dislike me.'

His double turned from the window. 'We're not the same person.'

'But we are. You're a copy of me.'

The double shook his head. 'I'm a recording of what you *were*, what you used to be. The man you used to be before the accident. You've changed. Lister's changed you.'

Lister? Changed him? Preposterous.

'I haven't changed. In what way have I changed?'

'Well, for a start, you've just apologized.'

What was it his father used to say? 'Never apologize – never explain.'

'I'm sorry,' Rimmer apologized again; 'it's just – I want us to get on.'

'Oh, don't be pathetic.'

Rimmer closed his eyes and leaned back on his chair. Was it just him? Was it some dreadful flaw in his personality that prevented him from having a successful relationship even with his own self? Or would it be the same for most people? Would *most* people find their own selves irritating and tire-somely predictable? When he saw his face in the mirror in the morning, that was the face he carried around in his head: he never saw his profile; he never saw the back of his own head; he didn't see what other people saw. It was the same with his personality. He carried around an idealized picture of himself; he was the smart, sensitive person who did this good thing, or that good thing. He buried the bad bits. He covered up and ignored the flaws. All his faults were forgiven and forgotten.

But now he was faced with them; all his shortcomings, personified in his other self.

Rimmer had never been aware how awesomely petty he was. How alarmingly immature. How selfish. How he could, on occasion, be incomprehensibly stupid. How sad he was; how screwed-up and lonely.

And he was seeing this for the first time. It was like the first time he'd heard his own voice on an answering machine. He expected to hear dulcet tones, clear, articulate and accentless, and was embarrassed and nauseated to discover only inco-herent mumblings in some broad Ionian accent. In his head he sounded like a newsreader; in reality, he sounded nasal and dull and constantly depressed. And meeting himself was the same, only worse, raised to the power 1000.

And there were other things. He was at least thirty per cent worse-looking than he thought. He stooped. His right leg constantly jiggled, as if he wanted to be somewhere else. He snored! Not the loud buzz-saw hunnnk-hnnnunk of Lister; his own snore was, if anything, more irritating – a high-pitched whiny trill, like a large parrot being strangled in a bucket of soapy water. It was a terrible thing to admit, but he was reaching the devastating, inescapable conclusion that he, as a companion, was the very last person he wanted to spend any time with.

Was this the same for everybody? Or was it just him? He didn't know.

So lost was he in this train of thought that he was only vaguely aware of Lister coming into the room and announcing that *Nova 5* could only sustain one hologram, and so one of the Rimmers would have to be switched off. Who was it going to be? he was asking.

'Who what?' asked Rimmer.

'Who's going to come on *Nova 5*, and who's going to be turned off?'

'Well, obviously I'm coming,' said Rimmer.

'Why "obviously"?' said his double.

'Because I'm the original. I was here first.'

'So what? We should toss for it.'

'Nooo,' said Rimmer through a disparaging laugh. 'Why should I want to toss for it? I might lose.'

Lister took out a coin. 'Heads or tails?'

'What?' said Rimmer.

'Fair's fair. You call.'

'You expect me to call heads or tails as to whether or not I get erased?' Rimmer's features fled to the perimeter of his face. 'No way. I stay.'

'You're the same person. It's only fair. Call.' Lister flipped the coin, caught it, and covered it with his hand.

'I'm not calling.'

'I'll call,' said the double.

'*I'll* call,' Rimmer said firmly. 'Heads . . . no, tails. Tails, I mean. No, wait, heads, heads.'

'It's tails,' said Lister. 'You get erased.'

'I haven't finished deciding yet. I think I was going to choose tails. Yes, I was. "Tails," in fact.'

'Too late,' said the double. 'Erase him.'

'But I was here first,' protested Rimmer. 'In a way, I created you.'

'What difference does it make? You're identical,' Lister said; 'you're the same person.'

'But we're not,' Rimmer whined balefully. 'Not any more, we're not.'

THIRTY-TWO

It was four in the morning and Rimmer sat on the bunk, his long arms wrapped around his spindly knees, his brain fighting off sleep. It was ironic, he thought, that he'd just about come to terms with having died, and now here he was, about to be erased forever.

On the toss of a coin.

But that was life, he thought. Life was the toss of a coin. You're born rich; you're born poor. You're born smart; you're born stupid. You're born handsome; you're born with a face like a post office clerk.

Heads you are, tails you aren't.

Rimmer felt that most of his life had come up 'tails'. Relationships with women: tails. Career success: tails. Friendships: tails. His life, best out of three: tails, tails and tails.

He'd never been in love, and now he never would be. He'd never been an officer, and now he never would be. He'd never be anything, because he was about to be erased.

All right, there still would be an Arnold Rimmer, but it wasn't him, it was his so-called double. But he wasn't a double – they were different.

He allowed himself an ironic snicker. He couldn't even succeed at being Arnold Rimmer – there were two of them and he'd come second. Unbelievable.

Unbe-smegging-lievable.

What had he learned from his life? What? Except 'keep your face out of the way of atomic explosions'? Nothing.

He'd learned nothing. What had he achieved? Again, nothing. His life was a goalless draw.

In his entire life, thirty-one years alive and one year dead, he'd made love with a real live woman once. One time only. Uno. Ein. Une. Once. One raised to the power of one. What Planck's Constant can never be more than. Pi divided by itself.

We are talking one here, me old buckeroo, he thought. *Once.*

Yvonne McGruder. A single, brief liaison with the ship's female boxing champion. 16th March, 19.31 hours to 19.43 hours.

Twelve minutes.

And that included the time it took to eat the pizza.

In his whole life he'd spent more time vomiting than he ever spent making love. Was that right? Was that fair? That a man should spend more time with his head down a lavatory than buried in the buttocks of the woman he loved?

He'd always deluded himself that the problem was he hadn't met the right girl yet. Now, given that the human race probably no longer existed, coupled with the fact that he had passed on, even he had to admit there was more than a possibility he was leaving it a *little* bit on the late side.

He'd never had a break. Never. And so much of life was luck.

Luck.

If Napoleon had been born Welsh, would his destiny have been the same? If he'd been raised in Colwyn Bay, would he have been a great general? Of course he wouldn't. He'd have married a sheep and worked in the local fish and chips shop. But no – he'd had the luck to be born in Corsica, just at the right moment in history when the French were looking for a short, brilliant Fascist dictator.

Luck.

Van Gogh. Wasn't it sheer good fortune that Van Gogh was born raving mad? Wasn't that why his cornfields looked like they did? Wasn't that why he did several hundred paintings of his old boots? Wasn't that why his paintings were so innovative? Because he had the happy chance to be born with a leak in the think tank?

Luck!

And what about John Merrick? The jammy bastard – born looking like an elephant. How can you fail? You just stand around while people goggle at you, and you rake it in.

He was too normal, that was his problem. Too ordinary, and normal, and healthy and bland. A bit of madness, a spot of deafness, the looks of an elephant, a birthplace like Corsica, and he could have been somebody. He could have been the deaf, mad, elephant Frenchman for a start.

He stood up and paced around the room. His body wanted to sleep, but his mind wanted to rant. This was torture. It was Death Row. It was Hell. If it was going to happen, he wanted to get it over with. He couldn't tolerate the agony of a day knowing everything he did he would be doing for the last time.

Forget tomorrow, he wanted to be erased now.

'Forget tomorrow,' he said, 'I want to be erased now.'

'It's half past four in the morning,' croaked Lister, scraping the fuzz off his tongue with his top teeth.

Rimmer's duplicate sprang out of his bunk. 'Great! Let's get it over with.'

'What d'you think you're doing?' Lister asked.

'I'm coming to watch.'

Lister shook his head. 'It's not a freak show.'

The double forced air through his teeth disappointedly. 'There's precious little entertainment on this ship. If you can't attend the odd execution, what've you got left?'

Lister started to get dressed. 'I'll see you in the disc library in ten minutes.'

Rimmer nodded and left.

*

When Rimmer arrived Lister was already there, sitting in front of the generating console clutching a mug of steaming black coffee and a jam doughnut brushed with sugar.

Great, thought Rimmer. *Come to my execution. Light refreshments available.*

'Fancy a drink?' said Lister, sipping at his rum-laced coffee.

Rimmer grunted in the negative. He was wearing his best blue First Technician boiler suit, with a row of worn-looking medals dangling over the spanner pocket.

'I didn't know you had any medals. What are they?'

Rimmer pointed to the first medal with his forefinger: 'Three years' long service.' He tapped the second: 'Six years' long service.' He touched the third: 'Nine years' long service, and . . .' he hesitated, his finger over the final medal, as if remembering, 'and . . . uh . . . twelve years' long service.'

Lister didn't smile.

'Come on – one drink.'

Rimmer capitulated. 'I'll have a whisky.'

Holly simulated a large shot of Glen Fujiyama, and Rimmer took it in one belt.

'Another?'

Rimmer nodded, unable to speak, feeling as if the lining of his larynx had been stripped like wallpaper.

A second malt arrived in a hologramatic glass. He tipped it into his mouth.

Rimmer was totally unused to drink. His face glowed brightly. His hair seemed to uncoil and hang onto his face. He swept it back with both his hands, and sighed a long, world-weary sigh. A sigh that had been inside him, trying to get out, for thirty-one years.

'Gaaahhhhhhhhhhhhhhhhhhhhhhhhhhhhhhhhhhhhhhhhhhhhhh.'

He unfurled himself into a spare monitor seat and jiggled his right leg impatiently. 'Come on – let's go! Let's do it! Come on – turn me off. Let's do it! Erase me. Wipe me clean. Let's go.'

Lister finished his doughnut and dusted the sugar off his hands. 'So what's this big thing about gazpacho soup?' he said, casually taking a throatful of coffee.

'How do you know about gazpacho soup?'

'I heard the end of the argument. And you've been yelling about it in your sleep ever since I joined up. I just wondered what it was.'

'Aahh! Wouldn't you like to know?'

'Yeah. I would like to know.'

'I bet you would, Listy. I bet you would.'

'Are you going to tell me?'

Rimmer wagged his finger. 'Secret.'

'Go on – tell me.'

'I can't. It's too terrible.' Rimmer clasped his hands and rested them between his splayed knees, his back hunched, his eyes fixed on the rubber-matting floor. He shook his head. 'I can't tell you. I'd like to tell you but I can't.'

'Why?'

Rimmer's eyebrows plaited. 'You're right. What's the difference? What does it matter now? Now I'm going to be erased? You want to know about gazpacho soup? I'll tell you.' He flung his head back and closed his eyes, and started to tell Lister about the greatest night of his life.

THIRTY-THREE

'It was the greatest night of my life,' he began. 'Every Friday evening the Captain held a formal dinner in her private dining room, in her quarters. Just a few of the top officers and their partners, and one, maybe two, of the boys and girls to watch. The young Turks. The up-and-comers. The people who were happening. I'd only been with the company five months and the invitation hit the mat. I knew what it was before I opened it.

'"*The Captain requests the pleasure of the company of Mr A. J. Rimmer and guest. 8.30 for 9.00. Black tie, evening dress. RSVP.*"

'We were in orbit round Ganymede; it was a long-term dock for repairs. I didn't know what to do – I didn't have a partner, and I didn't know any women well enough to ask them. So, on the Friday morning, I caught the shuttle, found the best escort agency on Ganymede, and hired . . .' Rimmer's eyes milked over '. . . She was gorgeous. Nothing I can say now can begin to indicate how truly dynamite this girl was. She made Marilyn Monroe look like a hippo. She was at the university, doing a Ph.D. in stellar engineering, and did the escort thing for extra money. She had *four* degrees. One of the degrees was in something I couldn't even pronounce – that's how smart she was. I paid the agency fee, which was a lot. I mean, a *lot* lot. And then I tipped her double to pretend we were dating on a regular basis, and to act as if she was crazy about me. Only in public,' Rimmer waved his hand, as if to ward off evil thoughts, 'there was no funny business.

Oh, how I longed for the funny business! But that wasn't the deal. It was all above board.

'We went shopping, and I bought her a dress. Not just a dress.

'A drrrrrrrrrrrressssssssssssssss.

'It probably cost about the same as the entire NASA budget for the twenty-first century. I had to write extra small to fit all of the numbers into the box on my chequebook. Then,' he made a trilling sound with his tongue, 'then we went out and picked a tuxedo for me.

'She went home to get changed, and we arranged to meet at the shuttle port at six.

'Seven o'clock, she still hasn't shown up. I phone the escort agency, which in the meantime has turned into a Chinese restaurant. I try the university. What do you know? There is no university on Ganymede. I've been had. I've been taken. I've blown three months' salary and I haven't even got a date. I can't believe it. I catch the seven-thirty shuttle back to *Red Dwarf*. I ask all five air hostesses, but they say they're all on duty and can't come. So there's nothing for it: I have to go on my own. I'm humiliated before I walk in the door.

'So, I turn up at the Captain's quarters completely by myself. Everyone else has got partners. The table is all set with place cards. I have to spend the whole evening sitting opposite an empty chair. They ask me where my date is, and I panic and tell them she was killed in a road accident earlier in the evening, but I'm over it now.

'We sit down, and dinner begins. I'm feeling like I've got off to a really bad start, so I'm trying desperately to be charming as smeg, but no one's warming to me. Then I remember the joke. Ledbetter had told me this joke about a bear trapper in Alaska. It was funny, it was clean; it was perfect for the dinner party. Originally I was going to save it for the mints and coffee, but by this time I'm feeling I might not even *make* it to the mints and coffee; the empty chair's staring back at me, and the rest of the guests are convinced my girlfriend's lying in some morgue somewhere while I go out to a dinner party. So I decide now is the time to tell the joke. And I'm telling the joke, and it's a long joke, and I'm suddenly aware no one's talking and everybody's watching me telling the joke, and I'm very self-conscious all of a sudden, and I can feel my ears – I'm suddenly really aware of my ears – and the back of my neck's starting to prickle. Suddenly, for no reason at all, I forget the end. I forget the punch line. I forget how it finishes. I just stop talking, and everyone's still looking at me. I have to say: "I'm very sorry, but that's as much as I remember." There's this pause. Horrible pause. Horrible. Horrible. And I can see the Captain's boyfriend looking at me with pity in his eyes, because he thinks I'm half-crazy with grief. And everyone starts talking. But not to me. Then the stewards wheel in the first course.

'It's soup.

'Gazpacho soup.

'While they're serving, I'm studying the cutlery. I'd bought this etiquette book, and I know two things. One: never wear diamonds before lunch, and two: with cutlery, start from the outside and work your way in. I start from the outside. I start so far from the outside, I inadvertently take the spoon of the woman sitting next to me. Eventually we sort it out, and start to eat.

'My soup is cold. I mean, stone cold. I look up. Everyone else's appears to be fine. Here's my chance to make a mark. I call over the steward and very discreetly tell him my soup is cold. He looks at me like I'm something he's just scraped off his shoe. He takes the soup away and brings it back hot. Everyone starts laughing. I start laughing too. And the more I laugh, the more they laugh.'

He stopped, and turned his closed eyes to the ceiling. He smiled through clenched teeth and then, as if every word were punctuated by the pulling of a dagger from his heart, inch by agonizing inch, he said:

'I . . . didn't . . . know . . . gazpacho . . . soup . . . was . . . meant . . . to . . . be . . . served . . . cold.'

His head slumped forward again, and he carried on.

'And by now they're hysterical, uncontrollable. I still think they're laughing at the steward, when all the time they're laughing at me as I eat my piping-hot gazpacho soup.' The memory washed over him like a wave in an acid sea. He bathed in its flesh-stripping agony. He cleared his throat. 'That was the last time I ate at the Captain's table.' Rimmer opened his eyes. They'd been closed throughout the entire story. 'That evening was pretty much the end of my career.'

There was a silence.

'Is that it?' Lister said eventually. 'Is that what you've been torturing yourself with for the last seven years? One dumb mistake that anybody could have made?'

'If only they'd mentioned it in basic training. Instead of climbing up ropes and crawling through tunnels on your elbows. If just once they'd said "Gazpacho soup is served cold", I could have been an admiral by now. I could. I really could.'

'Come on – everybody has memories that make them wince. And ninety-nine per cent of the time the only person who remembers the incident is you.'

'Oh, what does it matter *now*? Come on. Let's get it over with. Erase me.'

'And those things nearly always happen with people you don't know very well, and don't see very often, so who gives a smeg anyway?'

'Just turn me off. Get on with it.'

Lister swigged at his now cold coffee. 'I've already done it. I wiped the other one.'

Emotions wrestled for space on Rimmer's brow. 'You wiped . . . the duplicate? When?'

'Before you walked in.'

'And you let me stand here . . . and . . . spill my guts?'

'Yeah.' A big, broad grin.

'Why?'

'I wanted to find out about gazpacho soup, and I knew you'd never tell me.'

'Of course I wouldn't tell you — because you'd make my life hell with gazpacho soup jokes for the rest of eternity.'

'Rimmer — I swear I will never mention this conversation again.'

Rimmer regarded him dubiously.

'I don't break my word. I'm a lot of things, but I'm not a liar.'

Rimmer looked at him through one eye. 'All right, then. I believe you. You're a disgusting rancid slob, but you keep your word.'

'Thank you.'

Rimmer got up from the chair. 'So I'm going back to Earth, then?'

Lister nodded. 'We're all going back to Earth, then.'

Rimmer motioned drunkenly towards the hatchway. 'Come on. Let's go down the Copacabana, have a real drink.'

Lister got up to follow him.

'Souper,' he said.

THIRTY-FOUR

Strange, but years later, whenever Lister remembered it, he always remembered it in black and white. And something else; the memories came in a rush: there were no insignificant details, only significant ones. He remembered his scalp tingling as the cargo bay doors boomed open.

He remembered his giddiness as *Nova 5* taxied across the cargo deck and blasted into the blackness of space.

He remembered the silvery light that preceded each jump, and the incomparable feeling of existing simultaneously at two points in the universe – and then the jolt as all his cells 'decided' to be in the new position.

Perhaps a thousand jolts.

And there it was – on the navicomp screen.

The planet Earth.

They were home.

Part Three

Earth

ONE

The big clock on the wall tocked round to five o'clock, and Lister lifted up the flap on the counter and turned the sign on the door to 'Closed'. Bailey's Perfect Shami Kebab Emporium was shutting for the day. Lister rang up 'no sale' on the old-fashioned wrought-iron till, and counted the week's takings. Fourteen dollars and twenty-five cents. Another great week.

He dipped his hand into the penny candy jar, picked out a liquorice shoelace, then grabbed his overcoat and scarf, pulled on his fur-lined deerstalker and mittens, and walked out into the crisp white snow. The bell on the door jangled behind him; there was never any need to lock the shop, not here in Bedford Falls. There was only one cop for the entire population of three thousand, and he spent most of his day asleep in his patrol car.

Lister crunched across the eiderdown street, chewing happily on his liquorice, and headed for the bank. A group of carol singers were standing round the war memorial, belting out *God Rest Ye Merry, Gentlemen*, accompanied by a four-piece brass band. They all waved a cheery greeting, and Lister stood with them and helped them finish his favourite carol.

'Merry Christmas,' he said, and dropped two dollars into their can as Ernie, the cab driver, produced a hip flask from the bell of his tuba and gave Lister a nip of brandy.

It being after five o'clock, and Christmas Eve, the bank was closed, of course. Lister tried the door. It jangled open.

'Hello? Anybody home?'

Money was stacked in neat piles on the wooden counter – obviously Horace hadn't got round to putting it in the safe yet.

'Horace? Are you there?'

Horace stepped through the back door, holding a sheet of wrapping paper and some string.

'Sorry, Mr Bailey, I was just wrapping presents for the kids up at the orphan home. You ever tried to wrap a Hula-Hoop? I'll be a monkey's uncle if I can figure it.'

Lister handed over ten dollars and asked Horace to put it in his account.

'Ten dollars! Business is *good*, Mr Bailey.'

Lister smiled, and pulled out a handful of candy walking sticks from his huge overcoat pocket. 'I didn't have time to wrap them. Hope the orphanage doesn't mind.'

'They won't mind, George. Merry Christmas.'

'Merry Christmas, Horace,' said Lister, and turned to go. 'You know – you should get a lock for this bank door or something.'

'That's what everybody says, but I figure what the heck – I'd only lose the key.'

Lister laughed, and walked back out into the street.

Last minute shoppers exchanged Merry Christmasses with him as he crossed back to the Emporium, where his rickety old model 'A' Ford was covered in snow. He took the hand crank from the bench seat and jerked the engine into spluttering life. As he turned left at Martini's Bar his arms started to hurt again, so he pulled over outside Old Man Gower's drugstore.

His arms had been giving him problems for a few weeks now. It was like a burning sensation down both his forearms – excruciatingly painful at times, but Doc MacKenzie couldn't find anything wrong with them. There were no marks, nothing showed up on the X-ray: it was a complete mystery.

He grabbed a tub of cooling ointment from Old Man Gower's shelves and dropped twenty-five cents into the open till, then hopped back in his old Ford and headed for home: 220 Sycamore.

A couple of birds — robins, Lister guessed — were singing in the snow-laden lilac trees that lined the avenue. Life was good. Everything seemed . . . well, perfect. But, God, did his arms hurt.

It had been two years since they returned to Earth. Two years since *Nova 5* had completed the duality jumps which brought them back to their own solar system. Two years since they'd skidded to a landing in the middle of the Sahara desert. As they'd opened the airlock and stepped out into the baking heat, there, like a mirage over the brow of a vast dune, an army of jeeps and helicopters had descended on them.

The world's press went crazy! The three-million-year-old men! Space adventurers!

Things hadn't changed that much. The human race were still there, a foot or so taller, but still there. And so was everything that went with the human race: advertising, commercialism, marketing, huge dirty cities and people on the make. And it had turned into a freak show: interviews, book offers, chat shows, endorsements, sponsorship deals . . . Lister had hated it. He was a piece of meat that people wanted to package and sell.

'*I'm three million years old — what's my secret? I eat Breadman's Fish Fingers.*'

'*I've been all around the universe, and I've never come across anything quite as good as Luton's Carpet Shampoo.*'

Rimmer lapped it up, the Cat adored it, but Lister just wanted to get away. He'd turned down all the offers, changed his name and opted for the peaceful anonymity of this backwater town in the American mid-west. He couldn't believe it when he'd discovered there actually *was* a town called Bedford Falls. He'd gone there on a whim, to take a look, and was stunned how similar the place was to the Bedford Falls in *It's a Wonderful Life*. It seemed like fans of the film had all collected there to live out their lives in a self-created 1940s American Shangri-la.

Of course he couldn't keep his secret from the townfolk for long; his face had been plastered all over magazine covers and newspapers for six months, so he guessed more or less everyone knew who he was and where he'd come from. But they pretended they didn't. They all called him 'Mr Bailey', or 'George', which was the pseudonym he'd chosen. They respected his privacy, and guarded his secret, and he was left in peace to live out the rest of his life in this quiet idyll.

But something was wrong with his arms, and it was beginning to worry him.

He turned the Ford into the tree-lined drive of his old house and honked his horn three times. The snow lay thick and deep on the lawn, and a huge, eight-foot snowman was grinning a welcome in coal. Lister grabbed the Christmas presents off the back seat and staggered under their weight up the drive to the porch. As he pushed open the door with his back, he could hear a carol being mutilated on a clapped-out old piano. He loved that sound. To Lister it was better than the London Phil.

He walked into the parlour. A log fire was burning merrily in the grate. Jim and Bexley were smashing *Silent Night* out of the complaining piano, while Krissie was standing on a stepladder, putting tinsel on the Christmas tree. She turned and smiled, and blew him a kiss.

When the kids were in bed they sat snoozily in the big leather armchair with the springs poking through the back, watching the fire splutter and splurt, and listening to Hoagy Carmichael on the wind-up phonograph. After Krissie climbed the stairs to their draughty bedroom with the leaky roof, he took out the ointment – he didn't want her to know about his arms – and began to apply it to the sore areas.

It came as something of a shock that, when he'd put the cream specifically on the areas that throbbed and hurt, it spelt out a word. A word written in pain down his forearm.

The word was 'DYING'.

TWO

The black stretch Mercedes with the tinted, bullet-proof glass glided along the Champs Elysées, and pulled up outside the canopy of the hundred-and-forty-floor skyscraper. Rimmer finished his phone call to his publicist, then stepped out of the limo. A string of bodyguards kept at bay the group of teenage girls who'd camped out on the steps overnight, in the hope of catching a glimpse of A.J.R. He allowed them a thin smile as he walked under the canopy and up the marble steps into the Rimmer Building (Paris). The Rimmer Building (Paris) was an identical copy of the Rimmer Building (London) and the Rimmer Building (New York). He was happy with the towering glass and steel architecture, so he saw no need to vary the design. The electric doors purred open and he strode across the thick white mink carpet, trailed by the gaggle of accountants and financial advisers who seemed to follow him everywhere.

As he walked across the massive lobby, he dismissed his financial advisers for the evening, and nodded almost imperceptibly at Pierre, the Sorbonne graduate he'd hired exclusively to press the button that summoned the lift. While he waited, he swung round to look at the colossal white marble statue of himself, captured in the middle of a Full Double-Rimmer, which the Space Corps had long accepted as its standard official salute. The lift took a full ninety seconds to arrive, so he fired Pierre and pressed the button himself for floor 140 – his luxury penthouse suite. The fact that he could actually press the button at all was, in a way, the key to the immense fortune he'd amassed since his return to Earth two years previously.

After the hero's welcome, his cunning business brain had taken full advantage of the offers which flooded in daily. With the money he culled from advertising and the publication of his memoirs, he'd set up various multi-national corporations which had sponsored the Rimmer Research Centres, which had finally invented the Solidgram – a solid body that housed his personality and intellect. He was now exactly like any normal living person, with the added bonus that he was more or less immortal. The Solidgram had sold in such quantities, his income from that alone allowed him to buy the Bahamas for 'somewhere to go at the weekends'.

It amused him no end that he was now one of the three or four richest men in the world, while Lister was stuck in a dead-end burger bar in a dead-end town somewhere in the middle of nowhere.

He'd hired a private investigator who had taken fourteen months to track him down. Rimmer was now well into the complicated negotiations to buy up the entire town, which he intended to turn into a huge maggot farm. Just for the hell of it.

He got out of the lift and walked past the salute-shaped pool on the roof garden. Hugo, one of the gardening staff, was aquavac-ing cherry blossoms from the surface of the water.

'Monsieur Rimmer!' he called, 'Madame Juanita – she is unwell again.'

Rimmer sighed. 'Unwell' was the code for throwing a major Brazilian wobbly. His wife was having one of her regular tantrums. Juanita Chicata was unquestionably the most beautiful woman in the world. Everything about her was classic, from the tip of her perfect nose to the toes of her beautiful feet. Eyes the colour of fire, panther-black hair, dangerous lips. Dangerous woman. She'd made two fortunes, the first as the world's number one model, the second as the world's number one actress. And she was a great actress – she wasn't a model who got by on her looks, she really was the finest actress in the world. And she was nineteen years old. She had beauty, brains, talent, everything. God had finally got it right.

Every man, *every* man desired her.

And she'd married Rimmer two summers earlier. This was another source of amusement for Rimmer. While Lister had ended up with a very ordinary girl-next-door type, he'd acquired the 'Brazilian Bombshell'.

Right now the Brazilian Bombshell was exploding in the master bedroom of their penthouse apartment. Rimmer wandered through the exotic Chinese roof garden, while four hundred catering staff prepared for the customary Saturday night party. The marquee had been erected over-looking the glistening Seine, the forty thousand fireworks were all in place and primed, the three-hundred-yard-long buffet table was crammed to overflowing with food which had been flown in from around the world earlier that day, the centrepiece of which was a replica of Juanita's naked body in caviar. He paused to admire it. Even like this, even sculpted from little black fish eggs, it was a body that drove him crazy. He couldn't help himself – he leaned over and nibbled at the splendid right breast – the real ones were insured for ten million each, and she hadn't let him near them for over a year and a half. Which was why right now Rimmer had his face buried deep in the ice-cold caviar.

Suddenly, from above, there was a shattering of glass as a Louis XIV grand piano crashed out of the french windows of their master bedroom and landed on the roof garden, crushing one of the catering staff.

It had amused Rimmer when the private detective reported

that Lister had a piano — a clapped-out tuneless wreck with dry rot which Lister had bought at a second-hand shop in Bedford Falls for four dollars and thirty cents. Rimmer's piano, which now lay in pieces on top of a screaming servant, had cost him a million. It was a lot to pay for a piano that nobody played, but his wife thought it would look 'kinda neat' in the bedroom, so he'd got it. Now, of course, it wasn't worth the price of a cup of tea, because she'd hurled it out of the window because she was . . . 'unwell'.

Juanita was regularly 'unwell' — perhaps two or three times a week — and on each occasion it cost Rimmer upwards of three hundred thousand. Still, he could afford it. And she *was* the most beautiful woman alive. And she was married to him.

As he walked into the master bedroom he found Juanita hurling dollops of cold cream at an original Picasso, while two maids swept up the remains of the fifth-century Ming vase that she'd used to smash the nose of the Michelangelo statue he'd bought her as a kiss-and-make-up gift.

Rimmer sighed and shook his head. Why had she gone crazy this time? What was the reason for today's little sulk? Was it because for the second month in a row she wasn't on the cover of *Vogue*? Was it because she *was* on the cover of *Vogue*, and she didn't like the photograph? Was it because she'd put on a pound in weight? Or had she *lost* a pound in weight? Both, of course, were disastrous. Had the maid accidently brought up Lapsang tea instead of Keema? Last time she did that it had cost Rimmer three Matisses and his entire collection of Iranian pottery. Was the telephone dirty again? Was there nothing on TV she wanted to watch?

Whatever it was she was obviously upset, because now she had taken down Rimmer's twelfth-century samurai sword and was hacking away at the water bed. The liquid gurgled happily over the irreplaceable Persian rug.

'Nita, Nita,' he cooed soothingly as he sploshed over

towards her, 'what is it? What has disturbed my little turtle dove?'

She turned to face him, ferocious, the samurai sword clasped above her head. 'I can't tell you. You wouldn't understand eet!' She skewered a Cézanne hanging above the bed, and sliced it into thin shreds.

'You can tell me anything,' Rimmer said softly.

'Not thees! I can't tell you thees!'

'Please. Tell me what's made you so angry.'

'Hugo!' she screeched and, at the mention of his name, she hurled the Koh-i-Nor out of the window and down onto the Champs Elysées below.

'What about Hugo?' said Rimmer, picking up the phone to make arrangements for the pool man's dismissal.

'He won't make love to me any more,' she bawled. Then she collapsed into a sobbing heap in the soggy mess of the demolished water bed. 'Not ever. He's afraid you'll find out and sack heem.'

'Well, he's got a point,' Rimmer found himself saying.

Then it hit him.

What she'd said. He was stunned. He felt sick.

He was nauseated. His wife unfaithful! Juanita and Hugo! His hairy-shouldered pool attendant had caressed that fabulous bosom! What would the insurance company say?

His wife had slept with his pool attendant. No wonder the water was never at the right temperature!

Rimmer felt . . . numb.

THREE

Lister sat in the red glow of the firelight, looking down at his arms and the messages in ointment on each of them. How was it possible for pain to 'spell out' words? What was it? Was it something inside him? The message on his left arm: 'DYING'. What did that mean? *He* was dying? The something *inside* him was dying?

He looked across at his right arm: four letters and a symbol, but he didn't know what they meant. Could it be that it was just a coincidence that the pain happened to spell out two messages that happened to be in English on his forearms? Unlikely, but not impossible. After all, some fairly bizarre things had happened since he returned to Earth. Finding Bedford Falls the way he'd always imagined it. Finding someone who was the exact duplicate of Kristine Kochanski. Exact. Down to the pinball smile. Down to the laugh. Down to the tiny mole on her bottom. Who just happened to be a direct descendant of the Third Console Officer he'd had an affair with aboard *Red Dwarf* three million years ago. Who just happened to fall in love with him almost instantly, and give him twin sons.

And the boys. Both beautiful, both perfectly-formed, never any trouble. They never cried, they never whined; they even changed one another's nappies.

Wasn't that a bit odd? Self-nappy-changing babies? Lister didn't know much about babies, but Krissie had always accepted it as normal behaviour, so he had too. Also, he didn't know exactly when babies started to walk and talk, but Jim and Bexley were only fifteen months old yet they could play the piano, converse like adults, and even toss a Zero–Gee ball about with him in the back garden.

Previously, he'd never given these things much thought. His life was pretty much perfect. He had everything he wanted, and what was the use in worrying about how lucky he'd been?

The Emporium – that was another peculiar thing. Now he came to think of it, every week he always took fourteen dollars and twenty-five cents. Which, as it happened, was the exact amount he needed to pay for his mortgage, three dollars; food, two dollars; petrol, twenty-five cents; the rent on the shop, a dollar fifty; savings, five dollars; leaving three dollars fifty, which he could give to people in trouble.

He got up and started pacing the threadbare carpet. He didn't like where his thoughts were leading him. How many times had it been Christmas Eve since he arrived at Bedford Falls? Five, six hundred? In fact, wasn't it *always* Christmas Eve? How was *that* possible?

Bexley padded down the stairs in his Donald Duck sleepsuit and Goofy slippers.

'Hi, Dad. Jim wants a drink of milk. We've run out – is it OK if I get some?'

Lister looked at his fifteen-month-old son as he struggled into his quilted jump suit. He was big for his age, there was no question. Fifteen months, he could talk and dress himself. He was precocious.

'I'm just going to pop down to Old Man Gower's,' he said, tugging on his wellingtons. 'D'you want anything?'

Lister shook his head. Bexley stood on tiptoe and opened the front door.

Lister heard the model 'A' Ford start up and Bexley roared off into town. Everyone thought it was funny that Bexley could drive Lister's car. Obviously it was illegal, but Bert, the cop, thought it was funny too. 'He's a better driver than I am,' he used to say; 'why should I stop him?'

Now that *was* weird. A fifteen-month-old baby driving into town to get some milk for his brother. It was barely believable. Well, it *wasn't* believable. It was impossible.

Lister looked down at the message on his right arm. Four letters, one symbol. A chill passed through him. He knew what it meant. 'U = B T L'.

He knew what it meant.

FOUR

It was a gloriously warm summer's evening with just enough breeze to make it perfect. The Rimmers were having a party. Arnie and Juanita were entertaining. And anybody who was anybody, and anybody who was one day going to *be* anybody, was there.

The four-hundred piece New York Philharmonic Orchestra, flown in specially for the evening, were playing a tribute to James Last. The prima ballerinas from all the European Ballets were arranged around the roof garden in gilded cages, spinning and pirouetting to entertain the guests.

Five thousand guests in all.

The men in black DJs, and the women in fabulously outrageous ball gowns, mingled among the flocks of pink flamingos Rimmer had hired for the evening.

Rimmer sat in his white dinner suit under the shade of a giant parasol, sipping a glass of 1799 Château d'Yquem, holding court to only the most famous and influential. A waiter was serving soup from a giant golden tureen. One of the guests, a member of the British Royal family, was complaining that the soup was cold. Rimmer leaned over and whispered discreetly in his ear that it was gazpacho soup, and gazpacho soup was always served cold – it was Spanish.

'Well, I didn't know that,' said the Prince of Wales. Rimmer waved his hand in a desultory fashion to dismiss the poor man's embarrassment.

'Not many people do.'

Rimmer caught sight of the swimming pool, and it plunged him back into his depression. A fluttering started in his stomach. He loved his salute-shaped pool, but he'd never be able to look at it again without thinking of Hugo, the pool attendant. Hugo, the caresser of twenty-million-dollar bosoms. He'd dismissed him, of course, then made a few phone calls. Never again would Hugo be able to use a credit card. Never again would he shop at any Marks & Spencer's branch in the entire solar system. And buying shoes from any of the companies in the Burton group he would find strangely impossible. Getting his haircut anywhere in France would be out of the question. And a certain canned food company beginning with 'H' had guaranteed that a certain individual, also beginning with 'H', would never be sold any of their products in the future. Never again would the wretched man ever enjoy beans on toast. At least, not really good beans on toast. Only inferior supermarket brands. Not in itself punishment to rival the *auto de fes*, but Rimmer had barely begun pulling the strings and calling in the favours which would ensure Hugo's life became unbearable.

Rimmer heard Juanita's tinkling laugh and, as he peered through the milling party guests, he caught a tantalizing glimpse as she stood on the Chinese bridge over the pool, dazzling some producer with her wit and beauty. He froze.

She was wearing *that* outfit! The one he'd expressly forbidden her to wear. The glass brassiere with the live goldfish swimming inside, the thin red belt, and *nothing else*! Just the diamond high heels and the gold anklet.

A red belt! That's all she was wearing. He shook with rage. She was uncontrollable. Everything was on display! Everything! For all the guests to see.

'But it's so chic!' she'd argued. 'Adrienne created eet especially for me. You're such a prude.'

The more he'd screamed at her to put some clothes on, the more determined she'd been to wear it. To wear it and humiliate him. Her only gestures to modesty were the two goldfish – one in each bra cup – and they could hardly be relied on to stay in a nipple-covering position all the time. He hated her. But he loved her.

The Brazilian Bombshell.

What could he do? She drove him crazy. But he was stuck with it. The third richest man in the whole of the world had a wife who wore a couple of goldfish at dinner parties.

He tried to rip his eyes away from her and back to the game of RISK he was playing with his three favourite dinner guests. It was Julius's go. With his yellow counters he'd established a foothold in Africa and was poised to throw the dice and attack Southern Europe, where Rimmer's blue counters had their second front. The third player, the Frenchman with the kiss curl, looked on earnestly. If the yellow assault should succeed, he could break out of South America with his red counters and swamp George's green counters, which were massed in the USA.

Julius shook the dice and rolled three threes. Rimmer rolled two fours. Julius attacked and Rimmer defended, until the yellow hordes had been reduced to only two counters. The Italian rolled his eyes skywards. He was finished, and he knew it.

'Well, Julius, me old fruit,' Rimmer grinned, 'looks like you're a gonner.'

Caesar took off his laurel wreath and scratched his balding head. 'I'm going to get a drink!' he stormed, and stalked off to the poolside bar.

'So –' Rimmer turned to his two remaining adversaries – 'just Messrs Patton and Bonaparte left in.'

'God damn you, you dirty son of a bitch!' General Patton threw his huge cigar into the pool. 'Throw the dice and get it over with.'

One of the waiters – Rimmer couldn't remember his name – leaned over and whispered discreetly.

'There's a gentleman in the main reception who insists on seeing you, sir.'

'Send him away.'

'He *insists*, sir.'

'Send him away. I'm busy.'

'He says his name is "Lister", sir. Claims he was your cohort on *Red Dwarf*.'

Lister stood in the mahogany-panelled library, where the man in the penguin suit had finally ushered him. He helped himself to a foot-long Havana cigar, and sat in the huge leather reading chair, his legs crossed on the polished walnut table. The twelve feet high double doors swung open and Rimmer strode in, grinning.

'Listy! Long time no see. I was going to invite you, but . . . I didn't really think it was your scene.'

'You've done pretty well for yourself. What are you now, the second richest man in the world?'

'Third,' said Rimmer, modestly. 'Long way to go before I'm second.'

'And married to Juanita Chicata.'

'I'm getting by,' Rimmer nodded. He reached into the drawer behind his desk. 'So, two years. Has it really been two years?'

'Yup.'

'I've missed you. First six months of my marriage I couldn't get to sleep because, for some unfathomable reason, Juanita doesn't snore like an adenoidal pig.'

Lister lassoed Rimmer with a huge grey smoke ring, and grinned back.

'So,' said Rimmer, taking out a cheque book a yard long, with more pages than a James Clavell novel, 'you finally came to see me. How much do you want? One, two, three, four pounds?' Rimmer threw back his head and brayed loudly.

'You're a smeg head, Rimmer, you really are a smeg head.'

'But a rich smeg head, eh?' Rimmer brayed again. 'Seriously, what do you want?' he poised his pen over the cheque, 'a couple of mill? What do you want?'

'I want,' Lister said, leaning forward, 'to go back to Earth.'

'Come again?'

'This isn't Earth.'

Rimmer smiled uncomprehendingly.

'I'm afraid, Arn,' Lister continued, 'we've taken a wrong turning. We are in another plane of reality. Somehow we've wound up playing Better Than Life. We're just a couple of Game heads.'

FIVE

It couldn't be. It was ... well, it just couldn't be. Rimmer followed Lister down the narrow white stone steps to the roof garden, where the party was still in full swing. Lister was jealous, plain and simple. Rimmer didn't like to say it to his face because it would be like rubbing it in. But it was only natural he should feel jealous. Rimmer had everything. He'd amassed a fifty billion dollarpound fortune, whereas Lister had amassed a leaky house, a silly car, and a wife and two kids. The poor boy had flipped! He couldn't accept he was a failure and Rimmer was a hit, so he was trying to persuade everybody they were in the wrong dimension of reality. Totally fliparoonied.

'Heard from the Cat?' Lister was asking.

'No. He's on some island off Denmark. Haven't heard from him since we got back to Earth. You?'

Lister shook his head, grabbed a bottle of Dom Perignon from a passing ice bucket, and they sat down. He rolled back his sleeves. 'Let me show you my arms.'

'Your arms?'

'Both my arms look perfectly normal, don't they?'

Rimmer looked at his perfectly normal arms and nodded. He started looking round for his bodyguards.

'But they hurt like hell. And when I put ointment over the spots that hurt, it spells out a message.'

Rimmer shook his head, smiling. 'Amazing.'

'Watch.' Lister took a jar of cold cream out of his jacket

277

pocket and daubed 'DYING' on his left arm and 'U = BTL' on his right.

'Now, I don't want to sound like I'm a sceptic,' Rimmer rubbed the flat of his hand against his face, 'but you have to concede that the effect I've just witnessed could just as easily be produced by an insane person with two arms and a pot of cold cream.'

'Yes, but I'm just covering the areas of pain! It's the pain that spells out the message.'

'The pain?'

'In my arms. Someone's trying to get a message to us.'

'On your arms, through the cold cream.'

'Look, if we *are* in the Game, we won't *know* we're in the Game. It protects itself – it won't let you remember that you've started to play it.'

'But we *didn't* start to play it.'

'No, we don't remember starting to play it. That's different.'

Rimmer flopped back in his seat and looked round the roof garden. He looked at the two thousand people dancing a conga round the pool. He looked at the phalanx of waiters holding the silver platters above their heads as they glided about, serving the second course of the banquet. He looked across at the sous-chef, atop a ladder, carving generous portions of meat from the barbequed giraffe which slowly rotated on the forty-foot spit. Could this really not be real?

'If we're in the Game,' Lister continued, 'we're wandering around somewhere with electrodes in our brains, totally oblivious to the real world. Someone in that real world is trying to tell us where we are by burning or cutting or scratching a message into my arms: "U = BTL": "You are in Better Than Life", and "DYING": in reality, I'm dying! I'm a Game head.'

'But it doesn't make sense! I thought when you're in the Game all your fantasies were supposed to come true. But look at you – stuck in some hick town in the back end of nowhere with a wife and two kids, and no money.'

'Money isn't important to me.'

Rimmer snorted.

'Bedford Falls and everything else,' Lister shook his head wistfully, 'that was everything I always wanted.'

There was a series of explosions and forty thousand fireworks burst in the night sky, forming a portrait of Rimmer and Juanita in a pink Valentine's heart. While the awe-struck guests gazed in open-mouthed wonder, the fireworks portrait animated: Rimmer's face winked down at them, then turned and kissed Juanita's image. Then two huge bangs – and the two faces transformed into the Rimmer Corporation company logo.

The standing ovation lasted for ten minutes.

'Come on, Rimmer – face facts. Look at this place. The Rimmer Building? Overlooking the Champs Elysées? Your company inventing the Solidgram? You're married to the most famous actress in the world? Is *any* of it even *remotely* credible?'

Lister stood up and pointed across the pool, his voice raised an octave in incredulity. 'Who the hell are they?'

Rimmer looked round.

Lister was waving his arms excitedly. 'The guys under the parasol, applauding?'

'Napoleon Bonaparte, Julius Caesar and General Patton.'

'And what are they doing here?'

'Oh, that. There's a perfectly rational explanation for that,' Rimmer nodded vigorously.

Lister grabbed another bottle of champagne. 'Which is?'

'It's a bit hush-hush at the moment. I'm not really at liberty to say.'

'Un-hush-hush it.'

Rimmer mulled it over. Well, it would be public knowledge in a week or so. Couldn't do any harm. He leaned over conspiratorially. 'Rimmer Corporation Worldwide plc have developed a Time Machine. I've been playing around with it for a few months, inviting famous people from different eras in Time to pep up a few dinner parties.'

Lister was looking at him in a strange way.

'What's wrong with that?' Rimmer protested. 'You don't think that's believable?'

'No, I don't. I think you just wanted to meet these people, so your imagination had to cook up a nearly credible explanation to bring them here.'

'Nonsense!' said Rimmer, but without conviction. Could it be true? Could he have fantasized the invention of a Time Machine just so he could bring back Caesar, Bonaparte and Patton – the three greatest generals in history – simply in order to beat them at 'RISK', the strategic war game for ages fifteen and over? Could he really be that small-minded?

'Come on –' Lister stood up and drained the bottle – 'we've got to find the Cat.'

Rimmer picked up a phone and punched in three numbers. 'Harry? Put the Lear Jet on stand-by. Mr Rimmer and guest will be going to Denmark this evening.' He put the phone down and turned to Lister. 'Wait in the car – I'd better say goodbye to, uh . . .' And he wandered off.

'Een the middle of our party, you are going off weeth your stupid friend to Denmark?!'

Juanita, still naked from the waist down apart from the diamond stilettoes, stormed up and down the parquet floor of the roof garden's white balustraded gazebo. Rimmer thrust his hands deep in his pockets and squirmed.

'Darling, I know it's awful, but the thing is: there's an outside chance . . .' Rimmer didn't know quite how to put this '. . . there's a tiny little possibility that you don't exist.'

'I don't what?'

'It's only a slight chance, and there's probably nothing to

worry about. But if Lister's right, you're just a figment of my imagination.'

'And for this reason you are leaving my party and flying to Denmark?'

'Yes,' said Rimmer, 'it's a sort of metaphysical emergency.'

'Thees man comes here thees evening, with his stupeed furry hat, and tells you your wife doesn't exist, and you go waltzing off weeth heem to Scandinavia?'

'You're right, I won't go. I won't go. Of course you exist. I'll go down to the car and explain that we've talked it through, and we've come to the conclusion that we all *do* exist, and we don't want anything more to do with him.'

'You're crazee! My mother was right. She always warned me against marrying a dead man!'

Rimmer watched her naked, tanned bottom as she clomped down the summerhouse steps and wandered over to a group of people eating their barbequed giraffe steaks. He scanned the group. Lenin, Einstein, Archimedes, God and Norman Wisdom. Wisdom was staggering around, laughing hysterically, with his jacket half off his shoulders. Suddenly, without warning, he threw himself up into the air and landed on the floor. Lenin, Einstein and Archimedes looked down rather disdainfully. God splurted out his mouthful of Cinzano Bianco and bellowed uncontrollably, tears streaming down his face.

'That's comedy!' God was saying. 'That is comedy!'

Let's face it, Rimmer thought, there was at least a marginal possibility that Lister was right.

SIX

The black stretch Mercedes with the tinted, bullet-proof glass purred onto the shiny black tarmacadamed runway of Rimmer International Airport (AJR), and drew up along-side the black Lear Jet, Rimmer One.

The twenty-minute journey had been conducted mainly in silence. Lister had been watching MTV on one of the car's TV sets, where a poll had proclaimed Rimmer the Sexiest Man Of All Time. Second was Clark Gable, and third was Hugo Lovepole. Rimmer had smiled wanly. It was turning into a nightmare. If this was indeed his fantasy – and he was still clinging onto a faint hope that Lister was wrong – if it *was* his fantasy, it was suddenly hideously embarrassing. His psyche lain bare for all to see.

The chauffeur clicked round the car and opened one of the eight passenger doors, and they got out. Lister looked at the chauffeur and almost said 'hello', because at first he thought he knew him. Then he realized he didn't, but he'd seen his face somewhere.

'Who's the driver?' he whispered to Rimmer as they walked across to the Lear Jet's steps.

'It's a lovely evening, isn't it?'

'Is he somebody famous?' Lister persisted.

'Who?'

'The driver.'

'No.'

'Who is he, then?'

Rimmer started to climb the steps. 'He's my dad,' he said quietly. 'I brought him back in the Time Machine.'

'To be your chauffeur?!' Lister wrinkled his cheeks in disbelief.

'Yes!' Rimmer hissed.

'I'm very proud of you, Son,' his father called. 'I'm so proud I'm fit to burst.'

'Shut up,' said Rimmer.

As they got to the top of the Lear Jet's steps, the screaming started. Rimmer had been dreading it. He'd hoped they might be able to slip aboard unnoticed. But even this small mercy was denied him. As Lister turned, hanging over the observation balcony of the airport terminal building, twenty thousand teenage girls caught in the helpless throes of Rimmermania waved intimate garments and banners, screamed and chanted uncontrollably.

'Arnold! We love you!'

'Arnieeeeeeeeeeeeeeeeeeeeeeeeeeeeeeeeeeee!'

Rimmer shook his head in humiliation, his cheeks glowing baboon-bottom red.

They screeeeeeeeeeamed as he half-nodded at them. Lister squinted, trying to read the banners. 'Arnie is brave' he could make out. 'Arnie has had lots of girlfriends'. 'Arnie is FAB'. He turned to Rimmer.

'Basically,' he grinned, 'you just want to be adored, don't you?'

'Thank you, Sigmund,' said Rimmer without parting his teeth.

'It's really quite cute.'

'Look – we're still not a hundred per cent sure that this *is* a fantasy. And if it turns out it's not, you're going to feel plenty silly as you drive your clapped-out old banger back to Nowhere City.' Rimmer ducked his head and disappeared into the body of the plane.

*

Rimmer wasn't really watching the in-flight movie, but he was wearing the headset as a kind of sanctuary to avoid Lister's accusing grin. The film was *Darkness At Noon*, which had culled Juanita her first Oscar. How well Rimmer remembered that evening – the twenty-five minute thank you speech she'd made, saying it was all down to him. He watched her play the scene in the apartment – the famous 'olives on the cocktail stick' scene. Could he really have fantasized this woman? It was absurd! Why would he fantasize a woman, no matter how beautiful, who was Trouble with a capital 'T' the size of the G P O tower?

Because he wanted the most exciting woman in the world. The most desired, the most beautiful, the most . . . dangerous. But, having got her, why would he then fantasize she was unfaithful? With Hugo the hairy-shouldered pool attendant! What the hell did that say about the state of his mind? Mentally unwell, that's what it said. And why had he fantasized his wife's refusal to make love with him for the past eighteen months? Why on Earth did he want *that* to happen?

Was it that even in his fantasies Rimmer couldn't bring himself to believe anyone could truly love him? That inevitably she would reject him, giving him those pathetic excuses that the insurance company wouldn't allow him to touch her bosom? And inevitably she would take a lover – a lover who was more masculine than he? More manly? Oh, my god.

My god, my god, my god.

He moaned softly. The innards of his psyche were there for all to see: putrid and rotten and rancid. His neuroses parading like grinning contestants in the Mr Universe contest!

He glanced over at Lister, who had taken out a well-worn leather wallet and was looking sadly at some dog-eared photographs of his family back in Bedford Falls.

Hadn't Lister's fantasy been even more ridiculous? A leaky house? A clapped-out car? A little shop? It was so . . . corny. A girl-next-door type wife, two kids. If they were playing Better Than Life, he could have had anything he wanted.

Absolutely anything he wanted. And this was his choice? Something so ordinary, so small, so . . . normal?

Oh my god, my god, my god.

That was the truth, wasn't it? Lister's fantasy was so much more mature than his. Lister didn't need mega-wealth to make him happy. He needed fourteen dollars and twenty-five cents. He didn't need a stunning-looking actress desired by all. He just wanted someone who cared for him. Even the car. Rimmer had a twenty-five-foot black penis extension. Lister had a clapped-out old banger. What did that mean, then? That Lister had a limousine inside his Y-fronts, while Rimmer had a 1940s Ford that needed hand-cranking?

Lister's was the fantasy of a man at peace with himself. A man who felt he had nothing to prove. Rimmer's was twenty-five foot cars, hundred and forty storey buildings, airports, Lear Jets, a twenty million dollar bosom, a forty billion dollar fortune, his father as his own chauffeur . . . It *couldn't* be a fantasy. No one could be *that* screwed-up!

Lister sat there looking at the black-and-white dog-eared snaps which Mr Calhoon, the photographer, had taken last Christmas Eve with his old box Brownie on its tripod, with the magnesium flare. There was one in particular of him and Kochanski with big cheesy grins.

So you don't exist, he thought. I just made you exist and fall in love with me.

He was still hung up on Kristine Kochanski. A girl he dated for five weeks and two days, three million years ago. In a way he was kind of jealous of Rimmer. If he'd have known it was a fantasy, he'd have become Jim Bexley Speed and dated Ida Lupino. He'd have played with the Beatles: the Fab Five – John, Paul, George, Ringo and Dave. But he hadn't. He'd settled down in Bedford Falls and married Kristine Kochanski. He wanted to live his life in a movie. What a jerk! What an even bigger jerk for falling in love with someone who, if she'd been alive and real and with him now, probably would give him a sweet little smile and sit down at the back of the plane with one of her wacky mates.

Sure, they'd had a great two years; but it hadn't been real – none of it. Counterfeit delights. A pathetic hankering on account of a crazy obsession. Unreal. Impossible. Ridiculous.

The air hostess leaned over him.

'Can I get you anything?' she smiled. It was Ida Lupino. Ida Lupino was standing in the aisle, dressed as an air hostess. 'Anything at all?' she twinkled.

Lister shook his head. 'I'm married. I'm married to someone who doesn't exist, with two non-existent kids. I can't get involved with someone else who doesn't exist. Life would get too complicated.'

The Lear landed in Copenhagen. The Danish government laid on a power boat to get them across to the Cat's island.

They sat in the back of the boat as it cut through the billowing waves of the foul-tempered sea. The island loomed through circles of mist, towering above the stormy waters: a single, sea-ringed mountain, tapering into the clouds. As they moved slowly closer, something at the very summit caught the sunlight and glimmered.

They moored the boat at a crumbling wooden jetty, and looked around, trying to find a route up the unclimbable mountain. They heard a sound: a creaking steel chain. And crashing out of the soggy mist, a cable car lurched to a halt in front of them.

They sat, rocking in the dangerous wind, as the cable car slowly squeaked its way up the mountain. The trip took three hours. They went through cloud. The atmospheric pressure changed. Whatever the Cat's fantasy was, it certainly didn't involve entertaining a great many visitors.

Finally the cable car wheezed into its mooring, and they got out. Standing on a narrow mountain track were two rickshaws attended by eight-foot tall, huge-breasted Amazon Valkyries in scanty armour. Lister shook his head.

'I've really got to have a word with the Cat about his sexual politics.'

Worse was to follow because, as Lister climbed aboard the rickshaw, he realized that the two wing mirrors he'd assumed were for the giantesses to see behind them were in fact strategically placed so the passenger could spend the short trip to the mountain top watching their cartoon-sized boobs jiggling up the track. He shook his head again.

'Who did he get this place from? Benny Hill?' He climbed out. 'Forget it – we'll walk.'

Rimmer tried to hide his disappointment as they trudged up the curving track. As they reached the crest, they saw it.

Any faint hopes that Rimmer still entertained that they were on Earth and in the world of reality gurgled noisily down the plug hole as they gazed up at the Cat's home.

It was a thirty-towered golden castle surrounded by a moat filled with milk.

SEVEN

The tip of the highest golden tower was almost invisible to the naked eye. The battlements were patrolled by more of the horn-helmeted, skimpily armoured Valkyries.

Lister and Rimmer clumped noisily across the wooden drawbridge.

'Halt! Who goes there, buddy?' one of the Valkyries shouted from the gate house.

'We've come to see the Cat!' shouted Lister, his voice sounding weak and ineffectual by comparison.

They were led into the castle and through a maze of chambers. The Cat's portrait hung on every wall: here clad in gleaming armour, there grinning from a rearing horse; there wrestling a lion, here draped on top of a pink piano. They followed the guards out into an ornamental garden that made the grounds of the Palace of Versailles look like a window box. Rimmer began to regret the smallness of his own imagination.

The guards were marching double time, and Lister and Rimmer felt compelled to keep up. They were getting quite tired by the time they reached the end of the gardens, which let out onto a courtyard surrounded by stables.

The Cat, in a red riding jacket, gleaming white jodhpurs and black leather boots, was mounted on a cream-coloured, fire-breathing, racing yak. There was a smell of sulphur hanging in the air as the yak reared and tried to bolt. The Cat, laughing, deftly wrestled it under control as it haughtily spouted two more jets of fire from its nostrils.

A dozen hunting dogs yapped and bayed and snapped at the leashes held by four Valkyries. As the dragon yak ceased its protestations, the Cat turned and caught sight of Rimmer and Lister.

'Hey! What's happening?' He waved his black riding cap and tooted his hunting horn, driving the dogs berserk. 'Sydney!' he called to the tallest of the Valkyries, 'Saddle Dancer and Prancer! Guys,' he turned to Rimmer and Lister, 'grab a yak!'

Rimmer mounted his flame-coloured yak with more than a little trepidation, and held timidly onto the reins.

'I've never really ridden a . . . fire-breathing racing yak before,' he said unnecessarily.

Lister patted the neck of his beast, and used the resultant jet of flame to light one of the foot-long Havana cigars he'd stolen from Rimmer's study back in Paris. Then he hooked a foot into the stirrup and clambered into the saddle.

The Cat tooted his curved hunting horn and called to the Valkyries restraining the hounds: 'Release the dogs!'

The dozen hunting dogs streamed out of the courtyard. The Cat reared on his yak and bellowed 'Tally ho!', and all three of them thundered over the cobblestones and out into the dank, misty wasteland that surrounded the castle.

Lister clung desperately to the neck of the bouncing yak, the reins hanging free as it splashed through the bog land which was covered in a carpet of mist. Before him, whenever he dared to open his eyes, he could see the Cat, straight-backed, holding onto the reins with his left hand, a silver shooting pistol in his right, while behind him he could hear the occasional low moans of Rimmer as he recited various incantations from a number of different religions.

They came to a low hedge. The dogs burst through it and the yaks leapt over. As they hammered across the hard, frosty ground, Lister saw the Cat level his pistol. He couldn't see the quarry, and he wasn't particularly keen to. They were riding fire-breathing dragon yaks. What on Earth would they be hunting? He saw the Cat's shoulder jerk back, and a puff of smoke, before he heard the crack of the pistol. In the distance, one of the dogs cartwheeled twelve feet into the air and landed, dead, on the floor.

'No!' Lister yelled as the Cat quickly picked off the eleven remaining dogs. He reined in the yak, raised his horn and tooted a victory call.

'You shot all the smegging dogs!' said Lister, gulping for air.

'They're vermin,' laughed the Cat; 'what did you think we were shooting?' He raised himself in his saddle and called to the entourage of Valkyries galloping up on horses some way behind them. 'More dogs, Sydney!'

They stood before the roaring fire in the vast inglenook fireplace of the Cat's baronial dining hall, drinking hot milk laced with cinnamon from pewter mugs.

The Cat stood, a spat-covered foot resting on the gold fender, his elbow crooked above his head on the marble mantelpiece, shaking his head, staring into the fire.

'You mean none of this is real? None of this actually exists?'

'Of course it doesn't!' Rimmer snorted in disgust. 'Fire-breathing yaks? Eight-foot tall Nordic goddesses? A castle surrounded by a moat of milk? Is any of it even *remotely* tinged with credibility? I don't understand how you could even believe it was!'

Lister thought of the Rimmer Buildings, Paris, New York, and London, but he didn't say anything.

'I mean,' Rimmer shook his head, 'at least our fantasies were possible! Perhaps not likely, but possible. But yours is just totally preposterous. It's like a Gothic fairy tale. How come you didn't suspect anything? Didn't you think it was a little bit odd the way you just *acquired* all this?'

'No. I just thought I deserved it.'

'Deserved it?' Lister tilted his head.

'Because I'm so good-looking.'

A naked, oiled Valkyrie banged the enormous gong and announced it was supper.

As they took their places at the long oak banquet table, the lights dimmed and a spotlight picked out Sydney holding a large silver platter at the top of a stone staircase which led up to the balcony skirting the baronial hall.

The flagstones in the middle of the hall slid apart, and from beneath a seven-piece band rose up on a hydraulic pedestal. Mozart on piano, Jimi Hendrix on lead guitar, Stéphane Grappelli on rhythm, Charlie Parker on sax, Yehudi Menuhin on violin, Buddy Rich on drums, and Jellybean on computer programs. They began to play.

'Listen to these boys,' the Cat confided; 'they really kick ass.'

They had never heard the tune before, but it was so .. perfect, so instantly classic, Lister and Rimmer immediately started tapping along with the heavenly beat.

Sydney danced down the stairs, flanked by forty lurex-clad Valkyries, all bearing platters and singing:

> *'He's going to eat you little fishies,*
> *He's going to eat you little fish,*
> *He's going to eat you little fishies,*
> *Because he likes eating fish!'*

Three platters were placed before them, each containing a large aquarium packed with writhing shoals of vividly-coloured fish.

Rimmer eyed his dinner with disgust. 'Don't you prefer them caught and cooked?'

'No, sir!' said the Cat, picking up the mini-fishing rod which was laid out with the cutlery by his plate. 'I like my food to *move*.'

'I think,' said Rimmer, draping his napkin over the fish tank, 'we've established beyond all reasonable doubt that we are playing Better Than Life.'

'Right,' Lister agreed, 'but the question is: how do we get out?'

'Why do we have to get out?' asked the Cat as he sucked a squirming angel fish off the hook of his rod.

'Because it's a computer-induced fantasy, because it's not real, and in the real world our bodies are wasting away. We're dying.'

'What are you talking about?'

Lister explained about the messages on his arms, and how it meant that someone was trying to get through to them.

'Which someone?' asked the Cat.

'Holly, obviously,' said Rimmer.

Lister shook his head. 'Maybe. We don't know. We don't know exactly at what point we started playing the Game. How much of this has been real? Did we get back to Earth? Did we fix *Nova 5*? Did *Nova 5* exist? Maybe I started playing BTL back on Mimas, and *you* two don't exist. Maybe our whole relationship and everything that's happened has been part of my fantasy.'

'No, no, I exist,' said Rimmer. 'Honestly.'

'Yeah, but you'd say that even if you didn't exist,' said Lister.

'He's right, said the Cat; 'maybe I don't exist either. That would certainly explain why I'm so unbearably good-looking.'

'Oh, I don't believe this!' said Rimmer. 'Not only am I dead, I don't exist either! Thanks a lot, God!'

'No, look, I think we have to assume' – Lister punctuated 'assume' with a circled thumb and forefinger – 'that we all exist, and that we got into the Game before *Nova 5* left *Red Dwarf*.'

'OK,' said Rimmer, 'how do we get out?'

'I think I can answer that,' said a fourth voice.

A familiar figure waddled through the stone archway and up to the banquet table.

And he started to explain everything.

EIGHT

Rimmer lurched happily down Corridor 4: gamma 311. 'It's a funny thing,' he slurred, 'even though I've had so much to drink I'm in total comfac of my mandulties.'

'Where is he?' said Lister, poking his head into another of the sleeping quarters on the habitation deck. 'Where the smeg is the Cat?'

'Master Holly says he's on this deck,' said Kryten, peering through the hatchway of another empty sleeping quarters.

'Then why the hell doesn't he answer?' said Lister, tugging the ringpull on another bottle of self-heating saké.

Rimmer's duplicate had been erased that morning, just before the gazpacho soup confession. Nova 5 was reconstructed, fuelled and ready to go. They would be back at Earth in three months, and they'd spent the day celebrating down in the Copacabana Hawaiian Cocktail Bar. The evening had gurgled by in a blurry haze of ever-more elaborate cocktails before either of them had realized the Cat had been missing for two days. Lister had led the drunken safari up to the habitation deck to find him.

There were over three thousand separate sleeping quarters on this deck alone, and they had looked through more than half of them before they staggered into Petrovitch's old room.

The two lockers had been pulled away from the wall, and in a crudely chiselled recess was a stack of Game headbands. Petrovitch, the high-flying, career-minded leader of A Shift had been smuggling Better Than Life, the illegal hallucinogenic brain implant. He'd been smuggling it to the richly paid, insanely bored terraforming engineers of Triton.

The rumours were true.

This correct officer, this model, this paragon, was a low-life, scumbag Game dealer! At a glance Lister estimated there must have been a hundred headbands. Petrovitch could safely have expected to make ten years' wages if he found a hundred suckers who were prepared to buy the cripplingly addictive nirvana offered by the deadly Game. And there always were suckers: plenty of them. Not one person ever entered the Game without believing he could take it or leave it. Once inside, few ever made the painful journey back to reality.

The Cat gently rocked on the sleeping quarters armchair, giggling insanely. The silver headband glimmered menacingly on his head, the electrodes buried deep inside his brain. His face was painted with the harrowingly familiar vacant grin of the lost soul of a Game head.

The three of them sat around the banquet table in the baronial hall of the Cat's fantasy as Kryten recounted how Lister had followed the Cat into the Game.

'But Better Than Life's addictive! I *knew* that.'

'You were drunk, Mister David; you thought you'd be OK just to go into the Game and tell the Cat what danger he was in. But once you'd linked up to the Cat's headband, you didn't come out.'

'What about me?' said Rimmer. 'Why did I go in?'

'You were drunk too. You said you had the willpower to drag them both out. You got Holly to splice you into the Game. And that was the last we saw of you.'

Kryten told how they had wandered around *Red Dwarf* in the twilight zombie state the Game induced. How he'd done his best to feed them, and keep them from harming themselves. But over the months the Cat's and Lister's bodies had begun to wither. Sometimes they'd spend weeks in a single position and develop huge bedsores. They'd tumble down stairs and get up, bloody and laughing, believing they'd made a parachute jump or some such thing. How he'd once seen Lister eat his own vomit with delight, obviously believing he was enjoying some sumptuous delicacy. How, in desperation, he'd begun lasering the messages into Lister's arms to warn him of the danger. This had distressed Kryten greatly. It was built into his software that he mustn't harm human beings. Months of cajoling by Holly had finally persuaded him that *not* to do it would hurt Lister even more.

But still the three of them remained in the Game. In the end, Kryten had no choice but to enter himself.

'But that's stupid,' said Lister. 'You'll get addicted too.'

Kryten shook his head. 'Holly was right. I'm immune. I could have come in right at the start and rescued you.'

'Immune?' said Rimmer. 'Why are you immune?'

Kryten cracked his face into a hollow grin. 'I'm a mechanoid. I don't have dreams. I don't have fantasies the way you do. I have very few expectations or desires.'

'Very few?' said Lister. 'Then you do have some?'

A Valkyrie appeared, bearing a brand-new, freshly wrapped squeezy mop.

'Only one,' said Kryten, accepting the gift and tearing off the paper. 'Oh, wonderful. A squeezy mop! Just what I've always wanted.'

'O K', said Lister, leaning forward, 'the sixty-four million dollarpound question: how do we get out?'

NINE

The windscreen wipers patted the snow into neat white triangles on the model A's window as the car grunted past the white-coated sign: 'Bedford Falls – 2 miles'.

Lister banged at the dashboard with a gloved hand, and the faltering heater whirred back from the dead, and unenthusiastically started to de-mist the windscreen. Lister craned over the steering column and tried to make out the grey ruts in the snow which served as a rough indication as to where the road might be.

He was leaving the Game. It was easy to leave the Game. Easier than he'd have thought.

First you had to want to leave. And, of course, to want to leave you had to know you were in the Game in the first place. That was the hard part, realizing that this wasn't reality. Then it was only a matter of finding an exit. Just that. A door marked 'EXIT'.

'And where are these doors?' he'd asked Kryten.

'It's your fantasy,' Kryten had replied; 'they're wherever you want them to be.'

So there it was. All he had to do was imagine an exit, and go through it.

He'd pass through the exit and find himself back on *Red Dwarf*, probably thin and gaunt and wasted from his two years in the Game but, nevertheless, back in reality. Once back, he could remove his headband – no, *destroy* his headband! Destroy them all! – then start the long haul back to health.

But it was an individual matter. They all had to create their own separate exits. Alone. You're born alone, you die alone, you leave the Game alone.

The glimmering lights of Bedford Falls twinkled in the valley below as, for the last time, he made his way down the hill to his personal Shangri-la.

Ever since he'd left Earth, every step he'd taken had led him further away from the dirty polluted world he loved. First Mimas, then the outer reaches of the solar system, then Deep Space, and finally here – in the wrong dimension of the wrong plane of reality. It was hard to imagine how he could ever be further away from home.

The Ford juddered down the main street under the strings of lights that hung between trees down the avenue. He passed Horace's bank, and through the window saw the money still stacked in neat piles on the counter. He passed Old Man Gower's drugstore. How could he have believed it existed? He passed Martini's Bar, alive inside with joyful revellers celebrating Christmas Eve. He headed the old car down Sycamore Avenue, and slid to rest outside no. 220.

There, in the middle of the street, a pink neon sign hung over a shimmering archway. There was his exit, just as he'd imagined it. On the other side was reality.

It started to snow. Christmas Eve.

How could he leave them on Christmas Eve?

What harm was one more day? He turned away from the dissolving exit and crunched up the drive to 220.

One more night of that pinball smile.

Just one.

He couldn't leave them on Christmas Eve.

But, of course, in Bedford Falls it was always Christmas Eve . . .